DARKNESS AT NOON

ARTHUR KOESTLER

PHILIP BOEHM, TRANSLATOR
MICHAEL SCAMMELL, EDITOR

SCRIBNER
NEW YORK   LONDON   TORONTO   SYDNEY   NEW DELHI

Scribner
An Imprint of Simon & Schuster, Inc.
1230 Avenue of the Americas
New York, NY 10020

This book is a work of fiction. Any references to historical events, real people, or real places are used fictitiously. Other names, characters, places, and events are products of the author's imagination, and any resemblance to actual events or places or persons, living or dead, is entirely coincidental.

Copyright © 1941 by The Macmillan Company
Copyright renewed © 1968 by Mrs. F.H.K. Henries (Daphne Hardy)
German language copyright © 2019 by The University of Edinburgh,
the Trustee for the Estate of Arthur Koestler
English language translation copyright © 2019 by Philip Boehm
Introduction © 2019 by Michael Scammell

The translator thanks TOLEDO, a program of the Robert Bosch Foundation and the Deutscher Übersetzerfonds, for their support of this project.

This Scribner trade paperback edition September 2019

SCRIBNER and design are registered trademarks of The Gale Group, Inc., used under license by Simon & Schuster, Inc., the publisher of this work.

For information about special discounts for bulk purchases, please contact Simon & Schuster Special Sales at 1-866-506-1949 or business@simonandschuster.com.

The Simon & Schuster Speakers Bureau can bring authors to your live event. For more information or to book an event, contact the Simon & Schuster Speakers Bureau at 1-866-248-3049 or visit our website at www.simonspeakers.com.

Interior design by Carly Loman

Manufactured in the United States of America

10 9 8 7 6 5 4 3 2 1

Library of Congress Cataloging-in-Publication Data

Names: Koestler, Arthur, 1905–1983, author. | Boehm, Philip, translator. | Scammell, Michael, editor.
  Title: Darkness at noon / Arthur Koestler ; Philip Boehm, translator ; Michael Scammell, editor.
  Description: Scribner hardcover edition. | New York : Scribner, 2019.
  Identifiers: LCCN 2019018703 (print) | LCCN 2019022052 (ebook) |
ISBN 9781982135225 (ebook) | ISBN 9781982123734 | ISBN 9781982123734?
(hardcover :?alk. paper) | ISBN 9781501161315?(paperback :?alk. paper) |
ISBN 9781439188453?(ebook)
  Subjects: LCSH: Moscow Trials, Moscow, Russia, 1936–1937—Fiction. | Soviet Union—History—1925–1953—Fiction. | Political prisoners—Fiction. | Totalitarianism—Fiction.
  Classification: LCC PR6021.O4 (ebook) | LCC PR6021.O4 D3 2019 (print) | DDC 823/.912—dc23
  LC record available at https://lccn.loc.gov/2019018703

ISBN 978-1-5011-6131-5
ISBN 978-1-9821-3522-5 (ebook)

CONTENTS

INTRODUCTION

Michael Scammell

I.

Arthur Koestler's *Darkness at Noon* is an intellectual and political thriller about the life and death of a fictional revolutionary leader, Nikolai Salmanovich Rubashov, told as he languishes in prison accused of treason. After repeated interrogations by his two prosecutors—Ivanov, a veteran revolutionary and former colleague of Rubashov's, and Gletkin, a younger, more ruthless party apparatchik—Rubashov is forced to confess to a series of crimes he has not committed. After a public trial, he is sentenced to death and summarily executed in the prison basement.

Koestler doesn't identify the country where the story is set. There are several allusions to Nazi Germany, but the names of the characters are mostly Russian and the political system he describes is obviously the Soviet one. His inspiration for writing his book was the show trials of Soviet Communist Party leaders in the late 1930s, when the world was startled by the news that more than half the Soviet leadership had been charged with treason. Koestler had been a loyal member of the party himself until then and on his first and only visit to the Soviet Union in 1932, had met some of the government ministers who were being imprisoned and put on trial. One whom Koestler particularly admired was Nikolai Bukharin, a popular and highly intellectual Bolshevik leader, who had been in and out of power since the October Revolution and was regarded as one of Stalin's most formidable ideological rivals.

By the time Bukharin was imprisoned, Koestler had had a taste of political prison himself. In 1937, during the Spanish Civil War, he had been sent to Madrid as a communist agent, gathering enough material to publish a volume of strident, anti-Franco propaganda entitled *L'Espagne Ensanglantée* (Bloodstained Spain). He returned to Spain as a foreign correspondent for a liberal British newspaper, *The News Chronicle*, but was arrested during the Battle of Málaga and placed in solitary confinement in the city of Seville. He remained there for three months, seeing other prisoners led out for execution and constantly fearing he might be next. He was released after some influential British friends intervened on his behalf and immediately wrote *Dialogue with Death* about his experiences. His book was highly praised by Thomas Mann, Walter Benjamin, and George Orwell, who praised it as "of the greatest psychological interest" and "probably one of the most honest and unusual documents that have been produced by the Spanish War," among others.

Koestler also resigned from the Communist Party and delivered a passionate speech to the communist-controlled German Writers' Association in Paris, in which he explained his reasons, quoting André Malraux: "A life is worth nothing, but nothing is worth a life," and Thomas Mann: "In the long run, a harmful truth is better than a useful lie," two aphorisms that directly contradicted communist ideology. Soon afterward, the third big Soviet show trial got under way. Bukharin and twenty of his Soviet government colleagues were accused of a host of fantastic crimes, among them plotting to assassinate Lenin and Stalin, carve up the Soviet empire, and restore capitalism. Few people outside the Soviet Union believed these accusations, but after first denying the charges, Bukharin and his comrades inexplicably pleaded guilty. Bukharin's ambiguous words seemed to concede that he was "objectively responsible" for his criminal behavior, but not for any particular crime cited in the indictment (see Appendix), leaving onlookers to debate the true extent of his confession.

Koestler was electrified by these confessions. How could such a large portion of the Soviet establishment have spent months plotting against the government and Stalin without being discovered? How had powerful leaders such as Bukharin been transformed into impotent defendants and manipulated to confess to crimes they had clearly not committed? How had Stalin managed to pull off his monstrous coup de théâtre so successfully? And why had the victims played their parts so willingly and gone so obediently to their deaths?

2.

Darkness at Noon was Koestler's attempt at answering these questions and his answers were controversial. It was taken for granted, for example, that torture must have been used to extract these confessions from the Soviet leaders. Koestler by no means ruled out the use of torture in Soviet jails and there are many instances of torture in *Darkness at Noon*. Rubashov himself is denied sleep and has a blinding light shone in his eyes during his interrogations, but Koestler never shows Rubashov undergoing direct physical torture. He plays it down, not, as some critics have alleged, to soften the crimes of the communist authorities, but because he was more interested in something else. Rubashov represented the old guard of the Bolshevik Party, and Koestler had concluded that after thirty to forty years of suffering every kind of adversity, including various types of torture, they couldn't be broken by torture alone.

Spain had taught Koestler that the idealistic form of communism that had inspired these men in their youth and had also attracted him to enlist in the party had all but disappeared, giving way to a harshly oppressive regime in which all power was concentrated in the hands of one man—Joseph Stalin. The result was widespread corruption and the establishment of a dictatorship that brutally crushed the people, especially the peasants and workers in whose name the revolution had been carried out. The show trials were both a symptom of this corruption and proof of the rot that was undermining the whole system, and the most loyal party members among the accused had confessed because the ideological ground beneath their feet had been cut away and they had nothing more to believe in. It was their resulting psychological collapse that Koestler wished to explore, rather than the mechanisms of the trials themselves.

Koestler postulated that some of the government's leaders, such as Bukharin, while conforming outwardly, had never entirely abandoned their revolutionary creed and had retained many of their original communist ideals. Cocooned in their privileged party positions, they had been slow to grasp the radical corruption undermining the country from within, and when they finally acknowledged this truth, were unable to hide their disillusionment. Their instinctive resistance in a police state made their arrests inevitable, and the combination of isolation, exhaustion, disillusionment, and psychological disintegration did more, in Koestler's view, to bring about their demise than physical mistreatment alone would have done. In turning against the party they had lost their sole source of support and, unable to resist any further, confessed to their "crimes" as a "last service to the party."

In response to his critics, Koestler cited a book called *I Was Stalin's Agent* by General Walter Krivitsky, which had described in detail the interrogation and trial of one of Bukharin's former colleagues, Sergei Mrachkovsky, who had said he was publicly confessing to his crimes out of a sense of duty to the party. Koestler added that he didn't think all the defendants who confessed had avoided torture, only "a certain type of Old Bolshevik with an absolute loyalty to the party," who would succumb without it.

To this theory Koestler attached another, equally controversial suggestion that Rubashov might have undergone a kind of spiritual conversion in prison as well. During his long hours alone Rubashov uses a prison tapping code to make contact with a White Russian prisoner in the cell adjoining his. The code itself was also grounded in reality. Koestler had learned of it from a childhood friend, Eva Zeisel, who had just been expelled to the West after serving sixteen months in a Soviet jail for allegedly plotting to assassinate Stalin. In Koestler's novel, Rubashov's tapping exchanges with his neighbor persuade him that the latter is a buffoon, a conventional moralist who prattles on about old-fashioned notions such as honor, decency, and conscience. As time passes, however, Rubashov begins to doubt himself. "Looking back, it seemed he had spent forty years in a mad frenzy . . . of pure reason. Perhaps it wasn't healthy . . . to cut off the old ties, to disengage the brakes of 'thou shalt not.' "

This biblical phrase seems highly uncharacteristic for the communist, Rubashov, but it dovetails with echoes of Dostoevsky's *Crime and Punishment* that appear from time to time in Koestler's book. Ivanov mentions the novel during his first interrogation of Rubashov and their arguments often resemble Porfiry Petrovich questioning Raskolnikov. While ruminating in his cell, Rubashov recalls the image of a pietà he once saw in a European art gallery while in effect sending one of his party subordinates to his death. These Christian motifs point to themes of martyrdom and absolution, and Koestler suggests that by the time he is ready to confess, Rubashov is prompted by a deeper sense of guilt than simply disloyalty to the party. His crimes are violations of traditional morality and when he finally confesses to Gletkin, it is for reasons Gletkin cannot possibly understand.

Koestler refrains from portraying Rubashov as a full-fledged Christian, however, and at his execution leaves him an agnostic. "A dull blow struck the back of his head. It was long expected but nevertheless took him by surprise. . . . A second, shattering blow hit him on the ear. Then all was still. The sea rushed on. A wave gently lifted him up. It came from afar and traveled serenely onward, a shrug of infinity."

3.

Koestler wrote his novel with astonishing speed, starting it in the South of France in the summer of 1939 and finishing it in Paris in April 1940. The last eight months coincided with the time of the Phoney War, a period of calm before the German invasion of France in May 1940, but there was no calm for Koestler. Still in the midst of writing, he was arrested by the French police as an "enemy alien" and imprisoned in Le Vernet internment camp in the South of France. He thought it was because of his German citizenship, but later learned he had been classified as a Soviet agent, this at a time when he had left the Communist Party and was writing his anti-Soviet novel. The camp regime was lax enough for him to be able to continue writing and after four months, for lack of evidence, he was allowed to return to Paris.

He was condemned to house arrest and ordered to report regularly to the nearest police station, but even so, he was subjected to unannounced police raids and the occasional confiscation of his papers. Once or twice the unfinished text of *Darkness at Noon* sat on his desk and a carbon copy rested on top of his bookcase, but the French police overlooked them.

Koestler's English girlfriend, a twenty-one-year-old art student named Daphne Hardy, was sharing the apartment with him at the time and unbeknownst to him, had translated some short passages from the novel to while away the time while Koestler was in Le Vernet. "I had started to translate his book for my own consolation," she later wrote. "He chanced to find it and read the first few pages while I squirmed in bed. . . . After a minute or two he turned around and said, '*Also Schätzchen, das ist sehr gut. Wir werden ein Geschäft machen.*' " (Well, darling, it's very good. We'll make some money out of this.)

Hardy had no prior experience in translation and was nervous about her abilities, but agreed to give it a try. "After breakfast each day," she later recalled, "we would draw the curtain, which partitioned the apartment in two. He would sit at his table in the bigger room with the bookcases, I would sit on the edge of the divan at the round table . . . imprisoned there until lunchtime . . . while he worked with concentrated fury about ten feet away." She completed her work at top speed and mailed her translation to publisher Jonathan Cape in London, and Koestler mailed the carbon copy to a German-language publisher in neutral Switzerland. Days later, when German troops moved to occupy Paris, Hardy and Koestler fled south to escape arrest. Koestler joined the French Foreign Legion to hide his identity while Hardy, a British citizen, made her way to London. Nothing was heard from Switzerland and she believed that to all intents and purposes, her translation was the only copy of the book to survive.

Koestler's original title for the novel, *The Vicious Circle*, didn't appeal to Cape and he asked Hardy to supply a new one. Abashed by the responsibility and fearing Koestler's wrath if she got it wrong, she consulted a variety of literary sources and settled on *Darkness at Noon*, a vivid and apt metaphor that proved to be a stroke of genius. Koestler fully approved and was under the impression that the title came from a well-known line in Milton's *Samson Agonistes*, "Oh dark, dark, dark, amid the blaze of noon," an attribution that persists in some circles today, but Hardy's inspiration was the book of Job: "They meet with darkness in the daytime, and grope in the noonday as in the night."

4.

Darkness at Noon was published by Cape in London in December 1940, just as German bombs were raining down on the city and there was serious talk of a possible German invasion. Koestler was back in jail again—in England now, having arrived illegally from Lisbon—and again as a suspected agent, this time of the Germans. It was hardly an auspicious moment to launch a political novel about show trials in the prewar Soviet Union. A world war had just broken out and Stalin's show trials were largely forgotten. Sales of the book were slow to begin with and only a few critics, most of them on the left, understood its importance.

"Who will ever forget the first moment he read *Darkness at Noon*?" wrote Britain's future Labour Party leader Michael Foot, reviewing the book. "For socialists especially, the experience was indelible." Other reviewers deemed the novel "the most devastating exposure of Stalinist methods ever written," "one of the few books written in this epoch which will survive it," and "a bitter pill to swallow." George Orwell thought the book "brilliant as a novel" and accepted its explanation of the show trials, but was even more impressed by the accuracy of its analysis of communism. Four years later, when writing *Animal Farm*—inspired in part by Koestler's ideas—Orwell went further and pronounced *Darkness at Noon* a masterpiece.

The English public, distracted by the war, was slow to be convinced. In the United States, not yet at war, sales were better, helped by a glowing review in *Time* by Whittaker Chambers, the former Soviet spy, who knew what Koestler was talking about. Its selection by the Book of the Month Club also boosted sales, but they were still modest compared with what happened after the war, when sales of the English-language edition exploded. A French translation came out and sold 100,000 copies in its first year. Lines of people formed outside the French publisher's office in Paris waiting for the book to come off the presses and copies were changing hands at eight times their original price. By the middle of the following year it had sold 300,000 copies and went on to sell two million in two years, then a record in French publishing.

This phenomenal success was due in large part to the turbulent political scene in Europe during and after World War II. When Koestler's novel first appeared, Stalin had just signed a non-aggression pact with Nazi Germany and was regarded as an enemy by the Allies, but after Germany invaded the Soviet Union, Stalin switched sides and his armies were instrumental in helping to secure the Allied victory. The Soviet Union's stock soared and communists in Western Europe suddenly found themselves seriously competing for power. In France, they were the largest party in the Constituent Assembly and were expected to win the first postwar general election with ease. In this context, the anti-Soviet message of *Darkness at Noon* erupted with shattering force. There were rumors of a communist delegation visiting the French publisher to demand he cease publication, and of party members being dispatched to bookstores to buy up all available copies. When a constitutional referendum was held in May 1946, the Communist Party narrowly lost by 48 to 52 percent, and experts agreed with the future Nobel Prize winner François Mauriac that the tipping point was the publication of *Darkness at Noon*.

When Koestler returned to Paris in late 1946, he was greeted as a hero, embraced by Sartre, de Beauvoir, Camus, and Malraux as a literary equal. In the United States, which Koestler visited for the first time two years later, he was regarded as the most potent anti-communist writer of his time. Arriving in New York for a US lecture tour on the British luxury liner the *Queen Mary*, with Clark Gable, Dizzy Gillespie, and Admiral Richard E. Byrd as fellow passengers, Koestler was hailed as "Celebrity of the Day" in that day's *Celebrity Bulletin*.

5.

Within a few years *Darkness at Noon* had been translated into more than thirty languages and become a worldwide bestseller. For decades it was widely read in American high schools and assigned in undergraduate political science courses, and the accepted English version has always remained in print, despite a falloff in readers since the collapse of Soviet communism. This raises the question of why make a new translation almost eighty years after the novel was written and why publish it now?

One reason is circumstantial. When Koestler and Hardy fled Paris to escape the Germans, they lost their copy of the original German typescript and the carbon copy had apparently disappeared into thin air, leaving Hardy's translation as the only text in existence. Her English version had introduced *Darkness at Noon* to the English-speaking public all over the world and had become the ur-text from which all other translations were made, a rare occurrence in modern literature.

This situation changed some four years ago, in 2015, when Matthias Wessel, a German graduate student working on Koestler's German writings, stumbled across the carbon copy of *Darkness at Noon* that had seemed to disappear in 1940. He found it in the archive of Emil Oprecht, founder of the Europa publishing house in Zurich, but it wasn't labeled as such. The name on the title page was simply *Rubaschow* (the German spelling of "Rubashov") and the author's name was given as A. Koestler. Every page, including the title page, had been stamped by the French censor's office, confirming that it had come from Paris in wartime, but the title had still meant nothing to Swiss editors at the time. Koestler was little known and it was only when Wessel, well versed in Koestler's work, came across it that it was recognized as the only copy of the original German text in existence.

The unearthing of the manuscript led to a reconsideration of Koestler's prose in German and a reexamination of Hardy's key translation into English. Despite her youth and lack of experience, her version has been properly acknowledged as idiomatic and fluent, serving the novel well for over seven decades, but it also reveals signs of the difficulties she had encountered. She had been forced by circumstances to work in haste, with no dictionaries or other resources available for consultation, which exposed her understandable lack of familiarity with the Soviet and Nazi machinery of totalitarianism. Obliged to improvise, she occasionally employed terminology—such as "hearing" for "interrogation"—that made these regimes look somewhat softer and more civilized than they really were. The text she worked on was not quite final either, for the Zurich typescript reveals changes Koestler made at the last minute and passages not found in the Hardy translation (such as a paragraph on masturbation in prison), items that Hardy couldn't possibly have known about or foreseen.

It seemed that a fresh and up-to-date translation of the novel would be helpful, preferably by a seasoned translator with the knowledge and experience to clarify the jargon of Marxism-Leninism and present it in terminology that is both accurate and makes sense to an English-speaking reader. Philip Boehm, a noted translator of over thirty books and plays from German and Polish, who lived for several years behind the Iron Curtain, has proved the ideal choice for the job. In Boehm's translation, Koestler's novel is a crisper read than before. The prose is tighter, the dialogue clearer, the tone more ironic, and the intricacies of Marxist-Leninist dialectics more digestible. Boehm captures nuances of status and hierarchy in the relationships between party members and their leaders that weren't always evident before, along with aspects of the regime's calculated cruelty that have only been understood in recent years. The effect for the reader is of chancing upon a familiar painting that has had layers of varnish and dust removed to reveal images and colors in a much brighter light.

6.

Twenty years ago, the editors of the Modern Library in New York ranked *Darkness at Noon* at number eight on its list of the hundred best English-language novels of the twentieth century.

Setting aside the irony of a translated novel appearing on a list of English-language books, the choice was farsighted, a tribute to the novel's high quality and to its success in transcending its historical moment.

The historical dimension is important, of course. Though Koestler refused to name the country where his story takes place, it most closely resembles the Soviet Union and Number One is clearly based on Stalin. The novel was highly topical from the moment it first appeared, and it remained so for a long time, thanks in part to its adoption as a weapon in the Cold War. Today, we have only to look at authoritarian regimes in China, North Korea, and scattered across the globe to be reminded that its basic message is still relevant, and that current dictatorships operate in essentially the same way they always have—by terrorizing their subjects and depriving them of their most important freedoms.

It's important to remember that Koestler was also writing fiction, however, and as the times have changed, contemporary details have fallen away and the novel's allegorical dimension has moved to the fore. *Darkness at Noon* is also a dystopia in the mold of Orwell's *Nineteen Eighty-Four*, and Rubashov is an archetypal political prisoner, a flawed everyman in search of salvation. *Darkness at Noon*'s message remains topical but also timeless, a warning to readers that is not to be ignored.

THE FIRST INTERROGATION

It is impossible to reign innocently.

                                        Saint-Just

I.

The cell door clanged shut behind Rubashov.

He lingered for a few seconds leaning against the door and lit a cigarette. To his right was a cot with two tolerably clean blankets and a straw tick that looked freshly stuffed. The washbasin to his left was missing the stopper, but the faucet worked. The bucket next to that had just been disinfected and did not smell. The side walls were solid brick, so they didn't resonate, but the heating and drainpipe exits were sealed with plaster and tapping there produced a passable tone. The heating pipe itself also seemed to conduct sound quite well. The window began at eye level and Rubashov could see down into the yard without having to hoist himself up by the bars. So far so good.

He yawned, took off his jacket, rolled it up, and set it on the mattress as a pillow. He looked down into the yard; the snow had a yellowish gleam from the double light of the moon and the electric lanterns. A small circular lane for walking had been shoveled out close to the walls. It was still dark, and the stars shimmered brightly in the cold air despite the lanterns. A sentry posted on the outer wall opposite Rubashov's cell had shouldered his rifle and was counting out his hundred paces. He stamped his feet with every step, as if on parade, and Rubashov couldn't decide whether he was doing this because of regulations or because of the cold. Now and then his bayonet shaft flashed with the reflected light from the lanterns.

Standing at the window, Rubashov took off his shoes. He put out his cigarette, placed the stub next to the foot of the cot, and sat down on the straw tick for several minutes. Then he returned to the window. The yard was quiet; the sentry was in the middle of an about-face; Rubashov could make out a patch of

Milky Way just above the machine-gun tower. He stretched out on the cot and wrapped himself in the top blanket. It was five in the morning; wake-up probably didn't happen before seven, not in the winter. He was very sleepy; he figured the interrogations wouldn't begin for another three or four days, so he took off his pince-nez and set it on the stone tiles next to the cigarette stub, then smiled and shut his eyes. Wrapped in the warm blanket, he felt secure: for the first time in months he wasn't afraid of his dreams.

A few minutes later, when the warder switched off the light from the outside and peered through the spy hole into the cell, former people's commissar Rubashov was asleep, with his back turned to the wall. His head lay on his left arm, which jutted out of the bed, straight and stiff but for his hand, which dangled limply at the wrist and twitched as he slept.

2.

One hour earlier, when the two men from the People's Commissariat for Internal Affairs sent to arrest him had begun pounding on the door to his apartment, Rubashov had been dreaming that he was being arrested.

The pounding grew louder, and Rubashov struggled to wake up. He had practice in jolting himself out of a nightmare; for years the recurring dream of his first arrest would run its course like clockwork. Now and then he managed by sheer will to stop the clockwork and pull himself out of the dream, but this time it didn't work: the past weeks had worn him down; he sweated and gasped in his sleep, the clockwork went on humming, and he went on dreaming.

As always, he dreamed that three men had come to arrest him and were pounding on his door: He could see them through the door as they stood outside, banging against the frame. They had brand-new uniforms, the handsome dress of the German

dictatorship's Praetorian Guard; the aggressively barbed cross
that was their party's emblem adorned their caps and sleeves. In
their free hand each held a cumbersomely large revolver; their
belts smelled of fresh leather. All of a sudden they were inside
his room, right in front of his bed. Two were strapping country
boys with thick lips and fishlike eyes; the third was short and
rotund. They loomed over his bed, brandishing their pistols, so
close he could feel their breath. Everything was quiet but for
the short fat man's asthmatic wheezing. Then someone flushed
a toilet in one of the upper stories; the water went coursing
smoothly through the pipes in the walls.

The clockwork was receding. The pounding on Rubashov's
door grew louder; the two men outside who had come to arrest
him took turns pummeling and blowing into their frozen hands.
But even though he knew the next part of the dream was particularly excruciating, Rubashov could not wake up; the dream
kept going: The three men loom over his bed as he struggles
to put on his robe, but one sleeve has turned inside out and he
can't get his arm inside. He tries in vain but he cannot move, he's
completely paralyzed even though everything depends on getting his arm into the sleeve in time. This agonizing state lasts for
several seconds, Rubashov groans, he feels his temples breaking
out in a cold sweat, the pounding at his door invades his sleep
like a distant drumming, his arm under the pillow twitches in a
feverish attempt to slip into the sleeve—until at last he feels the
pistol butt smashing against his ear.

That first blow always brought release. That was also the
moment when he typically woke up, for no matter how many
hundreds of times he relived the scene, the pistol always hit him
anew. That was the blow that had damaged his hearing. Then
he would usually shudder for a bit, while his hand, still stuck
under the pillow, would go on twitching as it fumbled for the
sleeve, because most of the time before he awoke completely he
had to get through the last and worst part of the nightmare—
the dizzying, ambiguous feeling that the waking and release

were also nothing but a dream, and that in reality he was still lying on the damp stone floor of the dark cell, with a bucket at his feet and a jug of water by his head, along with a saved crust of bread.

The same dazed state lasted several seconds this time as well, since he didn't know whether his groping hand would touch the bucket or find the switch for the lamp on the nightstand. Then the fog lifted; the light flashed on; Rubashov took a few deep breaths and used his blanket to blot his forehead and the bald spot that was emerging on top. He lay still, his hands folded on his chest, and enjoyed the exhilarating feeling of freedom and safety like someone recuperating from an illness. With re-awakened irony he looked up and winked at the oil print of Number One, the leader of the party, which hung over the bed in his room, as well as on the walls of all the neighboring rooms, above or below him, and on all the walls of the building, the city, and the inordinately vast land for which he had fought and suffered and which had now taken him back into its mighty harboring bosom. At this point he was fully awake—but the pounding at his door continued.

3.

The two men from the interior ministry who had come to arrest Rubashov stood in the dark stairwell, deliberating. Vasily, the caretaker who had brought them upstairs, stood in the open elevator, panting with fear. He was a gaunt old man; a broad red scar protruded from the torn collar of the military coat he'd pulled over his nightshirt, giving him a scrofulous appearance. The neck wound came from the civil war, where he'd fought to the end in Rubashov's partisan regiment. Later Rubashov was posted abroad and Vasily only heard about his former commander from the occasional article in the newspaper that his daughter read aloud in the evening. She recited the speeches

Rubashov gave at the party congresses; they were long and difficult to understand, and Vasily could never quite hear in them the voice of the little bearded partisan commander, the Rubashov who could curse so beautifully that even Our Lady of Kazan would have smiled with joy. The caretaker typically dozed off in the middle of these speeches, but he always woke up when his daughter solemnly raised her voice for the closing declarations and the applause. After each of these proclamations—long live the Internationale, long live the world revolution, long live Number One—Vasily would add an "amen," heartfelt but barely audible so his daughter wouldn't hear, then he would take off his jacket, cross himself in secret and with a guilty conscience, and go to bed. The oil print of Number One hung over his bed, too, next to a photograph of Rubashov as partisan commander. If they found the photograph they would likely come for him as well.

The stairwell was cold, dark, and very quiet. The younger of the two agents suggested shooting the lock. Vasily propped himself against the elevator door. In his haste he hadn't put his boots on properly; now his hands were shaking so badly he couldn't tie the laces. The older of the two men opposed shooting the lock; the arrest should be as inconspicuous as possible. They blew into their frozen hands and resumed their pounding, the younger man using his pistol butt. A woman a few stories down started screaming in a shrill voice. "Tell her to shut up," the young man said to Vasily.

"Quiet!" Vasily called out. "The authorities are here."

The woman quieted down at once. The young man proceeded to kick the door with his boot. The whole stairwell boomed; at last the door sprang open.

The two officials in their uniforms stood at Rubashov's bed, the young one holding his revolver, the old one at attention as before a superior officer. Vasily stayed a step behind them, leaning against the wall. Rubashov was still blotting the sweat off his head; he looked at them with bleary, nearsighted eyes. "Citizen Nikolai Salmanovich Rubashov, we arrest you in the name of the law," said the younger. Rubashov groped under his pillow for his pince-nez and sat up. With his glasses back on, his eyes had the same expression Vasily and the older official knew from the faux oil prints and photos made during the revolutionary years. The old official stood even more erect; the younger, who had grown up hearing other names, stepped closer to the bed: the other three could see that he was on the verge of committing some brutality—in speech or deed—in order to mask his insecurity.

"Put that revolver away, comrade," Rubashov said to the young man. "What's this all about?"

"You just heard: you are under arrest," said the younger official. "Now stop talking and get dressed."

"Do you have a warrant?" asked Rubashov.

The older official took a paper from his pocket, handed it to Rubashov, and resumed his stance.

Rubashov read it carefully. "I see," he said. "But then these things never do tell you anything, do they? To hell with you."

"Get dressed and make it quick," said the young man. It was clear that his coarseness was not something he was affecting but part of his character. *Well, that's a fine generation we've brought on ourselves*, thought Rubashov. He recalled the propaganda posters that always portrayed this younger generation of people with laughing faces. He felt very tired. "Hand me my robe instead of waving your gun about," he said. The young man turned red but didn't say anything. The older official handed Rubashov his robe. Rubashov wrestled his arms into the sleeves. "At least this time I managed," he said with a twisted smile. The other three didn't understand and said nothing. They watched in silence as Rubashov slowly climbed out of bed and rummaged around for his rumpled clothes. Ever since the woman's shrill scream the building had been quiet, but they had the feeling the residents were lying awake in their beds, holding their breath.

Then they heard a toilet flush in one of the upper stories; the water passed through the pipes in the walls with a steady rush.

4.

The car that had brought the officials was waiting downstairs outside the entrance—a new American model. It was still dark; the driver had switched on the headlights; the street was asleep or pretending to sleep. They climbed inside—first the young official, then Rubashov, followed by the older man. The driver, also in uniform, set off. As soon as they left the apartment blocks the road ceased to be paved. Even though they were in the middle of the city, completely surrounded by nine- and ten-story high-rises with modern facades, the streets were essentially straight out of the countryside—frozen dirt cart paths scarred with ruts that were filled with powdery snow. The chauffeur drove at a crawl, and the car creaked and groaned like an oxcart despite the high-quality shock absorbers.

The young man couldn't stand the silence. "Drive faster," he told the driver.

The driver shrugged his shoulders without turning around. When the three men had climbed in, he had given Rubashov a callous, indifferent look. Rubashov had seen that same expression once before, from an ambulance driver who had picked him up after an accident. The slow, bumpy ride through the dead streets, guided by the jittery beam of the headlights, was hard to bear. "How far is it?" asked Rubashov, without looking at his escorts. He almost added: to the hospital and the operating room. "A good half hour," said the older official. Rubashov fished some cigarettes out of his pocket, stuck one in his mouth, and automatically offered the pack to the others. The young man declined brusquely; the older took two and handed one to the driver. The driver reached to his cap for a lighter and lit all three, keeping one hand on the steering wheel. Rubashov was annoyed to feel his heart ease a little. *Getting sentimental at a time like this*, he thought. But he couldn't resist the temptation to speak and create a modicum of human warmth around him. "A shame about these nice cars," he said. "They cost a fair amount of hard currency and after half a year on our roads they're shot to hell."

"You're right, our roads are very much underdeveloped," said the older official. From his tone Rubashov realized the old man had recognized his helplessness. He felt like a dog who'd been tossed a bone, and chose not to speak anymore. But the young man suddenly decided to challenge him: "Are you saying the capitalist countries have better roads?"

Rubashov had to grin. "Have you ever been outside the country?" he asked.

"That doesn't matter. I know how things are there," said the young man. "Don't bother trying to feed me some kind of story."

"Who do you really take me for?" asked Rubashov very calmly. But he couldn't help adding: "You really ought to study your party history a little."

The young man went silent and kept his eyes fixed ahead. All three were quiet. The motor gasped and stalled for the third time and the driver cursed as he restarted it. They bumped along through the outskirts of town, where, judging from the appearance of the wooden shanties, nothing here had changed. The moon hung over their crooked silhouettes, pale and cold.

5.

All the corridors of the magnificent new prison were equipped with pallid electric bulbs that barely lit the iron walkways, the stark whitewashed walls, the cell doors with the names, and the black holes for spying. The dull, lackluster light and the shrill acoustics of their steps on the stone tile floor seemed so familiar that for a few seconds Rubashov toyed with the illusion that he was once again dreaming. He tried to persuade himself that he actually believed this. *If you can convince yourself you're only dreaming, then it really will be just a dream*, he thought. He wanted this so badly that he nearly got dizzy—but then right away he felt a suffocating sense of shame. *I have to swallow it all with decency, down to the end*, he thought. *Even if I wind up choking on the last crumb.* Meanwhile they had reached cell number 404. A card was hanging over the spy hole, with his name: Nikolai Salmanovich Rubashov. The sight of his name on the card moved him deeply. *They've prepared everything beautifully*, he thought. He wanted to ask the guard for an extra blanket on account of his rheumatism, but the cell door was already clanging shut behind him.

6.

The warder squinted through the spy hole at regular intervals, but Rubashov lay still on his cot, except for his hand, which occasionally twitched in his sleep. On the tiles beside the cot were his pince-nez and a cigarette butt.

At seven in the morning—two hours after being taken to his cell—Rubashov was awakened by a blast from a bugle. He had slept straight through the two hours without dreaming and was immediately alert. The bugle sounded three times, the same blaring notes in a minor sequence. The tones reverberated for a long time, then faded out, giving way to a hostile silence.

The day was just beginning; the predawn light softened the contours of the tin bucket and the washbasin. The bars on the window were silhouetted black against the dull glass; a broken pane on the top left had been covered with newspaper. Rubashov sat up, reached for his pince-nez and the cigarette stub, and lay back down. He put on his pince-nez and lit the stub. The silence persisted. All the men in this whitewashed hive of cells were undoubtedly getting up from their bunks, cursing and feeling their way across the floor, but no sound reached the prisoners in the isolation unit, except for the occasional steps echoing down the corridor. Rubashov knew he was in an isolation cell and that he'd remain there until they shot him. He ran his fingers through his short, pointed beard, smoked, and lay still on his cot.

So they're going to shoot you, he thought. He blinked and stared at his foot, which was sticking straight up at the other end of the blanket. He noticed his big toe was moving. He felt warm, snug, and secure—and very tired; he didn't mind the idea of dozing off into death, as long as they let him lie under the warm blanket. *So they're going to shoot us*, he repeated in his thoughts. He slowly wiggled his toes inside his sock, and was reminded of a poem that compared Christ's feet to a white deer in a thornbush. He rubbed his pince-nez on his sleeve in his usual manner—a gesture well-known to his followers. Under the warm blanket his happiness was near complete; the only thing he feared was having to get up and move. "So they're going to snuff us out," he said to himself quietly, and lit a new cigarette, although he only had three left. Sometimes the first cigarettes on an empty stomach gave him a slight surge of pleasure, and he was already feeling a little giddy—a sensation he knew well from earlier brushes with death. He also realized that this sensation was objectionable, and from a certain perspective impermissible, but for the moment he had no desire to embrace that point of view. Instead he watched the play of his stockinged toes and smiled behind his pince-nez. He felt a warm wave of sympathy with his body, which he otherwise did not love, and his impending destruction filled him with a compassionate lust. "The old guard is dead," he said out loud, "we are the last ones." "They're going to snuff us out," he told himself. "Come, sweet death . . ." He tried to recall the melody of "Come, Sweet Death," but all that came to him were the words. "The old guard is dead," he repeated, and attempted to recall their faces. He only succeeded with a few. All he could remember of the first president of the Internationale, who had been executed as a traitor, was a patch of his checkered vest worn over a somewhat paunchy stomach. The man never wore suspenders, always leather belts. The first head of the revolutionary state—also executed—used to chew his nails in moments of danger. *History will rehabilitate you*, Rubashov thought without special conviction. What does history know of chewed nails? Rubashov smoked and thought about his dead comrades, about the humiliation that had preceded their death. Even so, he could not bring himself to hate Number One, although he had often looked at the oil print above his bed and tried. Among themselves they had given him many names, but in the end what stayed was Number One. The dread that eminated from Number One consisted above all in the possibility that he was right, and that all the people he killed had to concede he might be right—even as the bullet went into their neck. Absolute certainty did not exist, only a mocking oracle they called history, which would not deliver its verdict until long after the jawbones of the ones seeking counsel had turned to dust. Come, sweet death . . .

Rubashov sensed he was being watched through the spy hole. Without looking up, he knew that a pupil pressed against the glass was staring into the cell, and indeed just then a key grated in the heavy lock. It took a while for the door to open. The warder, a little old man in slippers, stood in the frame:

"Why didn't you get up?" he asked.

"I'm sick," said Rubashov.

"What's the matter? You can't see the doctor before tomorrow."

"Toothache," said Rubashov.

"Toothache," said the warder, "I see." Then he shuffled out and slammed the door shut.

Now I can lie down in peace and quiet at least for a little while, Rubashov thought, but the idea had lost its appeal. The stale warmth of the blanket began to annoy him and he tossed it aside. He tried watching his toes again but that bored him. Both socks had a hole above the ankle. He felt like sewing them up, but the thought of knocking on the door and asking the warder for needle and thread stopped him; they probably wouldn't let him have a needle anyway. He suddenly had a fierce craving for a newspaper. It was so strong he could smell the newsprint, hear the rustle and the crinkle of the turning pages. Perhaps a revolution had broken out in the night, a head of state had been murdered, or some American had discovered a way to defy gravity. There wouldn't be any news of his arrest—they would undoubtedly keep that secret for a while inside the country—but the sensation would soon leak out and people would rummage through the usual archives and print photos from ten years ago and scribble utter nonsense about him and Number One. His desire for the newspaper faded, but he did feel an equally strong craving to know what was going on in the brain of Number One. He pictured the man sitting at his desk, propped on his elbows, ponderous and unsympathetic, speaking slowly into a dictating machine. Others paced up and down when they gave dictation, blew smoke rings, or played with a ruler. Number One didn't move, didn't play, and didn't blow any rings . . . Rubashov suddenly noticed that he'd been pacing up and down the cell for a good five minutes himself; he'd risen from the cot without realizing it. He also caught himself following his old ritual of never stepping on the cracks between the tiles, and he already knew their pattern by heart. Nevertheless he hadn't taken his mind off Number One even for a second—as the man slowly transformed from the figure sitting motionless at his desk, dictating away, into the familiar oleograph portrait that hung over all the beds and dressers of the country and whose relentless, frozen gaze watched the people, day and night . . .

Rubashov paced up and down inside his cell, from the door to the window and back, between the cot, the basin, and the bucket, six and a half steps there, six and a half steps back.

Right-face at the door, left-face at the window—it was an old trick: if you didn't change the direction of the turn you quickly became dizzy. What was going on inside the brain of Number One? As he roamed up and down he imagined a cross section of this brain, neatly rendered with gray watercolor on a sheet of paper tacked to a drawing board. The convolutions of gray matter swelled like intestines; they coiled around each other like muscular snakes and frayed into an indistinct blur, like the spiral nebulae in astronomical charts. What went on inside the swollen gray bulges? We knew all there was to know about distant galaxies but nothing about that: the notion that history was more oracle than science must have had something to do with this. Perhaps one day, far in the future, people would teach history using painted tables of economic statistics, augmented with similar anatomical cross sections. The teacher would write an algebraic formula on the blackboard that described the living conditions of a specific nation in a specific epoch: "Here, citizens, you see the objective factors that determined the historical process." And then direct a pointer at a gray, nebulous landscape between the second and third cerebral lobes of Number One: "And here you see the subjective reflection of those factors. It is this that led to the ascendancy of the power principle . . ." Until mankind reached that point, politics would be confined to bloody dilettantism, nothing but superstition and black magic.

Rubashov heard several men marching in unison down the corridor. His first thought was that they were coming to beat him. He stopped in midpace, thrust out his chin, and listened. The steps halted in front of a cell, a quiet command was uttered, the key ring jangled. Then silence.

Rubashov stood rigid between his cot and the bucket, holding his breath and waiting for the first scream. He reminded himself that the first scream was usually the worst, when the horror still eclipsed the physical pain—what came later was easier to bear, you got used to it, and after a while you could even tell the type of torture from the tone and rhythm of the yelling. Toward the end most people behaved the same way, no matter how they might vary in temperament and voice: the cries would grow weaker and ultimately fade into whimpering and gulping air, which meant the torturers had let up. At that point the cell door would usually clang shut, the keys would jangle once again, and the first scream of the next victim would typically be heard even before they laid hands on him, the minute the torture patrol appeared in the door.

Rubashov stood still in the middle of his cell and waited for the first scream. He rubbed his pince-nez on his sleeve and told himself that this time, too, he would not scream, no matter what they did to him. He repeated this sentence soundlessly and evenly, the way you pray the rosary. He stood and listened; still no scream. Nothing but the stifled, naked silence of the prison corridor. Then he heard a quiet jangle, a voice mumbled something, the cell door shut. Again in unison, the steps headed to the next cell.

Rubashov went to the spy hole and peered into the corridor. The men had stopped diagonally opposite his cell, in front of Number 407. It was the breakfast procession, consisting of the old warder, two trusties pulling a vat with tea, a third carrying a basket with slices of black bread, and two uniformed guards with pistol belts. They weren't beating anyone, they were doling out breakfast. Number 407 was just receiving his bread. Rubashov could not see the man—he was probably standing in his cell in the regulation position, one step behind the door; all Rubashov could make out were his hands and forearms. The man's arms were naked and very thin; they stuck straight out of the doorframe into the corridor like two parallel sticks. The palms of the invisible Number 407 were turned upward and cupped into a bowl. Once they had received the bread, the hands closed and withdrew into the invisibility of the cell. The door of Number 407 slammed shut.

Rubashov left the spy hole and resumed his march through

the cell. He stopped rubbing his pince-nez on his sleeve, put it back in place, breathed deeply and with pleasure. He whistled as he waited for his breakfast, untroubled but for the disquieting sight of those thin arms and cupped hands, which vaguely reminded him of something he could not define. He didn't know what it was, only that it had been a long time ago, but the outline of those outstretched hands and even the shadows on them seemed familiar—some familiar image that had wafted in from his memory, like the scraps of a melody or the smell of a narrow harbor alley . . .

7.

The procession had already opened and shut a row of doors, but not yet his. Rubashov went back to the spy hole to see when they were finally coming; he was looking forward to the hot tea. He had seen steam rising from the vat and thin slices of lemon floating on the tea. He took off his pince-nez and pressed his eye to the peephole. He could make out four of the opposite cells: Numbers 401 to 407. Overhead was a narrow iron walkway that resembled a balcony; behind that were more cells, on the third floor. The procession was just coming back down the corridor, from the right; evidently they first took care of the odd-numbered cells, then the even. They were now in front of Number 408. All Rubashov could see were the backs of the two uniformed guards with the pistol belts; the rest were still outside his view. The door clanged shut and the procession moved to Number 406. Rubashov once again saw the steaming vat and the trusty with the bread basket; only a few slices were left. The door of Number 406 was immediately locked back up; the cell was uninhabited. The procession approached his cell, passed his door, and stopped at Number 402.

Rubashov started drumming on his door with his fists. He saw the trusties with the tea exchange glances and look in his direction. The warder busied himself with his keys outside Number 402 and acted as though he hadn't heard anything. The two uniforms stood with their backs to Rubashov's spy hole. Bread was being passed through the door of Number 402; the procession was bound to move on at any second. Rubashov drummed louder. He pulled off a shoe and used it to bang on the door.

The taller of the two guards slowly turned around, looked at Rubashov's door with no expression, and turned away. The warder locked the door of Number 402. The trusties with the vat of tea stood there, uncertain what to do. The guard who had turned around said something to the old warder, who shrugged his shoulders and shuffled to Rubashov's door, with jangling keys. The trusties with the tea followed, while the bread trusty stayed where he was and said something through the spy hole to Number 402.

Rubashov stepped back from his door and waited for it to open. The tension inside him suddenly broke off and he now didn't care whether he got tea or not. Besides, the tea had stopped steaming on the way back down the corridor, and the lemon slices on what remained of the bright yellow fluid had looked wilted and shrunken.

The key turned in his door, then a pupil stared through the spy hole and disappeared again. The door flew open. Meanwhile Rubashov had sat down on the cot and put his shoe back on. The warder held the door for the tall guard, who stepped into the cell. He had a round shaved skull and expressionless eyes. His stiff officer's uniform squeaked, as did his boots; Rubashov believed he could smell the leather of his pistol belt. The guard stopped beside the bucket and looked around the cell, which his presence made more cramped.

"You haven't straightened up your cell," he said calmly to Rubashov. "And yet you know the regulations."

"Why was I passed over at breakfast?" asked Rubashov, equally calmly, peering at the guard through his pince-nez.

"If you wish to discuss the matter with me you will have to stand up," said the officer.

"I don't have the slightest desire or reason to discuss anything with you," said Rubashov, and tied his shoe.

"Then next time don't hammer on the door, or else we'll have to apply the usual disciplinary measures," said the officer. He looked around the cell once again. "The prisoner does not have a rag for cleaning the floor," he said to the warder. The warder said something to the bread trusty, who ran off down the corridor. The other two trusties stood in the open door and peered into the cell with curious eyes. The second guard turned away from the door and positioned himself in the corridor, with his legs spread out and his hands behind his back.

"The prisoner also does not have a bowl for eating," said Rubashov, still busy tying his shoe. "Presumably you're trying to spare me the trouble of a hunger strike. I admire your new methods."

"You are mistaken," said the officer, and looked at him blankly. The man had a broad scar on his shaved skull and wore a ribbon in his buttonhole—a revolutionary banner of honor. *So he was in the civil war*, Rubashov thought. *But that was long ago and no longer makes any difference.*

"You are mistaken. You were passed over at breakfast because you had declared yourself sick."

"Toothache," said the old warder, who was leaning against the door. He was still in his slippers, and his uniform was wrinkled and stained with food.

"Have it your way," said Rubashov. He had a sharp retort on the tip of his tongue—about whether this was the latest achievement of the regime, treating the sick by withholding food, but all he said was "Have it your way." He was fed up with the whole scene.

The bread trusty came running back, panting and waving a dirty rag. The warder took the rag out of his hand and tossed it in the corner next to the bucket.

"Do you have any other wishes?" asked the officer without irony.

"Just drop your comedy and leave me in peace," said Rubashov. The officer turned to leave; the warder rattled his key ring. Rubashov went to his window and turned his back on them. After they had locked the door he remembered the most important thing and in one bound he was back at the door. "Paper and pencil," he yelled at full volume through the spy hole. He quickly took his pince-nez off and pressed his eye to the hole, to see if they turned around. He had shouted very loudly, but the procession kept moving down the corridor as if they hadn't heard. The last he saw of them was the back of the shaven-headed officer, with the broad belt and the holster containing his revolver.

8.

Rubashov resumed his march through the cell, six and a half steps to the window, six and a half steps back. The incident had troubled him; he replayed the details in his thoughts as he rubbed his pince-nez on his sleeve. He tried to hold on to the hatred he had felt for a few moments toward the officer with the scar, since that could help stiffen his backbone for the coming battle. Instead he once again succumbed to the familiar, fatal compulsion of placing himself in his opponent's shoes and viewing the scene through his eyes. There he—meaning Rubashov—sat on the cot, small and arrogant, with his pointy beard, pulling his shoe on over his sweaty sock, with the clear intention of provoking. Sure, this Rubashov had his merits and his great past, but the way he came across on his straw tick in the cell was a far cry from how he looked giving a speech at the party congress. *And that's supposed to be the legendary Rubashov?* Rubashov thought in the name of the officer with the expressionless eyes. *Yammering about breakfast like a schoolboy and isn't even ashamed. His cell not cleaned up. Hole in his sock. Pigheaded intellectual. Conspired against the system and the state; whether for money or sheer dogmatism, it's all the same. We didn't make the revolution for bellyachers. Of course, he helped make it, back then he was a regular guy, but now he's old and dogmatic, ripe for liquidation. Maybe he was even then; the revolution had its share of windbags that were deflated later on. If he had a smidgen of self-respect he'd straighten up his cell.*

For a moment Rubashov wondered whether he really ought to mop the floor. He stood in the middle of the cell, undecided, then put his pince-nez back on and went to the window.

The yard was now in daylight. The light was bright gray with a yellow tinge but even so not unfriendly; new snow was looming in the sky. He reckoned it might be near eight o'clock in the morning; it had only been three hours since he had first stepped into this cell. The walls that enclosed the yard resembled the walls of barracks; all the windows had the same iron grating, and the cells behind were too dark to see inside. It was impossible to tell if someone was standing right behind his window and looking down into the snow-filled yard, just like he was doing. The snow was pretty and slightly frozen over and undoubtedly crunched when stepped on. It was piled high enough to form a parapet on either side of the circular path that ran ten steps away from the wall. On the perimeter opposite Rubashov's cell the guard marched up and down. Once as he was making an about-face he spat in a wide arc down into the snow, then leaned over the wall to see where his spit had landed and frozen.

The old disease, thought Rubashov. *Revolutionaries aren't allowed to think through the minds of others.*

Or perhaps they are? Perhaps that's what they of all people should do?

How can you change the world if you're thinking through every brain at once?

Where can someone prone to understanding and forgiveness still find the motivation to act?

Where woudn't *he find the motivation to act?*

They're going to shoot me, thought Rubashov. *No one will care about my motives.* He leaned his head against the window-pane. The yard lay white and still.

He stood that way for some time, feeling the cool glass against his forehead, without thinking. Only gradually did he become aware of a ticking sound in the cell; it had been going on for some time, quiet but persistent.

He turned around and listened. The tapping was so faint that at first he couldn't tell which wall it was coming from. As he was listening it stopped. Rubashov tapped back, first on the wall next to the bucket, over near Number 406, but there was no reply. Then he tried the wall separating him from Number 402, next to the cot. This time he heard an answer. So he settled comfortably on the cot, from where he could keep an eye on the spy hole. His heart was pounding. He smiled—the first contact was always very exciting.

Number 402 was now tapping regularly: three times with short intervals, then a pause, then again three times, then another pause, then three more times. Rubashov repeated the same series to signal he was listening. He was eager to know if the other man knew the quadratic tapping alphabet, otherwise he was in for a lot of drudgery before he could teach it to his neighbor. The wall was too thick to carry sound well; he had to lean his head against it to hear clearly, while constantly keeping an eye on the spy hole. Apparently Number 402 was very practiced; he tapped clearly, without haste, and probably with a hard object such as a pencil. Since he was out of practice, Rubashov tried to visualize the letter square—five rows, each with five letters, with C also serving as K—as he memorized the numbers. Number 402 tapped five times—so fifth row, V to Z—then twice: second letter of the row. Then a pause, then twice—second row, F to J—then three times: the third letter of that row. Then three taps and four taps: third row, fourth letter, O. End.

WHO?

The man gets right to the point, thought Rubashov. *He wants to know who he's dealing with.* This was actually a breach of revolutionary tap etiquette, which called for a certain order: start with a political slogan, next transmit news, then turn to eating and tobacco, and only much later, often after days if at all, was there a personal introduction. Admittedly Rubashov's experience was limited to countries where the revolutionary party was the object of persecution and not the perpetrator, where conspiratorial reasons dictated that party members knew one another by first name only—and these were changed so often as to render all names meaningless. Apparently it was different here. Rubashov hesitated over whether he should give his name. Number 402 was getting impatient and repeated the question:

WHO?

Why not? thought Rubashov. He tapped out his complete name—NIKOLAI SALMANOVICH RUBASHOV—and waited for the effect.

For a long time there was nothing. Rubashov smiled; he could imagine his neighbor's shock. He waited one full minute, then another, then finally shrugged his shoulders and stood up from the cot. He resumed his walk through the cell, but at every turn he paused and went to the wall to listen. The wall stayed mute. He rubbed his glasses on his sleeve, then shuffled over to the door and peered through the spy hole.

The corridor was empty; the electric lamps spread their stale, flat light; not a sound could be heard. Why had Number 402 gone silent?

Probably out of fear. Presumably he was afraid that contact with Rubashov might compromise him. Perhaps Number 402 was an apolitical doctor or engineer who trembled at the thought of his dangerous neighbor. Clearly not a political, otherwise he wouldn't have asked for the name right away. He was likely caught up in some story about sabotage, had been inside for a good while, had perfected the tapping, and was consumed with the desire to prove his innocence. He was probably clinging to the naïve belief that his subjective guilt or innocence made any difference and had no idea of the greater context, the higher matters at stake. In all likelihood he was just sitting on his cot writing his hundredth petition to some official who never read them, or the hundredth letter to his wife, which would never reach her. In his despair he'd probably let his beard grow, a black Pushkin beard; stopped washing himself; and gotten used to biting his nails or indulging in private sexual excesses. Nothing was worse in prison than the awareness of one's own innocence; it made it harder to adapt and undermined the morale . . . All of a sudden the ticking resumed.

Rubashov quickly sat down on his cot, but he'd already missed the first two letters. Number 402 was now tapping hastily and less clearly, evidently very agitated:

. . . RVES YOU RIGHT.

"Serves you right . . ."

That was a surprise. So Number 402 was a conformist. He hated the oppositional heretics, as was proper, was convinced his own arrest was based on a misunderstanding, and that the foreign and domestic catastrophes of the recent years, from China to Spain, from famine to the extermination of the old guard, were either mere minor lapses or could be traced to the fiendish machinations of Rubashov and his oppositional friends. The Pushkin beard was gone; Number 402 now had a smooth-shaven, fanatical face, his cell meticulously clean and strictly maintained like in a military barrack. There was no sense in arguing with him; this type could not be reasoned with. Still, it made even less sense for Rubashov to relinquish his only and perhaps his last connection . . .

WHO? tapped Rubashov, very distinctly and slowly.

The answer came in fits and starts:

NONE OF YOUR BUSINESS.

HAVE IT YOUR WAY, Rubashov tapped slowly, then stood up and resumed his pacing, since he considered the conversation over. But the tapping came right back, this time very loud, resonant, and simultaneously scornful—Number 402 had evidently taken off a shoe to give his words greater emphasis:

LONG LIVE HIS IMPERIAL MAJESTY!

Voilà, thought Rubashov. *There still are some genuine bona fide counterrevolutionaries—and we thought the only place they existed was in the speeches of Number One, as scapegoats for some failure or another. Meanwhile here is the real thing, a flesh-and-blood alibi for Number One, shouting "Long live His Majesty," just as he should . . .*

AMEN.

Rubashov tapped and grinned. The answer came immediately, possibly even louder:

SWINE!

Rubashov was amused. He took off his pince-nez and tapped with the metal rim, to vary the tone, quietly and genteelly:

DON'T UNDERSTAND.

Number 402 seemed to be having a fit. DO— he hammered against the wall, but the G didn't come. Then his rage seemed to vanish abruptly and he tapped:

WHY DID THEY LOCK YOU UP?

How wonderfully naïve . . . Number 402's face went through another change. It became that of an imperial officer, handsome and stupid. Perhaps he wore a monocle. Rubashov tapped with his pince-nez:

POLITICAL DIFFERENCES.

Short pause. Number 402 was evidently cudgeling his brain to find an ironic reply. Then it came: BRAVO! THE WOLVES DEVOUR EACH OTHER!

Rubashov didn't answer. His need for company was satisfied; he resumed his wandering. But the officer from 402 now turned talkative. He tapped lightly:

RUBASHOV . . .

This was getting downright intimate.

YES? answered Rubashov.

Number 402 seemed to hesitate, then came a fairly long sentence:

WHEN DID YOU LAST SLEEP WITH A WOMAN?

Number 402 definitely wore a monocle; he was probably using it to tap, and the uncovered eye was blinking nervously. Rubashov did not feel disgusted. At least 402 was acting true to form, in any case more sympathetic than if he had tapped out editorials. Rubashov thought for a moment, then tapped:

THREE WEEKS AGO.

The answer came at once:

TELL ME!

This was going a little too far. Rubashov's first impulse was to break off the conversation, but then he considered the man might prove very useful, and hearing him out might incline him to connect Rubashov to Number 400 and the further cells. The cell to his left was evidently uninhabited, so the chain broke off there. Rubashov regretted that he had no practice in officers' casino conversation. He remembered an old chanson from before the war, one he had heard as a student somewhere in a cabaret, where ladies in black stockings had danced the French can-can; he sighed and tapped with his pince-nez:

BREASTS LIKE APPLES, ROUND AND FIRM.

Hopefully that was the right tone. Evidently it was, because Number 402 pressed for more:

GO ON. DETAILS . . .

Now the man was probably tugging nervously on his whiskers. He was sure to have a small moustache, with twirled ends. Damn him, he was his only connection; Rubashov had to play up to him. What do they talk about in the officers' casinos?

Women and horses . . . Rubashov rubbed his pince-nez on his sleeve and tapped painstakingly:

THIGHS LIKE A WILD MARE'S . . .

He stopped, exhausted. He couldn't possibly come up with more. But Number 402 was extremely pleased:

DEVIL OF A FELLOW! he tapped, excited. No doubt the man was now laughing raucously, but Rubashov couldn't hear anything; he was slapping his thighs and twirling his moustache, but Rubashov couldn't see anything. The abstract obscenity of the mute wall made him cringe.

MORE . . . , Number 402 urged.

He couldn't. FINIS— Rubashov tapped, exasperated, and immediately regretted it. He couldn't afford to antagonize Number 402. But the man refused to get annoyed and doggedly tapped with his monocle:

MORE—PLEASE, PLEASE . . .

Rubashov was now enough back in practice that he didn't have to consciously count out the taps but was able to transpose them directly into his audial perception. He believed he could make out the intonation that Number 402 was using to beg for more erotic material. The begging repeated itself:

PLEASE—PLEASE . . .

Number 402 must still be a young man and had to be suffering greatly. He had probably grown up in exile, the scion of an old officer family, sent back home with a false passport but nabbed right away. He was probably still tugging on his little moustache, had stuck his monocle back in, and was staring at the whitewashed wall, listening.

MORE—PLEASE, PLEASE . . .

. . . Staring and staring at the mute wall, whose moist stains gradually took on the outlines of the woman with the apple breasts and marelike thighs.

TELL ME MORE—PLEASE, PLEASE . . .

Perhaps he was kneeling on his cot, beseeching with his

hands, like the prisoner across the corridor who had received the bread.

And suddenly Rubashov remembered what that gesture had reminded him of, the outstretched, cupped hands of the invisible bread recipient . . . Pietà . . .

9.

Pietà . . . A Monday afternoon inside a museum in the middle of Germany. Not a soul was present apart from Rubashov and the young man he had traveled to meet. Their conversation took place on a round, plush sofa in the center of an empty gallery whose walls were draped with tons of heavy female flesh by Flemish masters. It was 1933, during the first months of terror, shortly before Rubashov's arrest. The movement was shattered, its members hunted down like game and beaten to death. The party was no longer a political organization but a thousand-armed, thousand-legged mass of bleeding flesh. Just as hair and fingernails continue to grow after death, individual cells, muscles, and limbs of the dead party continued to stir. Scattered throughout the country were little groups of people who had survived the catastrophe and continued to conspire underground. They met in cellars, forests, train stations, museums, and gymnasiums. They constantly changed their sleeping quarters, their names, their habits. They knew each other by first name only and did not ask each other for addresses. They placed their lives in each other's hands and didn't trust one another an inch. They manufactured leaflets in which they lied to themselves and to the others that they were still alive. At night they stole through narrow streets on the edge of town and scrawled the old slogans on the walls to prove that they were still alive. Before dawn they climbed the factory smokestacks and hung the old banners to prove that they were still alive. Few people saw the leaflets and those who did quickly threw them away, because they were terrified by the message from the dead; the slogans on the walls were erased at the first cockcrow, and the banners were pulled down from the smokestacks, but they kept reappearing. Because throughout the land were little groups of people who called themselves dead men on furlough and who devoted what was left of their lives to prove that they still had them.

They had no contact with each other; the nerve fibers of the party were torn, each group was on its own. Little by little they started putting out feelers once again. Respectable salesmen arrived from abroad, traveling on counterfeit passports and carrying suitcases with false bottoms—these were the couriers. As a rule they were caught, tortured, and beheaded; others took their place. The party stayed dead; it could neither breathe nor move, but its hair and nails continued to grow, and from abroad the central leadership sent galvanic currents through its rigid body, causing the limbs to twitch and convulse.

Pietà . . . Rubashov forgot about Number 402 and returned to his six and a half there, six and a half back. He was once again on the plush sofa in the empty gallery, which smelled of dust and floor wax. He had gone straight from the train station to the designated meeting place and arrived a few minutes early. He was fairly sure he wasn't being watched. His suitcase, which contained samples of novel dental devices from a Dutch company, was in the cloakroom. Rubashov sat on the round, plush sofa, stared through his pince-nez at the masses of soft flesh on the walls, and waited.

The young man, who called himself Richard and who at present was party leader in this city, arrived a few minutes late. Neither man had ever seen the other. Richard had already passed through two empty rooms when he spotted Rubashov on the round sofa. Rubashov had a book on his lap: the Reclam edition of *The Sorrows of Young Werther*. When he noticed the book, the young man glanced discreetly around the room, then sat down on the sofa next to Rubashov. He was a little embarrassed and sat about half a meter away from Rubashov, on the edge of the sofa, with his cap on his knees. He was a locksmith by profession and wore a black Sunday suit, since he knew his work coat would stick out in the museum. "So," he said, "you'll have to excuse my coming late."

"That's fine," said Rubashov. "First let's go through your people. Do you have a list?"

The young man named Richard shook his head. "I don't have lists," he said. "I keep it all in my head—addresses and everything."

"That's fine," said Rubashov. "But if you're caught no one will know what's what."

"Actually," said Richard, "just in case that happens I gave a list to Anni. She's my wife, you see."

He paused and swallowed, causing his Adam's apple to move up and down several times, and for the first time looked directly at Rubashov. Rubashov saw that his eyes were slightly bulging and bloodshot, streaked with red veins, and that his chin and cheeks showed stubble over the black collar of the Sunday suit. "You see, Anni was arrested last night," he said, and looked at Rubashov, and Rubashov could see in his eyes the vague and senseless hope that he, the emissary from the central leadership, could work a miracle and come to his aid.

"In other words," said Rubashov, rubbing his pince-nez on his sleeve, "the police have gotten hold of the entire list."

"No," said Richard. "My sister-in-law was in the apartment when they came for Anni, you see, and she managed to quickly hand it over to her. The thing is safe with my sister-in-law. You see, she's married to a constable but she's on our side."

"I see," said Rubashov. "And where were you when they arrested your wife?"

"It was like this," said Richard. "I haven't been sleeping at home for a few months now. I have a friend who's a movie projectionist, I'm able to get inside his place, and after the show's over I can sleep in the projection booth. You can enter straight off the street, using the fire escape. And all the movies I want, for nothing . . ." He paused and swallowed. "Anni used to get free tickets from my friend, and when it was dark, she would look up to the projection booth. She couldn't see me of course, but now and then I got a good glimpse of her face, when there was a lot of light on the screen . . ."

He went silent. Directly opposite Richard was a *Last Judgment*—curly-headed angels with ample buttocks were flying into a storm, blowing their trumpets. To Richard's left was an ink sketch by a German master, mostly obscured by the plush back of the sofa and Richard's head, so that Rubashov could only make out a small part—Mary's gaunt hands cupped upward, and a piece of empty heaven, with horizontal quill marks. He couldn't see any more because Richard's head stayed fixed as he spoke, his reddish neck bent slightly forward.

"I see," said Rubashov. "How old is your wife?"

"She's seventeen," said Richard.

"I see. And how old are you?"

"Nineteen," said Richard.

"I'm guessing you don't have children?" asked Rubashov, and craned his neck a little, but still couldn't see any more of the sketch.

"The first is on the way," said Richard, rooted to his chair.

Rubashov paused a moment, then asked Richard to recite the list of members. It contained some thirty names. Rubashov asked questions and entered a few addresses in his sales order book for the Dutch dental specimens—filling the blanks in a long row of local dentists, technicians, and respectable citizens taken from the telephone book. When they were done, Richard said:

"Now I would like to give you a brief report about our work, comrade."

"That's fine," said Rubashov. "I'm listening."

Richard reported. He sat slightly hunched over on the narrow sofa, away from Rubashov, and rested his large, red hands on the knees of his Sunday suit. He spoke without even once changing his position. As dry and matter-of-fact as an accountant, he described the banners on the smokestacks, the slogans on the walls, the leaflets left in the toilets at the factory. Across from him the trumpeting angels rushed into the storm, behind his neck the invisible Virgin stretched out her gaunt hands, and all around them prodigious breasts, thighs, and hips stared out from the walls . . .

Breasts like apples, Rubashov remembered. He stopped on the third black tile from the cell window and listened to see if Number 402 was still tapping. The wall was quiet. Rubashov went to the spy hole and looked across toward Number 407, who had stretched his hands out for the bread, but all he saw was the gray painted door and the small black socket of the peephole. The corridor was lit as always with electric light and so bleak and still that he couldn't believe that there were people living behind the doors . . .

As Richard gave his report, Rubashov did not interrupt. Out of the thirty men and women whom Richard had assembled following the catastrophe, seventeen were still around. Two, a factory worker and his girl, had flung themselves out the window when they were about to be arrested. One had deserted and fled the city and vanished without a trace. Two were suspected of being police informants, although it was unclear whether they really were. Three had left the party in protest against the policies of the central leadership; two of them had founded a new oppositional group; the third had joined the moderates. Five had been arrested, including Anni, last night—and of these two were known to be dead. That left seventeen, who were still distributing leaflets and writing on walls.

Richard reported very exactly so that Rubashov would understand all the personal connections, since these were especially important. Richard didn't realize that party headquarters had their own man inside the group and that Rubashov had already learned most of what had happened from this man. Nor did Richard know that this confidant was none other than the projectionist with the booth where he was sleeping, and who for a long time had been intimately involved with Anni, who had been arrested the night before. Richard didn't know all this, but Rubashov did. Because even though the movement was in ruins, the apparatus for surveillance and collecting information was still intact. That was perhaps the only thing that was still functioning, and Rubashov happened to be in charge of it at that moment—another thing that bullnecked young Richard with the Sunday suit didn't know. All he knew was that the police had come for Anni and that he and his comrades had to go on distributing leaflets and scribbling on walls and that he should trust the man from headquarters like a father, although he couldn't show this or betray any weakness, because whoever was soft and given to emotions wasn't up to the task and had to be cast out into the void, forsaken and alone.

Steps were coming down the corridor. Rubashov went to the door, removed his pince-nez, and pressed his eye against the spy hole. Two of the officials with leather holsters were leading a young man—from all appearances a country boy—down the corridor, followed by the elderly jailer with his keys. One of his eyes was swollen and there was blood on his upper lip; Rubashov watched him wipe his bloody nose on his sleeve, saw his dull and expressionless face. Further down the corridor, past Rubashov's field of vision, a cell door was opened and slammed shut. Then the officials and the warder came back down the corridor, this time unaccompanied.

Rubashov paced back and forth inside his cell. Once again he saw himself sitting on the plush sofa next to Richard, listening to the silence that had ensued after the young man had finished his report. Richard sat completely still, his hands on his knees, like someone who had confessed and was waiting for the priest to pronounce a penance. For a long time Rubashov didn't speak. Then he said:

"Are you finished?"

The young man nodded, his Adam's apple rising and falling.

"There are certain things in your report that aren't clear," said Rubashov. "You mentioned repeatedly the leaflets that you produced yourselves. We are familiar with them and their content was sharply criticized. They contained wordings that the party considers politically inadmissible."

Richard looked at him in shock, and his face turned red. Rubashov could actually see the skin above his jawbones getting hot and the bloodshot veins in his bulging eyes becoming even more pronounced.

"Meanwhile," Rubashov continued, "we have repeatedly furnished you with prepared printed material, including the thin paper edition of the official party organ. And you did receive what we sent."

Richard nodded. The heat did not leave his face.

"But you failed to distribute our material, you didn't even mention it in your report, and instead you handed out your own—without the party's approval or authorization."

"But we h-had to," Richard gasped, clearly under great strain. Rubashov looked at him carefully through his pince-nez; only now did he notice the young man was an occasional stutterer. *That's strange . . .* , he thought, *the third case in fourteen days. Our human material is very defective. It's either because of the circumstances we have to work in or else the movement fosters a defective selection.*

"Y-you have to understand, c-comrade," said Richard. He was sounding more and more agitated. "Th-the tone of your p-propaganda was wrong, b-because—"

"Lower your voice," said Rubashov suddenly and sharply. "And don't look at the door."

A tall young man wearing the black uniform of the dictatorship's special guard had stepped into the room, together with his girl. The girl was blond; the man had slung his arm around her broad hips, and her arm was draped over his shoulder. They

paid no notice to Rubashov and Richard and stopped in front
of the trumpeting angels, with their backs to the sofa.

"Keep talking," said Rubashov in a calm, muffled voice,
and reflexively fished his cigarette case out of his pocket. Then
he remembered that smoking was prohibited in museums and
stuck the case back in his pocket. The young comrade sat as
if paralyzed from an electric shock and stared at the couple.
"Keep talking," Rubashov repeated quietly. "Did you stutter as
a child? Answer and don't look."

"O-only s-sometimes," Richard managed to utter with great
difficulty.

The couple moved along the row of paintings and stopped in
front of a nude portrait of a very corpulent woman staring out
at the viewer as she reclined on a velvet chaise. The man whispered something apparently funny, because the girl giggled and
stole a glance at the two figures on the sofa. Then the couple
moved on to a still life with dead pheasants and fruits.

"Sh-shouldn't we leave?" asked Richard.

"No," said Rubashov. He was afraid the young man might
be so agitated he would attract attention if he stood up. "They'll
be going soon. Where we're sitting it's so dark they can't see us
clearly anyway. Take a few slow, deep breaths, that will help."

The girl giggled again; the couple strolled leisurely toward
the exit. As they passed they both turned toward Rubashov
and Richard. Just as they were about to leave the hall the
girl pointed at the ink sketch of the pietà and they stood in
front of the picture. "D-does it b-bother you much, wh-when
I s-stutter?" asked Richard quietly, and looked down at the
ground.

"One has to maintain control," said Rubashov dryly. At this
point he couldn't allow any familiarity to enter the conversation.

"It w-will get b-better in a m-minute," said Richard, his Adam's apple bobbing frantically up and down. "An-anni always
laughed at me."

As long as the couple was in the hall, Rubashov couldn't steer the conversation. Nor could he move; the man in uniform had backed so close that Rubashov was penned in next to Richard. The common threat did seem to help the boy get over his shyness; he even inched a little closer to Rubashov on the sofa.

"But she liked me in s-spite of that," he whispered. Now his agitation was different, calmer. "I n-never really understood her. She didn't w-want the child, but she couldn't get r-rid of it. M-maybe they w-won't do anything to her b-because she's pregnant. You can't r-really tell though. D-do you think they also b-beat pregnant women?"

He nodded with his chin in the direction of the man in uniform, who just then turned his head toward Richard. For a few seconds they looked at each other. The man said something to the girl and she turned as well. Once again Rubashov reached for his cigarette case, but he let go of it while his hand was still in his pocket. The girl said something and pulled the man away with her. The couple slowly left the hall, the man somewhat hesitantly. Rubashov and Richard heard the girl giggle again in the next room and her steps as she moved away.

Richard turned to watch them leave, and when he moved his head Rubashov could see a little more of the sketch—the thin arms of the Virgin, up to the elbow. They were the skinny arms of a little girl, reaching weightlessly toward the invisible cross.

Rubashov looked at his watch. The boy slid a bit further away without even realizing it.

"We have to finish up," said Rubashov. "If I've understood you correctly, comrade, you said you intentionally refused to distribute our material because you didn't approve of the content. Nor did we approve of the content of your leaflets. Of course you realize, comrade, that there must be certain consequences."

Richard turned to him with his bloodshot eyes. Then he again sank his head. "You know yourself it contained pure nonsense." His voice was quiet and flat, and he was suddenly no longer stuttering.

"I don't know anything about that," said Rubashov dryly.

"You wrote as though nothing had happened," said the boy in the same tired, sleepy voice. "They smashed the party to a pulp and all we got were empty phrases about the unbroken will for victory, nothing but a heap of lies, just like in the world war. Whoever we showed it to just spat. But you know all that yourself."

Rubashov observed the boy, who was now completely hunched forward, with his elbows on his knees and his chin on his red fists. He answered matter-of-factly:

"That's the second time you're ascribing to me an opinion I don't share. I have to ask you to desist."

Richard slowly turned, his bloodshot eyes gaping at Rubashov in disbelief. Rubashov continued:

"Our party is undergoing a difficult trial. Other revolutionary parties have been through more. The will of the party must remain unbroken. Whoever now turns soft and sentimental does not belong in our ranks. Anyone who contributes to a state of panic is playing into the hands of the enemy, no matter what he believes. His actions make him harmful to the movement and therefore he must be treated correspondingly."

Richard kept his chin propped on his fists, his face now fully turned toward Rubashov.

"So I'm harmful to the movement," he said. "I'm playing into the hands of the enemy. Perhaps I'm even being paid for that. Anni, too, no doubt."

"Your leaflets," Rubashov went on in the same dry tone, "which you admit to authoring, are full of sentences such as: 'we have suffered a defeat, we have been hit with a catastrophe, we have to start anew and change our politics from the ground up.' This is defeatism. It's demoralizing and cripples the fighting strength of the movement."

"I only know," said Richard, "that you have to tell people

the truth, because they know it anyway. Trying to feed them a lie is absurd."

"The party leadership," Rubashov went on, "has declared that the party has not suffered a defeat but has made a strategic temporary retreat, and that there is no reason to depart from its previous political course."

"That's rubbish," said Richard.

"If you continue in this tone," said Rubashov, "we will have to break off this discussion."

Richard was silent for a while. Inside the gallery the light was growing dim; the contours of the angels and the female figures on the walls were becoming even softer and more indistinct.

"Sorry," said Richard. "I mean: the party leadership is mistaken. You speak of a 'strategic retreat' when more than half of our people have been killed and the ones left are happy to be alive and are running to the others in droves . . . No one here understands all the hairsplitting that you people are coming up with over there, on the outside . . ."

Richard's features also began to blur in the dimming light. He paused a moment, then added:

"So I guess Anni was making a strategic retreat last night as well. But I understand—all of us here are living in a jungle . . ."

Rubashov waited to see if he was going to say something else, but Richard was silent. Dusk continued to fall. Rubashov took off his pince-nez and rubbed it on his sleeve.

"The party cannot be wrong," said Rubashov. "You and I can make mistakes—but not the party. The party, comrade, is more than you and me and a thousand others like us. The party is the embodiment of the revolutionary idea in history. History knows no vacillating and no consideration for feelings. It flows, powerfully and unerringly, toward its goal. On every bend it deposits debris and sludge and the bodies of the drowned. But—it knows its course. History doesn't make mistakes. Anyone who doesn't have this unconditional faith in the party doesn't belong in its ranks."

Richard stayed silent, his head propped on his fists, his face turned toward Rubashov, completely frozen. Because he said nothing, Rubashov continued:

"You impeded the distribution of our material, suppressed the voice of the party. You distributed leaflets in which every word was wrong and detrimental. You wrote: 'The ruins of the revolutionary movement must be gathered up and united to oppose the hostile forces of tyranny; we must forget the old internal conflict and together begin the fight anew.' That is wrong. For the party there can be no affiliation with the moderates. They were the ones who betrayed the movement countless times with their bourgeois morality, and they will do it again the next time and the time after that. Whoever engages in compromises with them is burying the revolution. You wrote: 'If the house is burning, everyone must put out the flames; if we continue to fight over doctrine we will all be burned to ashes.' That is wrong. We are fighting the fire with water, the others with oil. First it must be determined which method is correct, water or oil, before one unites the fire brigades. That is no way to make policy. No policy at all can come from despair and passion. The party's course is strictly marked out, an unswerving path in the mountains. The slightest misstep to the right or to the left results in a fall. The air is thin, whoever gets dizzy is lost . . ."

The light was now so far gone Rubashov could no longer see the hands in the sketch. A bell rang twice, emphatic and drawn out, signaling that the museum would close in fifteen minutes. Rubashov looked at his watch; he had yet to pronounce the decisive sentence, then it would be over. Richard sat next to him, still motionless, his elbows on his knees.

"Well, I have no reply to that," he said finally, and his voice was again toneless and very tired. "What you say is probably right. And the mountain path you are talking about is very beautiful. But all I know is that we've lost. And the ones left are leaving us. Maybe because it's too cold up there on the path. Maybe it's too cold here, comrade, in this country. The others have done a fine job warming up their own people. They have music and flags and they're sitting cozily around a warm stove. Maybe that's why they won. And why we're all finished."

Rubashov was silent. He wanted to hear if the young man had something else to add before he pronounced the decisive sentence. Nothing could change the content of the pronouncement, but he waited nonetheless.

Richard's heavy figure became less and less distinct. He had moved a little further away on the sofa, so that his back was now half turned to Rubashov; he sat hunched over with his face practically buried in his hands. Rubashov sat rigid and erect and waited. He felt a light, nagging pain in his upper jaw, probably the defective canine. After a while he heard Richard's voice:

"What's going to happen with me now?"

Rubashov probed the aching tooth with his tongue. He felt an urge to touch the place with his finger before pronouncing the verdict, but that was out of the question. He stated calmly:

"In the name of the leadership I am to inform you, Richard, that you are hereby expelled from the party."

Richard didn't move. Rubashov again waited awhile before he got up. Richard stayed seated. He lifted his head a little, glanced up at Rubashov, and asked:

"Is that why you came here?"

"Primarily," said Rubashov. He wanted to go but stood there and waited, with Richard sitting on the sofa.

"What will happen to me?" asked Richard. Rubashov said nothing. After a while Richard said:

"I guess I can't live in the comrade's projection room any longer."

After a slight hesitation Rubashov said:

"Better not."

He was immediately annoyed that he'd said that and wasn't sure whether Richard had understood the meaning. He looked down at the sitting figure.

"It's better if we leave separately. Farewell."

Richard sat up straight but stayed on the sofa. In the dim light of the room Rubashov could barely make out the bulging, bloodshot eyes, and yet it was this image—the seated figure with the blurred outlines—that was forever etched in his memory.

He left the gallery and crossed through the next one, which was just as empty and dim, with measured steps that creaked overly loud on the parquet. Not until he reached the exit did he realize he'd forgotten to look at the picture with the pietà; now all he would know was the cupped hands and two thin arms, cut off at the elbows.

Rubashov stopped on the stairs leading out to the street. His tooth had begun to hurt a little more. It was cool outside, and he wrapped his worn wool scarf more tightly around his neck. The lanterns on the grand, quiet plaza in front of the museum were already lit; only a few pedestrians were out at this hour; a narrow small-town tram came ringing down the avenue lined with elm trees. Rubashov looked around for a taxi.

Richard caught up with him on the bottommost landing. He was out of breath and must have gone running after Rubashov at the last moment. Rubashov kept moving without changing his speed and without turning around. Richard was half a head taller and much broader, but he hunched over and made himself smaller alongside Rubashov, and fit his gait to match the shorter man's. After a few steps he said:

"Was that supposed to be a warning, when I asked earlier if I could still stay at the comrade's and you said, 'Better not'?"

Rubashov saw a taxi with bright lights coming down the avenue. He stopped at the edge of the sidewalk and waited for it to come closer. Richard stood next to him. "I don't have anything more to say to you, Richard," he said. He waved to the taxi.

"Comrade—you can't possibly d-denounce me, comrade . . . ," said Richard. The taxi slowed down; it was only twenty steps away. Richard stood hunched over in front of Rubashov; he had grabbed the sleeve of Rubashov's winter coat and was speaking

straight into his face, so that Rubashov could feel his breath, the
moisture spraying on his forehead.

"You know that I'm not an en-enemy of the party," said
Richard. "You c-can't send me to the slaughter, c-comrade . . ."

The taxi stopped at the edge of the sidewalk; the driver must
have heard the last word. Rubashov quickly decided it was too
late to send the cab away; a policeman was posted a hundred
steps further down. The driver, an old man in a leather jacket,
looked at them with blank eyes.

"To the station," said Rubashov, and climbed in. The driver
reached back with his right hand and shut the door. Richard
stood on the edge of the sidewalk, holding his cap, his Adam's
apple bobbing quickly up and down. The taxi drove off toward
the policeman, then past the policeman. Because of the policeman Rubashov didn't want to look back, but he knew Richard
was still standing on the sidewalk's edge, watching the red tail-
lights of the taxi as it rode away.

For several minutes the streets were busy, and the driver
turned around a few times to look at Rubashov, as if he wanted
to make sure he was still there. Rubashov didn't know the city
well enough to tell if they were really heading toward the station. The streets were more and more deserted. At the end of a
boulevard a massive building came into view with a large illuminated clock, and they stopped in front of the station.

Rubashov climbed out. "What's the fare?" he asked—the
taxis in this town still didn't have a meter.

"Nothing," said the driver. His face was old and wrinkled;
he fished a dirty red cloth out of the pocket of his leather jacket
and took a long time to blow his nose.

Rubashov peered at him carefully through his pince-nez. He
was certain that he'd never seen the face before. The driver put
back his handkerchief. "For people like yourself it's always free,
sir," he said, and gripped the handbrake but didn't drive off.
All of a sudden he reached out his hand to Rubashov. It was an
old man's hand, with thick veins and black fingernails. "Have

a good trip, sir," he said, and smiled awkwardly. "If your colleague who was with you at the museum ever needs anything—my stand is in front of the museum, you can write down my number for him, sir."

Rubashov saw a porter to his right who was leaning against a pillar and watching. He placed a coin in the driver's outstretched hand and stepped into the station without saying goodbye.

He had to wait an hour for the train. He drank some stale coffee in the station cafeteria; his tooth was hurting badly. Once aboard the train he was so tired he dozed off. He dreamed that he was forced to run on the tracks ahead of the train. Richard and the driver were sitting in the train; they wanted to run him over because he'd cheated them out of the fare. The wheels rattled closer and closer, and his feet were crippled. He woke up feeling nauseous, with beads of cold sweat on his forehead; the people in the compartment were looking at him strangely. Outside it was night; the train was passing through the dark land of the enemy; the business with Richard had yet to be completed; his tooth ached. One week later he was arrested.

10.

Leaning his forehead against the window, Rubashov peered into the yard. His legs were tired and he felt a little dizzy from all the pacing. He checked his watch: eleven forty-five—he had been traipsing up and down his cell for nearly four hours straight, ever since he remembered the pietà. He wasn't surprised; he was familiar enough with prison daydreaming, the intoxicating effect of the whitewashed walls. He recalled hearing from a younger comrade—a barber's assistant—how in the second, most trying year of his solitary confinement the man had daydreamed for up to seven hours with his eyes wide open as he continued to pace. In that way he hiked more than seventeen miles in his cell, which was only five steps long, and hadn't even noticed the blisters on his soles.

Even so, it was happening a little fast this time; Rubashov had succumbed to this particular vice on the very first day, whereas it had taken weeks before. It was also strange that he'd been so focused on the past; chronically addicted prisoners almost always dreamed inside their cells about the future—and if they did dream about the past it was only to fantasize about how it *could have* transpired, never about how it actually did. Rubashov wondered what other surprises his brain held in store for him. He knew from experience that every confrontation with death changed the mechanism of thinking and triggered the most surprising reactions—like the needle of a compass close to the magnetic pole.

Snow was still looming in the sky, while down in the yard two men were taking their exercise around the shoveled path. One kept looking up at Rubashov's window: if this wasn't mere coincidence it meant that news of his arrest had already made the rounds. The man was thin, with a sallow complexion and a cleft lip. He had a flimsy raincoat wrapped tightly around his shoulders to ward off the cold. The other man was older and wore a blanket draped over his shoulders. They didn't speak to each other as they walked, and after ten minutes they were both called back inside by a uniformed official with a rubber truncheon and a pistol holster. The door where the official stood waiting was directly across from Rubashov's window; before it closed the man with the cleft lip cast one more glance up toward Rubashov. There was no way he could actually see Rubashov—the window was too dark viewed from the yard— but the man gazed at the window for some time, as though he was searching. Rubashov thought: *I see you and don't know you, meanwhile you don't see me and yet you know me.* Then he sat down on the cot, pulled out his pince-nez, and tapped to Number 402:

THE WALKER—WHO?

He didn't expect an answer, since he thought Number 402 might be offended. But the monocled officer didn't seem to carry a grudge and tapped back right away:

POLITICAL.

Rubashov was surprised; he had pegged the thin man with the cleft lip for a criminal.

YOUR KIND? he asked back.

NO—YOURS, tapped Number 402, undoubtedly grinning with a certain satisfaction. The next sentence came more forcefully, which meant he was probably again using the monocle:

HARELIP MY NEIGHBOR. CELL 400. TORTURED YESTERDAY.

Rubashov stayed quiet for a few seconds as he rubbed his pince-nez on his sleeve, even though he now used it only for tapping. At first he wanted to ask "why" but instead tapped:

HOW?

402 answered matter-of-factly:

STEAM BATH. NO BEATINGS HERE.

In that other country Rubashov had been beaten repeatedly, but he'd only heard about this particular method. It was his understanding that every known physical pain was bearable; if you knew in advance, then you could treat it like a surgical procedure—extracting a tooth, for instance. Far worse was not knowing what lay in store: because you had no way to gauge your ability to resist, there was no way to predict how you might react. And worst of all was the fear that you might do and say something that could never be rectified . . .

WHY? asked Rubashov.

POLITICAL DIFFERENCES, Number 402 tapped with clearly intended irony.

Rubashov put on his pince-nez and felt in his pocket for his cigarette case—only two left. Then he tapped:

AND HOW ARE THINGS WITH YOU?

EXCELLENT, THANK YOU . . . , tapped Number 402, cutting off any further questioning.

Rubashov shrugged his shoulders, lit his next-to-last cigarette, and resumed his pacing. Strangely, the prospect of what lay ahead seemed to brighten his mood. He felt the bland melancholy recede, his mind seemed refreshed, and his nerves seemed to tauten. He went to the basin and splashed the cold water on his face, arms, and torso, then rinsed his mouth and dried off with his handkerchief. He whistled a few bars of the toreador song from the famous opera and had to smile—his whistling had always been atrociously off-key. He remembered what someone had said to him a few days earlier: "If Number One were musical, he would have long since found some pretext to have you shot." "He'll find one anyway," Rubashov had quipped back, without seriously believing it.

He lit his last cigarette and began strategizing with a clear head. As he did, he felt the same calm, pleasant confidence he had experienced as a student before an especially difficult exam. He summoned everything he knew on the subject of "steam bath." He imagined the situation in detail, so he could analyze the expected physical sensations as technically as possible, in order to make them less unnerving. The main thing was not to get caught off guard. Now he felt certain they wouldn't manage to do that, just as the others hadn't managed over there, in the other country; he knew he wouldn't say anything that was irrevocable. He only wanted it to begin as soon as possible.

He remembered his dream with Richard and the old driver who had chased him because they felt he had betrayed them.

I'm going to pay the fare, he thought with an energetic smile.

He had smoked his last cigarette; it was still smoldering at his fingernails and he quickly dropped it. He started to stamp it out but then reconsidered, bent down, picked it up, and pressed the burning butt slowly into the back of his hand, between the winding, bluish veins. He stretched the procedure out for over half a minute, keeping an eye on the second hand of his watch. He was pleased with himself; his hand hadn't twitched once during the thirty seconds. Then he resumed his walk.

The eye that had been observing him for several minutes through the spy hole withdrew.

II.

A short while later the procession with the midday meal came down the corridor and once again bypassed Rubashov's cell. He did not go to the spy hole so as not to lose face. As a result he didn't discover what they served at midday, but the smell filtered into his cell, and it smelled good.

He felt an urgent need for a cigarette. It was clear he needed to get hold of some in order to concentrate; they were more important than food. He waited a half hour after the procession had passed, then began pounding on the door. The old warder took another fifteen minutes to get there. "What is it you want?" he asked in an unfriendly tone.

"I'd like someone to bring me cigarettes from the commissary," said Rubashov.

"Do you have any prison money?"

"They confiscated my money when I was brought in," said Rubashov.

"In that case you'll have to wait until it's converted into prison vouchers."

"How long will that take, here in your model institution?"

"You can write a complaint," said the old man.

"You know I don't have paper or a pencil," said Rubashov.

"You can't purchase writing materials without money," said the old man.

Rubashov distinctly felt his temper starting to rise—the pressure in his chest, the choking in his neck, the throbbing of the veins in his face—but kept himself under control. The warder saw Rubashov's eyes flash behind his pince-nez and was reminded of the oil prints he used to see everywhere, of Rubashov in uniform; he sneered and took half a step back.

"You little heap of dung," said Rubashov, slowly and clearly, then turned his back to the man and resumed his place at the window.

"I'm going to report that you insulted me," said the old man's voice to Rubashov's back, then the door clanged shut.

Rubashov rubbed his pince-nez on his sleeve and waited for his breathing to settle down. He absolutely had to procure some cigarettes—he needed them for the struggle ahead. He forced himself to wait ten minutes, then tapped to Number 402:

DO YOU HAVE TOBACCO?

Number 402 kept him waiting a little bit, then tapped, precisely and deliberately:

NOT FOR YOU.

Rubashov slowly returned to the window. He could picture his neighbor clearly: the young officer with the trim moustache had stuck his monocle back in and was now staring mindlessly at the wall that separated them; the eye behind the lens was glassy, the lid turned up and inflamed. What was going on inside his head? Maybe he was thinking: *We really gave it to you good.* And probably: *You scoundrel, how many of my kind have you had shot?* Rubashov gazed at the whitewashed wall; he could feel the other man facing him on the other side, even believed he could hear the man's agitated panting. *So, how many of your kind have I had shot?* In truth he couldn't remember exactly; it was long, long ago, during the civil war, perhaps between seventy and a hundred. What of it? That was fair enough, in a completely different category than Richard; he'd have done it all over again today. Even if he knew in advance that the revolution would put Number One in the saddle? Even then.

With you, Rubashov thought, looking at the whitewashed wall behind which the other man was standing—by now he'd probably lit a cigarette and was blowing smoke at the wall—*with you I don't have any accounts to settle. I don't owe you any fare. Between your kind and ours there's no common currency and no common speech . . . So now what do you want?*

Because Number 402 had resumed tapping, Rubashov stepped closer to the wall . . . SENDING YOU TOBACCO, he heard. Then right after that he sensed a more muffled noise, as 402 pounded on his cell door to call the warder.

Rubashov listened, breathing tensely; a few minutes later he heard the old man shuffling closer.

Without opening the door to Number 402, the warder asked through the spy hole:

"What do you want?"

Rubashov couldn't make out his neighbor's reply, though he would have liked to hear 402's voice. Then the old man said, loud enough for Rubashov to hear, "That's not allowed. Against regulations."

Once again Rubashov couldn't hear any answer. Then the old man said: "I'm going to report that you insulted me." His steps shuffled across the tiles and faded down the corridor.

For a while it was quiet. Then Number 402 tapped:

IT SEEMS THEY'VE GOT IT IN FOR YOU.

Rubashov didn't answer. He paced up and down; the craving for a cigarette was scratching at the dry membranes of his throat and sinuses. He thought about Number 402. *I would still do it again*, he told himself. *It was necessary and right. Still, is it possible that I owe you the fare as well? Do we also have to pay for our deeds that are necessary and right?*

The pressure in his forehead intensified. Rubashov paced restlessly back and forth, moving his lips as he thought.

Did one also have to pay for actions that were just? Was there some other measure of our actions outside reason?

And was it possible, according to this other standard, that the righteous man had to shoulder the heaviest guilt of all? Precisely the righteous man, the man who was just—because the others didn't know what they were doing? . . .

Rubashov stopped on the third black tile away from the window.

What was that? A touch of religious delirium? He realized

that he'd been talking quietly to himself for several minutes. Even now, as he was observing this, his lips moved of their own accord and said:

"I'm going to pay."

For the first time since his arrest Rubashov was scared. He reached instinctively for his cigarettes. But he had none.

Then he heard the fine ticking on the wall again, above his cot. Number 402 had a message for him:

HARELIP SENDS GREETINGS.

He saw the yellowish face of the man in the yard, looking up at his window; the message made him uneasy. He tapped:

WHAT'S HIS NAME?

Number 402 answered:

DOESN'T WANT TO SAY. BUT SENDS GREETINGS.

12.

Things got even worse over the course of the afternoon. Rubashov felt a slight chill, and his tooth began to ache again— the upper right canine, close to the infraorbital nerve. He hadn't been given anything to eat since his arrest, but he didn't feel hungry. He struggled to collect his thoughts, but between the shivers in his body and the scratchy itch in his throat they teetered relentlessly between the desperate craving for a cigarette and the sentence *I'm going to pay*.

Memories came crashing over him, ringing in his ears like a falling bell. Faces and voices faded in and out; it hurt when he tried to hold on to them. His entire past was full of festering sores that burst at every touch. It was the past of the movement, of the party—of course his present and future also belonged to the party and were inextricably intertwined with its fate, but his past was identical with that of the party. And suddenly this past was being called into question. The hot, breathing body of the party seemed riddled with ulcers, purulent lesions, bleeding stigmata pierced by rusty nails. When and where in history had saints ever been so flawed? When had a good cause ever been so badly represented? If the party was the embodiment of the will of history, then history itself was defective.

Rubashov stared at the damp stains on the walls of his cell. He yanked the wool blanket off the cot and wrapped it around his shoulders. He quickened his pacing, taking small steps and making abrupt turns at the door and the window, but the shivers kept running down his back. The ringing in his ears continued, mixing occasionally with muffled, blurry voices that could have come from the corridor or from his hallucinations—he couldn't tell. *The orbital nerve*, he told himself—from the fractured root of his tooth. *Tomorrow I'll tell the doctor about it, but there's a lot to be done before that. The cause of the defect within the party has to be located. Our principles were all correct, but our results were all wrong. This is a sick century. We identified the disease and analyzed its structure with microscopic acuity, but wherever we applied the scalpel as a cure, nothing but new ulcers arose. Our desire was pure, our will was firm; people ought to love us. But they hate us. Why do we deserve this hate?*

We brought you the truth, and in our mouths it sounded like a lie. We bring you freedom, and in our hands it looks like a whip. We bring you the living life, and wherever our word resounds trees wither and there is the rustle of shriveled leaves. We proclaim the brightest future, and our proclamations sound like vapid drivel and brutish barking.

An image appeared before his eyes, a large photograph in a wooden frame—the delegates to the first party congress. They were seated at a long wooden table, leaning on their elbows or with their hands in their laps while they gazed, bearded and serious, into the photographer's lens. Over each head was a little circle with a number; the names were noted down below. Only the old man presiding seemed amused, as he squinted slyly from his narrow Tatar eyes. Rubashov was seated at his right, his pince-nez perched on his nose. Somewhere at the lower end of the table sat Number One, burly and ungainly. They looked like the annual meeting of a small-town association of notaries, and yet they were preparing the largest revolution in the history of mankind. Back then they were just a handful of men in Europe, but they were the first of their kind—an elite of spirit and of deed, philosophers who acted. They were as familiar with the prisons of European cities as traveling merchants were with the hotels. They dreamed of achieving power with the goal of rescinding it, of ruling so that people would grow unused to being ruled. All their thoughts turned into action, and all their dreams became fulfilled. And where were they now? Their brains had changed the fate of the world and then each had received his dose of lead. Some in the forehead, others in the back of the neck. There were still one or two left, spent and scattered across the globe. And himself. And Number One . . .

He was very cold. He craved a cigarette. He saw himself again in the old Belgian port, with Little Löwy, who was short and funny and somewhat misshapen and smoked a sailor's pipe. He smelled the scent of the harbor, the mix of rotting seaweed, March wind, and fuel oil; he heard the carillon on the tower of the archers' guildhall; he saw the long, tapered alcoves perched above narrow streets, where the harbor prostitutes hung out their washing to dry during the day. It was two years after the affair with Richard, shortly after he'd been released from prison—they hadn't been able to prove anything against him. He had kept silent when they beat him, when they knocked his teeth out, damaged his hearing, shattered his pince-nez. He had kept silent and denied everything and lied coldly and carefully. He had marched up and down inside his cell or crawled back and forth across the stone tiles in the punishment block and he had been afraid and worked on his defense, and when he had blacked out and they had dumped cold water on him he had reached for his cigarettes and gone on telling lies. Back then he hadn't wondered why his torturers hated him, nor had he spent any time pondering why they considered him so worthy of their hate. The whole legal apparatus of the dictatorship gnashed its teeth but couldn't prove anything. After his release a plane picked him up and brought him here, to the country that was his homeland and the homeland of the revolution. There were grand receptions and jubilant public meetings and military celebrations.

He hadn't been in his homeland for years and found that much had changed. Number One made a point of frequently appearing with him in public. Half of the bearded men from the old photograph were no longer alive. It was forbidden to mention their names or to summon their memory except with curses. The single exception was the old man with the Tatar eyes, the former leader, who had died at the right time. He was revered as God the Father and Number One was his son— though it was rumored everywhere that Number One had falsified the old man's testament to assure his succession. The few bearded men left from the photograph were unrecognizable. They were now clean-shaven, used up, disappointed, full of cynical melancholy. From time to time Number One would snatch a new victim from among them. Then the others would loudly beat their breasts, repent their sins, and join the chorus acknowledging God the Father, the Son, and the Holy Ghost of the dogmatically petrified doctrine. After just one week—he still needed crutches to walk—Rubashov had requested another mission abroad. "You seem to be in a hurry," Number One said to him, peering at Rubashov through the billows of pipe smoke. They had served together in the party leadership for twenty years and still didn't address each other by their first names. Behind Number One's desk hung a portrait of the old man; at one point the photograph with the delegates had hung beside it, but that was gone. Their meeting was cold, lasting no more than a few minutes, but in parting Number One shook his hand particularly firmly. Rubashov had spent a long time agonizing over the meaning of this handshake and the way Number One had peered at him through his cloud of smoke—with a look of strangely knowing irony. Incidentally Number One had good, masculine hands. Then Rubashov had hobbled out of the room on his crutches; Number One did not see him to the door. The next day Rubashov left for Belgium.

Once on the ship he recovered somewhat and was able to focus on the task at hand. Little Löwy with his sailor's pipe was there to meet him. He was the local head of the dock-workers' section of the party, and Rubashov took an immediate liking to him. He led Rubashov through the docks and the winding harbor alleys with a pride as if he'd built it all himself. He knew people in every establishment—stevedores, sailors, and whores—and returned all greetings by tapping his pipe to his ear. Everywhere he stopped they treated him to a whiskey. Even a traffic cop at the market square gave Löwy a familiar wink, while some sailor-comrades off foreign ships who didn't speak his language gave him a sturdy, fond clap on his deformed shoulder. Rubashov took it all in, somewhat amazed. No, there was nothing deserving of hate in Little Löwy. The party dock-workers in this city were one of the best-organized sections in the world.

That evening Rubashov and Löwy went to a harbor pub and sat down with a few others. Among them was someone called Paul—the section secretary. Bald, pockmarked, with large, protruding ears, he was a former wrestling champion who wore a black sailor sweater under his jacket and a black bowler on his head. He could wiggle his ears and make the bowler rise and fall. And there was a man named Bill, a former seaman who had written a novel about life at sea. He had been famous for a year and then quickly forgotten; he now wrote articles for party leaflets, drank, and, like many former seamen, succumbed to the occasional homosexual relapse, which became the object of good-natured jokes. The others worked on the docks—heavy, hard-drinking men. New people kept showing up; they would sit down at the table or stand, pay for a round, and amble back out. The plump proprietor also joined them whenever he had a moment. He played the harmonica. Everyone drank quite a bit.

Little Löwy had introduced Rubashov as the "comrade from over there" and left it at that. He was the only one who knew Rubashov's true identity. The others noticed that Rubashov either was not talkative or didn't want to say much, so they limited their inquiries to the conditions "over there"—wages, the peasantry, industrialization. Their questions revealed an astonishingly detailed expertise, coupled with an equally astonishing ignorance about the situation as a whole and the general political atmosphere "over there." They asked about the progress of production in the light metal industry with the interest of children wanting to know the size of the grapes of Canaan. One old dockworker, who'd been standing at the bar awhile without ordering anything until Löwy treated him to a glass, shook Rubashov's hand and said: "You almost look like old Rubashov." "I've often heard that," said Rubashov. "Rubashov, now there's a good bloke," said the old man, emptying his glass. Scarcely ten days had passed since Rubashov had been released, and not quite two weeks since he'd learned he wasn't going to die in prison. The proprietor played his harmonica. Rubashov lit a cigarette and ordered a round for everyone. They all drank his health and raised their glasses to "over there," and Paul, the section secretary, wiggled his ears and made his bowler go up and down.

Afterward Rubashov and Löwy spent a little time by themselves in a harbor coffeehouse. The proprietor had lowered the blinds and set the chairs on the tables; he dozed leaning against the bar as Löwy told Rubashov his life story. Rubashov hadn't asked to hear it and immediately foresaw complications for the following day, but he couldn't help it that the comrades all felt an urge to tell him about their lives. He wanted to leave but suddenly felt very tired; evidently he had overestimated his strength, and he stayed seated.

It turned out that Löwy wasn't really from there, although

he spoke the language like a native and everyone knew him. He actually came from a city in southern Germany, where he had trained as a carpenter. On the Sunday outings of the revolutionary youth association he had played guitar and given lectures on Darwinism. In the turbulent months before the onset of the dictatorship, when the party urgently needed weapons and had none, a small group pulled off a reckless and daring caper. One Sunday afternoon they drove a furniture truck to the police station in the busiest precinct in town. There they produced some kind of document—two of the group were dressed as policemen who were supposedly escorting the transport. They loaded fifty rifles, twenty revolvers, and two light machine guns together with ammunition onto the truck and drove off. Eventually the weapons were discovered in another city when a garage belonging to a party member was searched. The case was never fully explained, but the next day Löwy left town. The party had promised him papers and a passport, but the arrangement fell through—the "comrade from above" who was supposed to deliver the papers and money for travel failed to appear at the appointed time.

"That's how it always is with us," Little Löwy added philosophically. Rubashov ignored the remark.

Nevertheless Löwy struggled along and ultimately managed to cross the border. Because he was a wanted man and his photo with the deformed shoulder was posted in every police station, he spent several months moving from place to place. When he had set out to meet the "comrade from above" he had had money for exactly three days. "I always thought it was only in books that people gnawed on tree bark," he noted. "Young plane trees taste best." Prompted by this memory he stood up and brought two knockwursts from the counter. Rubashov thought of prison soup and hunger strikes and they ate together.

Despite everything, Löwy did make his way into France and even found occasional work. Unfortunately he was arrested after a few days because he didn't have a passport and ordered to leave the country. "They might as well have sentenced me to climb up to the moon," he said. He turned to the party for help, but the local organization didn't know him and told him they'd first have to check with his comrades back home. So Löwy moved on; after a few days he was again arrested and sentenced to three months in jail. He sat that out, and took the occasion to lecture his cellmate—a tramp—on the resolutions of the last party congress. In return the tramp taught him how to earn money catching cats and selling their fur. One night, after the three months were up, the gendarmes took him to a forest on the Belgian border. They gave him bread, cheese, and a pack of French cigarettes. "Keep going straight," they told him, "and in half an hour you'll be in Belgium. If we catch you here again we'll smash your face in."

For a few weeks Löwy roamed around Belgium. He contacted the party but was met with the same response as in France. Since he'd had enough of gnawing on plane trees he tried his hand with the cats. Catching them was relatively easy, and if the animal was young and not mangy, a fur could be traded for half a loaf of bread and a bit of pipe tobacco. But between catching the cat and selling the fur, he had to perform a distressing operation. The quickest way was to grasp the animal by the ears in one hand and by the tail with the other and break its backbone over your knee. It was nauseating for the first few times but later he got used to it. Unfortunately after a few weeks he was arrested and jailed again because he didn't have any papers. And one night two Belgian gendarmes took him to a forest on the French border. They gave him bread, cheese, and a pack of Belgian cigarettes. "Keep going straight," they told him, "and in half an hour you'll be in France. If we catch you here again we'll smash your face in."

Throughout the following year Löwy was smuggled from one country to the other a total of three times, always with the complicity of the local French—or Belgian—authorities. He learned that they'd been playing the same game for years with hundreds of similar cases. He kept appealing to the party: his main worry throughout was that he might lose contact with the movement. "We don't have an endorsement from your organization," the party told him. "We have to wait for the reply to our inquiry. If you are a comrade then maintain discipline." And in the meantime, while Löwy went on skinning cats and getting shuttled across the borders, the dictatorship came to power in his homeland. Another year went by and Löwy, the worse from his wanderings, began spitting blood and dreaming about cats. He suffered under the notion that everything smelled of cats—his food, his pipe, the whores who occasionally took pity on him and let him sleep with them, and he himself. "We still haven't received any reply to our inquiry," said the party. By the time another year went by, all the comrades who could have provided information about Löwy's past had either been locked up or killed, or else gone missing. "There's nothing we can do," said the party. "You shouldn't have left without obtaining an endorsement beforehand. It's also conceivable you left without permission from the party. How are we supposed to know? There are many stool pigeons and provocateurs trying to infiltrate our ranks. The party must be vigilant."

"Why are you telling me this?" Rubashov asked. He wished he had left earlier.

Löwy poured himself a draft and saluted with his pipe. "Because it's instructive," he said. "Because it's just one example. I could tell you a hundred more. This is how the best of us get demoralized and worn out. Because everything is so ossified and calcified. The party has gout and all its limbs have varicose veins. That's no way to make revolution . . ."

I could tell you even more, Rubashov thought, but said nothing.

As it happened, Little Löwy's story had an unexpectedly favorable conclusion. After one of his countless arrests he was thrown in the same jail cell as the bald-headed Paul. By then Paul was working on the docks, and once when the police had tried to break up a strike he had called on his past life as a wrestler and put a policeman in a full nelson—a move made from behind where the holder thrusts his arms under his opponent's armpits, then raises them and locks his hands together while pressing against the opponent's neck until the cervical vertebrae start to crack. The full nelson had always earned him much applause in the ring, but in the class struggle the move was banned, as he noted with regret. Löwy and Paul became friends. It turned out that Paul was the lead organizer of the dock section of the party, and once they were released he furnished Löwy with papers and work and vouched for him to the party. So once again Little Löwy lectured on Darwinism and the last party congress to the dockworkers, as though nothing had happened. He was happy and forgot the cats as well as his ire toward the party bureaucrats. Half a year later he became the section political leader. All's well that ends well.

Rubashov wished with all his heart, as old and tired as he felt, that it would once again end well. But he knew why he had been sent, and there was only one revolutionary virtue he had never mastered: he was incapable of deceiving himself. He looked at Little Löwy quietly through his pince-nez and as Löwy, who didn't know how to interpret this look, smiled and saluted awkwardly with his pipe, Rubashov thought about the cats. He was disgusted to realize his nerves weren't functioning properly and that he might have drunk too much, because he couldn't rid himself of the insane idea that he had to take Löwy by the ears and legs and lay his misshapen shoulder across his knee. He felt himself getting nauseous and stood up. Löwy walked him home; noticing Rubashov's sudden bad mood, he was respectfully quiet. One week later Little Löwy had hanged himself.

◈

Between that evening and Löwy's death there had been a series of undramatic, businesslike sessions. The facts of the case were simple.

Two years earlier the party had asked the workers of the

world to fight the newly established dictatorship in the heart of Europe, and called for a political and economic boycott of the empire of tyranny. No goods should be purchased that were manufactured in the land of the enemy, and no transports should be let through that could benefit its powerful war industry. The party sections enthusiastically followed this directive. The dockworkers in the little port city refused to unload any freight from or to the enemy country. Other unions acted in solidarity with them. Waging the struggle with strikes was a serious, difficult business; there were clashes with the police, people were wounded, some were killed. The outcome of the struggle was still uncertain when one day a small flotilla of five old-fashioned black steam freighters pulled into the harbor. The peculiar boats bore the names of great revolutionary leaders, in the foreign lettering from "over there." The flag of the revolution fluttered from their bows. The ships were greeted with enthusiasm by the workers, who began unloading the freight. Several hours passed before they realized the cargo consisted of precious ores that were rare in Europe, and that they were being transported for the war industry of the empire of tyranny.

This realization set off an intense dispute within the section, which soon spread throughout the country to the party as a whole. The reactionary press took up the case with ridicule and scorn. The police, who had otherwise acted as strikebreakers, stayed neutral, leaving it up to the dockworkers whether or not to unload the freight from the odd black fleet. The party leadership ordered that the strike be broken off and the freight unloaded. They gave matter-of-fact explanations and clever reasoning for the conduct of the revolutionary fatherland and its leaders, but few were convinced. The section split; most of the old members left. For a few months the leadership maintained a tenuous connection with the remaining members. But in time, because the economy in the country was growing worse and worse, the party gained new adherents and recovered its strength.

Two years passed. A different dictator state in the south that was allied with the main enemy began a war of plunder and conquest in Africa. Once again the party called for a boycott, and the response was even greater, since this time practically every nation in the world had resolved not to deliver any raw materials needed for waging war to the peace-breaking invader. Without raw materials, and especially oil, the invader would be doomed. That was how things stood when the strange black flotilla set out once again. The largest of the ships bore the name of the only man who had spoken out against funding the world war and who had been killed, on their masts fluttered the flags of the revolution, and in their cargo holds was oil destined for the aggressor. They were just one day away from the port, and Löwy and his friends knew nothing of their arrival. It was Rubashov's task to prepare them. On the first day he had kept quiet as he assessed the terrain. On the morning of the second day, in the large room of the party office, the discussion began.

The room was bare, cluttered, and furnished in the cold, functional style that made all party offices in all cities of the world look alike. This was partly due to insufficient funds but more because of a life-averse puritanical tradition. The walls were covered with election posters, political slogans, and typewritten notes. In one corner was an old, dusty mimeograph machine; in another were piles of old clothes meant for the families of the striking workers; next to that were stacks of yellowed brochures and leaflets. The long table consisted of two parallel boards placed over two sawhorses. The windows were smeared with paint as at a new construction site. A bare bulb hung from the ceiling on a string over the table, and next to it a strip of flypaper. Löwy with his misshapen shoulder, Paul with his bare head, the editor Bill, and three others sat around the table.

Rubashov spoke at some length. The familiar ugliness of the setting made him feel at home. In these surroundings the correctness and appropriateness of his mission seemed obvious, and he didn't understand why he had felt so uneasy the previous evening in the noisy harbor pub. Without mentioning the practical reason for his coming, he explained the reality of the situation—carefully and objectively but not without warmth. The world boycott against the aggressor had effectively collapsed due to the hypocrisy and greed of the European regimes. A few still held to the resolutions for appearances' sake; others didn't even do that. The aggressor needed oil. Previously the land of the revolution had supplied a significant portion of that country's need. If it now stopped delivering, other countries would greedily leap into the breach—they were just waiting for a chance to drive the revolutionary homeland out of the world market. Such romantic gestures would only damage the constructive efforts under way "over there" and thereby endanger the revolutionary movement throughout the world. The implications were therefore clear.

Paul and the other three dockworkers nodded their heads. They were not quick thinkers, and what the "comrade from over there" had explained made sense; it was a theoretical discourse that didn't affect them directly. They didn't realize what he was driving at; not one of them thought about the black flotilla approaching their harbor. Only Löwy and the editor with the pinched face exchanged a quick glance.

Rubashov noticed. He then concluded his remarks more dryly, without warmth:

"That's basically all I had to convey to you. It is expected over there that you will carry out the resolutions of the party center and explain the context to the comrades who are politically less mature, if they should raise any doubts. That's all I have for now."

There was a pause. Rubashov took off his pince-nez and lit a cigarette. Then Little Löwy said in a casual tone:

"We thank the speaker. Who wishes to say something?"

No one responded. Then one of the three dockworkers responded, formulating his words slowly and deliberately:

"There isn't much to say. The comrades over there are bound to know what they're doing. Of course we have to continue supporting the boycott. You can rely on us. No cargo for those swine will get through here."

His two colleagues nodded. Then bald-headed Paul said, by way of reinforcement: "Not through here they won't." He made a warlike grimace and moved his ears for fun.

At first Rubashov thought he was confronted with an oppositional conspiracy; only gradually did he realize that in fact they hadn't understood him. He looked at Little Löwy to see if he would clarify the misunderstanding. But Löwy lowered his eyes and said nothing. Suddenly the editor spoke out, with a nervous grimace:

"Does this transaction once again have to take place right here in our harbor?"

The dockworkers stared at him in amazement; they had no idea what he meant by "transaction"—the black fleet with fluttering flags that was approaching under cover of fog and smokescreens couldn't be further from their imagination. But Rubashov was prepared for the question:

"It is the most favorable location geographically as well as politically. The cargo will pass overland from here. We have no reason to conceal things, but it is smarter to avoid exposing anything the reactionary demagogues might seize upon as political capital."

The editor again exchanged glances with Little Löwy. The dockworkers looked at Rubashov uncomprehendingly; clearly their mental gears were beginning to work away. Suddenly Paul spoke up—his voice now different, hoarse:

"What are we really talking about here?"

Everyone looked at him. His neck had turned red and he was staring widemouthed at Rubashov. Löwy said restrainedly:

"You're only just now catching on?"

Rubashov looked from one to the other and said calmly:

"I forgot to mention the details. Five cargo ships from the foreign trade commissariat are due to arrive tomorrow, weather permitting."

Once again it took several seconds before everyone understood. No one said anything. They all stared at Rubashov. Then Paul stood up slowly, tossed his cap on the floor, and strode out of the room. Two of his colleagues turned to watch him leave. No one spoke. Then Löwy cleared his throat and said:

"The speaker has just explained his reasoning for the transaction. If they don't deliver the oil from there, then others will. Who wishes to respond?"

The worker who had spoken earlier now said:

"We've heard that song before. In every strike you always find people who say: 'If I don't take the work then someone else is going to.' We've heard enough of that kind of talk. That's how scabs talk."

Once again there was a pause. They could hear Paul slam the door to the street. Then Rubashov spoke:

"Comrades, constructing socialism over there takes precedence over everything else. Sentimentalities will not move us forward. Consider that."

The dockworker thrust out his head and said:

"We've already considered it. We've heard enough. You over there have to set an example. The whole world is watching you. You talk about solidarity and sacrifice and discipline, and what you're really doing is using your fleet to break a strike."

Löwy suddenly raised his head. His face was pale. He saluted Rubashov with his pipe and said quietly and very quickly:

"What the comrade just said is also my opinion. Does anyone else wish to respond? I hereby close the session."

Rubashov hobbled out of the room on his crutches. The events took their prescribed, inevitable course. As the small, old-fashioned fleet pulled into the harbor, Rubashov exchanged telegrams with the authorities in charge over there. Three days later the harbor section leadership was ousted by decree of the relevant authorities, its members expelled from the party, and Löwy was denounced in the official party organ as an agent provocateur. Three days after that he had hanged himself.

13.

That night was even worse. Rubashov couldn't fall asleep before dawn. The shivers came at regular intervals, and his tooth was throbbing. He had the feeling that every association pathway in his brain was aching and inflamed; nevertheless he still succumbed to the embarrassing compulsion to summon image after image, reconstruct voice after voice. He thought about young Richard in his black Sunday suit, with his bloodshot eyes: "You can't send me to the slaughter, comrade . . . " He thought about Little Löwy with his misshapen shoulder: "Who wishes to say something?" Oh, there were plenty who did choose to voice their thoughts. But the movement made no allowances; it rolled unyieldingly toward its goal, piling up the corpses of the drowned wherever it changed course. And its course consisted of nothing but bends, according to its dictates. And according to its dictates, those unable to follow its meandering way needed to be flushed out onto the bank. The movement had no interest in individual reasons, motives, or morals: it was indifferent to what went on in any one person's head and heart. It recognized one crime only, deviating from the course, and only one punishment—death. Death itself was devoid of mystery, it had no sublime aspect; within the movement it was merely the logical consequence of political divergence.

Rubashov didn't fall asleep on his cot until early morning. Once again he was awakened by the bugle signaling the start of a new day; a short while later the elderly warder, accompanied by two uniformed officials, came to take him to the doctor.

Rubashov had hoped he'd be able to read the names of Number 402 and Harelip, but he was led in the opposite direction. The cell to the right of his own, Number 406, was empty. It was one of the last cells at this end of the corridor, and the whole isolation unit was closed off by a heavy concrete door the old man had difficulty opening. They passed through a long gallery of cells, Rubashov with the old warder in front and the two uniformed officials behind them. Here the cards listed several names above each door, and noises came pouring out of every cell—speech, laughter, even singing. Rubashov guessed right away that they were in a section reserved for criminals. They passed the barbershop; the door was open and the barber was shaving a prisoner with the sharp-eyed face of an old jailbird, while two peasants were having their hair shorn. They all turned their heads, curious, when Rubashov marched by with his escort. Next they came to a door marked with a red cross. The warder knocked respectfully, then he and Rubashov stepped in, while the two uniforms waited outside.

The clinic was small and stuffy; it smelled of tobacco and carbolic acid. A bucket and two basins were overflowing with cotton wool and dirty bandages. The doctor was sitting in front of a table with his back to them, reading a newspaper and chewing a butter sandwich. The newspaper was spread over a pile of instruments, tweezers, and syringes. The doctor didn't turn around until the old man had closed the door behind him. The doctor's head was unusually small and bald except for a light film of white fuzz—Rubashov was reminded of an ostrich.

"He claims to have a toothache," said the old man.

"Toothache?" said the doctor, looking past Rubashov. "Come here, you, and open your mouth."

Rubashov studied him through his pince-nez. "I would like to call your attention to the fact," he said, "that as a pretrial detainee I have the right to courteous treatment."

The doctor turned to the warder:

"Who is this bird?"

The old man gave Rubashov's name.

For a moment Rubashov felt the round ostrich eyes sizing him up. Then the doctor said:

"Your cheek is swollen. If you would open your mouth."

Rubashov's tooth wasn't hurting at the moment. He opened his mouth.

"You don't have any upper left teeth at all," the doctor said, his finger probing inside Rubashov's mouth. Rubashov suddenly turned pale and had to prop himself up against the wall.

"Right there's the problem," the doctor said. "The root of the upper canine has been broken off and is still lodged inside."

Rubashov took a few deep breaths. The throbbing pain ran from the jawbone by his eye all the way to the back of his head, and he cringed with every pulse, at even intervals. The doctor had sat back down and returned to his newspaper.

"If you want, I can extract the root," he said, taking a bite of his sandwich. "We don't have any anesthetic here. The operation will take thirty minutes to an hour, depending."

Rubashov heard the doctor's voice through a fog. He leaned against the wall and breathed deeply and evenly. "Thank you," he said with difficulty, "not now." He thought about Harelip and the "steam bath" and his ridiculous gesture of stubbing his cigarette on the back of his hand the day before. *It's going to be bad*, he thought.

Rubashov turned and moved toward the door, carefully placing one foot in front of the other, concerned with maintaining his balance. Once out in the corridor he thought he saw Richard's features in the face of one of the uniformed guards. As they headed back to his cell he had the impression that the tiles were giving way beneath his feet. For a moment he leaned on the shoulder of the old man, who immediately withdrew. "None of that nonsense," said the old man.

Rubashov managed to control his pain and make it to the cell. When the door shut behind him he threw up into the bucket, then collapsed on the cot, and immediately fell asleep.

◇

The midday meal procession no longer bypassed his cell; from now on Rubashov received his scheduled ration of food. The toothache subsided and stayed within manageable bounds—Rubashov hoped that the abscess had opened on its own. He resumed his marching across the cell, disallowed all daydreaming, and set to work on his defense.

Three days later he was taken to his first interrogation.

14.

They came for him at eleven a.m. Rubashov saw the warder's sullen-solemn expression and knew immediately where they were headed. He felt the same calm that had often appeared as a gift of mercy, the cheerful composure he had known as a student in the last minutes before his oral exams, and later, in the seconds before confronting some imminent danger.

They went the same way they had gone three days earlier to see the doctor. Once again the concrete door opened and closed with a loud creak—*Strange*, Rubashov thought, *how quickly we get used to intense environments.* It was as though he'd been breathing the air of these corridors for years, as though the atmosphere of all the prisons he'd ever known was contained right here. They walked past the barbershop and the clinic, which was closed; three inmates were waiting outside, under the supervision of a guard.

Beyond the clinic was terra incognita for Rubashov. They passed a spiral staircase that led to some lower floor—storerooms, dark cells, or something else? With the interest of an expert, Rubashov attempted to guess. They crossed a narrow courtyard where the walls had no windows; it was a blind shaft, fairly dark, but overhead was open sky. Beyond this courtyard the corridors were a little brighter, and the doors were no longer made of concrete but of everyday household wood, painted, with brass handles. Busy officials kept crossing their path; from behind one of the doors they heard radio music, and from behind another the sound of a typewriter—this was clearly an administrative section.

They stopped in front of the last door in the corridor; the old man knocked. Someone inside was on the telephone; a quiet voice called out, "Just a minute," and continued speaking in intervals: "Yes" and "Yes, sir" into the mouthpiece. Rubashov thought he recognized the voice, but he couldn't place it. It was a pleasant male voice, slightly blurred; he was certain he'd heard it somewhere before. "Come in," said the voice; the old warder opened the door and closed it as soon as Rubashov stepped inside. He saw a desk, and behind the desk was his former colleague from the university and eventual battalion commander Ivanov, who smiled as he hung up the telephone. "So we meet again," said Ivanov.

Rubashov lingered a moment by the door. "Allow me," he said, "to recover from the surprise."

"Sit down," Ivanov said, inviting him to do so. He had risen from his chair and was half a head taller than Rubashov. He smiled as he sized up Rubashov intently. The two men sat down—Ivanov behind the desk, Rubashov in front. They studied each other a long time without embarrassment—Ivanov with his near-tender smile, Rubashov cautious and alert. His eyes focused on Ivanov's right leg beneath the desk.

"That's all fine," said Ivanov. "Prosthesis with automatic joints, chrome plated so it won't rust. I can swim, ride horses, drive cars, and dance. Do you want a cigarette?"

He handed Rubashov his wooden cigarette case.

Rubashov looked at the cigarettes and recalled his first visit to the military hospital, after they had amputated Ivanov's leg. Ivanov had begged Rubashov to obtain some veronal and then spent the whole afternoon trying to prove that revolutionaries had the right to commit suicide. In the end Rubashov managed to convince Ivanov to give him some time to think it over, but that same night he was ordered to a different section of the front and didn't see Ivanov again until years later, and then only fleetingly. Rubashov looked at the cigarettes in the wooden case. They were hand rolled, with loose, blond English tobacco.

"Is this still an unofficial prelude or have the hostilities already commenced?" asked Rubashov. "In the latter case I'll have to decline. You know the etiquette."

"Nonsense," said Ivanov.

"Nonsense, then," said Rubashov, and lit one of Ivanov's cigarettes. He inhaled deeply, drinking in the smoke, anxious not to show his enjoyment. "And how's the rheumatism in the shoulder?" he asked.

"Thanks for asking," said Ivanov. "And how are your blisters?"

He smiled and pointed innocently at Rubashov's left hand. On the back of the hand, between the bluish veins where he had stubbed out his cigarette three days earlier, was a blister the size of a copper coin. For a moment they both looked at Rubashov's hand, which was lying in his lap. *How does he know that?* thought Rubashov. *He had me spied on.* He felt more shame than anger; took one last, deep drag; and tossed away the cigarette. "As far as I'm concerned the unofficial part is over," he said.

Ivanov blew smoke rings and observed him with the same tender smile. "Don't be silly," he said.

"If I'm not mistaken," said Rubashov, "you are the ones who are being silly. Did I have you arrested or vice versa?"

"We had you arrested," said Ivanov. He put out his cigarette, lit a new one, and held the box out to Rubashov, who didn't move. "To hell with you," said Ivanov. "Do you remember the business with the veronal?" He leaned forward and blew some cigarette smoke into Rubashov's face. "I don't want you to get shot," he said slowly. He leaned back in his armchair. "To hell with you," he repeated, and went on smiling.

"That's touching of you," said Rubashov. "And why exactly do you all want to shoot me?"

Ivanov let a few seconds pass. He smoked and doodled some figures on his blotter with a pencil. He seemed to be searching for a precise expression.

"Rubashov," he said at last, "I'd like to call your attention to something. Just now you said repeatedly 'you,' meaning the state and the party, in contrast to 'I,' Nikolai Salmanovich Rubashov. Naturally for the public there needs to be a trial and a legal justification. For me, and also for you, my friend, what I just said has to suffice."

Rubashov pondered this; he was a little puzzled. For a few moments he had the impression that his own voice was speaking out of Ivanov, as though Ivanov had hit a tuning fork that necessarily made his own thoughts resonate in the same key. Everything he had believed and proclaimed, the conviction that had guided his every action for the half century of his conscious life—all came washing over him like a wave. There was no "I" outside the "we" of the party; the individual was nothing, the party everything; the branch that broke off the tree must wither . . . Rubashov rubbed his pince-nez on his sleeve. Ivanov leaned back in his chair and smoked, no longer smiling. Suddenly Rubashov noticed a rectangular spot on the wall that was brighter than the wallpaper. He realized right away that the picture with the bearded heads and the numbered names had hung there—Ivanov followed Rubashov's gaze without changing his expression.

"Your argument," said Rubashov, "is somewhat anachronistic. As you very correctly noted, our kind used to speak in the 'we' form and avoided the first-person singular wherever possible. But who is this 'we' in whose name you are speaking today? Apparently it must be redefined. That is the crucial point."

"I completely agree," said Ivanov. "I'm glad that we have gotten so quickly to the heart of the matter. In other words: you are convinced that 'we'—meaning the party, the state apparatus, and the masses behind it—no longer embody the interests of the revolution."

"You better leave the masses out of it," said Rubashov.

"Since when have you had such contempt for the plebs?" asked Ivanov. "Does that also have to do with the transition to the first-person singular?"

He leaned over his desk and looked at Rubashov with a mixture of goodwill and derision. His head was now covering the bright spot on the wall, and suddenly Rubashov was again reminded of the scene in the painting gallery, where Richard's head had blocked his view of the outstretched hands of the pietà. At the same time he felt a tremendous jolt of pain shoot from his cheek up into his forehead and ears. He closed his eyes for a second. *Now I am paying*, he thought, and then wasn't sure whether he had spoken out loud.

"What do you mean?" asked Ivanov's voice. It rang close to his ear, taunting and somewhat surprised.

The pain gave way to a quiet, peaceful clarity. "Leave the masses out of it," he repeated calmly. "You don't understand anything about the masses. I probably don't either. Earlier, when the great 'we' still existed—back then we knew them, like no one had known them ever before. We had plumbed their depths, we were working in the anonymous bedrock of history itself . . ."

Without realizing it he had taken a cigarette out of Ivanov's case. Ivanov bent forward and gave him a light.

"Back then," Rubashov went on, "they called us the party of the rabble. Because we were working in the bedrock of history and the others merely plowing its surface. What did they know about history? Superficial ripples, little eddies, and breaking waves. They were surprised to see the transformation and didn't know how to interpret it. But we had plunged into the depths, into the formless, anonymous mass that had constituted the substance of history in every epoch, and we were the first to research the laws that governed their movement. What governed their inertia, their slow molecular shift, their sudden eruptions. That was the great insight of our doctrine. The Jacobins were moralists; we were empiricists. We dug up the primeval mud of history and there discovered the law that governed its structure. We knew more than people had ever known about mankind, and that's why we succeeded in enacting its greatest revolution. And now you have filled it all back in . . . ."

Ivanov leaned back in his chair, stuck out his wooden leg, and listened as he drew figures on the blotter. "Keep going," he said. "I'm anxious to see where you're headed."

Rubashov smoked, inhaling deeply and with pleasure. After his long abstinence he felt the nicotine was making him a little drunk.

"You can see I'm talking myself into trouble," he said, and smiled up at the bright spot on the wall, where the photograph had once hung. This time Ivanov did not follow his gaze. "Well," said Rubashov, "one more or less no longer makes any difference. It's all been buried, the people, the insights, the hopes. You have killed the 'we,' annihilated it. You think the masses are still behind you? There are a few other heads of state in Europe that think the same thing. The dictators invoke the masses the way the chaplains invoke Christ's stigmata in times of war."

He took another cigarette and lit it himself, since Ivanov didn't move this time.

"Pardon the sentimental form of expression," he continued. "After all, it's not every day you have a chance to engage in such risky conversations with an old comrade. Do you really believe that the people are still behind you? The masses are simply bearing you along, silent and submissive, just as they bear other regimes in other countries, but deep down they're no longer in tune with the party. They've become deaf and dumb once again, the great silent x of history, as indifferent as the sea that floats all ships. Every fleeting glance can be mirrored in its surface, but down below is silence and darkness. Long ago we managed just once to penetrate the depths, but that time is past. In other words"—Rubashov paused to put his pince-nez back on—"back then we were making history, today you are practicing politics. That is the whole difference."

Ivanov sat back in his armchair and blew smoke rings. "Excuse me," he said, "I'm not sure what the difference is. Perhaps you would be so kind as to explain it to me."

"I'd be happy to," said Rubashov. "A mathematician once said that algebra is the science of lazy people—you don't figure out the value of x but work with it as though you knew its value. In our case this x represents the anonymous masses, the people. Practicing politics means operating with this x without worrying about its properties. Making history means recognizing what the x stands for in the equation."

"Nice," said Ivanov. "Only unfortunately a little abstract. To get back to more tangible things: you are saying that 'we'—namely the party and the state—no longer represent the interests of the revolution, the masses, or, if you prefer, of history."

"Now you have it right," said Rubashov, smiling. Ivanov did not return the smile.

"Since when have you been developing this opinion?" he asked.

"Just gradually, over the course of the last years," said Rubashov.

"Can't you pinpoint the time more exactly? One year? Two years? Three years?"

"That's an absurd question," said Rubashov. "How old were you when you grew up? Seventeen? Eighteen? Nineteen?"

"You're the one who's acting dumb," said Ivanov. "Every step of mental development is tied to specific experiences. If you really want to know, I grew up when I was seventeen, the first time I was sent into exile."

"And back then you were a wonderful fellow. Forget it." Once again Rubashov glanced at the bright spot on the wall and tossed his cigarette.

"I repeat my question," said Ivanov, leaning forward slightly. "Since when have you belonged to the organized opposition?"

The telephone rang. Ivanov quickly picked up the receiver; said, "I'm not available"; and hung up without waiting for an answer. He leaned back in his chair again, with his leg stretched out, and waited silently for Rubashov's explanation.

"You know as well as I do," said Rubashov, "that I have never joined an organized oppositional group."

"As you like," said Ivanov. "But you're putting us both in an embarrassing situation that forces me to play the bureaucrat with you . . ." He reached into a drawer and pulled out a bundle of files.

"Let's start with 1933," he went on, spreading the files across his desk. "The onset of the dictatorship and the suppression of our party in Germany—the land where it seemed closest to victory. You entered the country illegally by order of the leadership, and were charged with purging and reorganizing the cadres . . ."

Rubashov had leaned back and was listening. He thought about Richard and the twilit avenue in front of the museum, where he had stopped the taxi.

". . . Three months later: arrest. Two years of prison. Exemplary behavior, no statements, nothing can be proven against you. Release and a triumphant return home . . ."

Ivanov paused, glanced briefly at Rubashov, and continued:

"You were greatly celebrated. We didn't meet back then; you were undoubtedly too busy . . . Incidentally I didn't hold it against you. After all, you couldn't look up every one of your earlier friends. As a matter of fact I saw you twice back then, at meetings, up on the podium. You were still on crutches and looked very banged up. The logical thing would have been for you to spend a few months recovering in a sanatorium and then take on a function in the state apparatus, considering you had spent four years on various postings abroad. Instead after just one week you applied for a new mission . . ."

He suddenly leaned forward, moving his face closer to Rubashov's.

"Why . . . ?" he asked, and for the first time his voice sounded sharp. "Maybe you didn't feel so well here? During your absence certain changes had occurred in the country that you apparently didn't agree with?"

He waited to see if Rubashov would say something, but Rubashov sat still in his chair, rubbed his glasses on his sleeve, and didn't answer.

"It was shortly after the first oppositional group was convicted and liquidated. You had close friends among them. When it became known just how far the opposition had degenerated, the whole country cried out in indignation. You were silent. Eight days later you left the country, even though you still couldn't walk without crutches . . ."

Rubashov felt he could smell the harbor in the small port city—the mix of seaweed and fuel oil. Bald-headed Paul was wiggling his ears; Little Löwy was saluting with his pipe . . . He had hanged himself from a beam in his garret, in a house so dilapidated it shook every time a truck drove by. Rubashov was told that Löwy had been spinning slowly around his own axis when they found him the next morning, so they first thought he was still moving.

"Having completed the mission with a good result, you are then appointed to lead our trade delegation in B. This time, too, everything is as it should be; the new trade agreement with B. is a clear success. Outwardly your actions continue to be exemplary, impeccable. But six months after you took up the post, your two closest workers, including your secretary Orlova, have to be called back on suspicion of oppositional-conspiratorial activity—suspicion that was confirmed in the investigation. It was expected that you would publicly distance yourself from them. Yet you said nothing . . .

"After another six months you yourself are recalled. The preparations for the second trial against the opposition are under way. Your name comes up repeatedly in the interrogations; Orlova keeps referring to you, thinking she will be exonerated. Your continued silence would be tantamount to a confession. You know that, and still you refuse to give a public declaration, until the leadership presents you with an ultimatum. Only then, since your own head is at stake, do you deign to make a declaration of loyalty, which at the same time seals Orlova's fate. That, I'm sure, is known to you."

Rubashov said nothing and noticed that his tooth was again beginning to hurt. Her fate was known to him. As was Richard's. And Löwy's. His own as well. He stared at the bright spot on the wall, the only trace left of the photograph of the men with the numbered heads. Their fate was also known. History had started down a course that at last promised some sensible change; now it was over. Why still all this talk, all this ceremony? If there was anything in humans that survived physical annihilation, then plump Orlova was lying somewhere in the great emptiness, her kind, cowlike eyes gaping in amazement at Comrade Rubashov, who had been her idol and who had sent her to her death . . . His tooth was hurting more and more.

"Shall I read you the statement you made at the time?" asked Ivanov.

"No, thank you," said Rubashov, noting that his voice sounded hoarse.

"As you remember, your explanation, which could also be called a confession of regret, closed with a sharp condemnation of the opposition and an unconditional declaration of support for the leadership's policy and faith in the person of Number One."

"Enough," said Rubashov hoarsely. "You know how such declarations came about. If not, all the better for you. Enough of this theater."

"We're almost finished," said Ivanov. "Now we're just two years away from the present. During these two years you were active as the head of the state aluminum trust. One year ago, during the third trial against the opposition, the main defendants refer to you repeatedly, in somewhat vague and cryptic terms. Nothing concrete can be proven, but mistrust against you grows in the party ranks. You offer a new declaration in which you profess even greater devotion to the policy of the leadership and criticize every opposition in even sharper terms as criminal . . . That was six months ago. And today you confess that for years you have considered the policy of the leadership wrong and harmful . . .”

Ivanov paused, leaned back comfortably in his chair, and straightened his prosthesis.

“Given that belief, your earlier declarations of loyalty,” Ivanov continued, “were nothing but means to a specific end. Please note that I am not moralizing. We both grew up in the same tradition and hold similar views in this matter. You were convinced that our policy was wrong and yours was correct. To state this out loud back then would have meant expulsion from the party, which would have made it impossible for you to continue working to advance your own agenda. You had to jettison ballast in order to be able to keep advancing—for the time being, conspiratorially—ideas you believed to be the only objectively correct ones. In your place I would have acted the same way. So far, so good.”

“And then what?” asked Rubashov.

The earlier, well-meaning smile had returned to Ivanov’s face.

“What I don’t understand,” said Ivanov, “is that today you openly admit that for years you have harbored the conviction that we are spoiling the revolution, and in the same breath you deny belonging to any oppositional organization or that you have conspired against us. Do you really want me to believe that you would have looked on idly while we, in your mind, ran the country and party into the ground?”

Rubashov shrugged his shoulders. “Perhaps I was too old and spent . . . Anyway, believe what you will,” he said.

Ivanov leaned forward again; he now spoke quietly and very emphatically:

"Do you really want me to believe you sacrificed Orlova and repudiated all of them"—he nodded at the bright spot on the wall—"simply to save your head?"

Rubashov was silent. A fairly long time passed. Ivanov kept moving his head closer and closer over the desk.

"I don't understand you," he said. "Just half an hour ago you gave the most passionate accusatory speech against us—a fraction of what you told me of your own free will would have sufficed to do you in. And yet you deny such a logical corollary as belonging to an oppositional group . . . Meanwhile we have all the evidence in our possession."

"Is that so?" asked Rubashov. "If you have all the evidence, then why do you need my confession? Evidence of what, by the way?"

"Among other things," Ivanov said slowly, "evidence of the planned assassination of Number One."

Another several seconds passed. Rubashov put on his pince-nez.

"Permit me," he said calmly, "now to ask you a question. Do you actually believe this nonsense or are you merely pretending to?"

The earlier, near-tender smile appeared in the corners of Ivanov's eyes.

"I told you, we have evidence. To be more precise: confessions. Even more precisely: the confession of the man who was supposed to carry out the assassination at your behest."

"Splendid," said Rubashov. "What's his name?"

Ivanov smiled. "An indiscreet question."

"May I read the confession? Or be confronted with the man?"

Ivanov did not stop smiling. He again blew smoke in Rubashov's face, with friendly taunting. Rubashov found it unpleasant but did not pull back his head.

"Do you remember the business with the veronal?" said Ivanov slowly. "I asked you about that at the beginning. Now the roles are reversed; today you're the one about to cast himself into the abyss. But not with my help, my friend. Back then you convinced me that suicide was petty-bourgeois romanticism. Now I'm going to make sure you don't succeed in doing yourself in. And then we'll finally be even."

Rubashov was silent. His head was now completely clear; he wondered whether Ivanov was lying or honest—but at the same time he felt the wish, like a physical impulse, to touch the bright spot on the wall with his fingers. *Nerves*, he thought. *Compulsion. Always stepping on black tiles, muttering senseless phrases, rubbing my pince-nez on my sleeve—I'm already doing it again . . .*

"I'm curious," he said out loud. "How do you imagine this rescue operation? Up to now the way you've been running the interrogation seems to have had the exact opposite goal in mind."

Ivanov smiled broadly and radiantly. "You old idiot," he said, and reached across the desk to grab Rubashov by a button on his jacket and pull him closer. "First I had to get you to explode—otherwise you would have done it at the wrong moment. Haven't you noticed that nothing's being taken down?" He took a cigarette from his case and stuck it forcefully into Rubashov's mouth, without letting go of his button. "You're behaving like an infant. Like a romantic infant," he added. "Now, let's fabricate a nice report and that will be all for today."

Rubashov finally managed to free himself from Ivanov's grasp. He looked at him through his pince-nez. "And what is this report supposed to say?" he asked.

Ivanov continued with his friendly smile. "It should say," he said, "that you confess to having belonged to such-and-such group of the opposition since the year such-and-such, but emphatically deny having organized or planned the assassination; that furthermore you broke away from the group when you learned about the criminally terrorist plans of the opposition."

Now Rubashov smiled, for the first time in the entire interview.

"If all the talk was aimed at *that*," he said, "then we can call it quits right here and now."

"Let me finish," said Ivanov without a trace of impatience. "I knew right away that you would balk. First the moral, sentimental side of the matter. What you confess will not frame anyone. To begin with they were all arrested long before you and in some cases physically liquidated; you know that yourself. And we can get confessions from the rest that are completely unlike this meaningless scrap of paper—any confession we want . . . I assume you understand me and are convinced by my frankness."

"In other words: you don't believe in this business of the assassination attempt either," said Rubashov. "So why don't you confront me with the mysterious X who made the alleged confession?"

"Think about it," said Ivanov. "Put yourself in my shoes—after all, the situation could just as easily be reversed—and you'll find the answer."

Rubashov pondered for a brief moment, then said: "You've been instructed from above to follow a specific approach in my case," he said.

Ivanov smiled. "That's putting it a little too harshly. The thing is that it hasn't been decided whether you belong to category A or T. Are you familiar with the designations?"

Rubashov nodded; he knew the designations.

"I see you're beginning to understand me," said Ivanov. "'A' stands for 'administrative' and 'T' stands for 'trial.' Most political cases—the ones where nothing is to be gained from a public appearance—are handled administratively. If you're placed in that category, then you'll be outside my jurisdiction. The hearing takes place in secret before the administrative collegium and, as you know, somewhat summarily. There's no opportunity for confrontations and the like. Think about . . ." He slowly named three, four names and glanced briefly at the bright spot on the wall. When he turned back around, Rubashov noticed for the first time a pained feature in his face, a slight rigidity in his gaze, as though his eyes weren't fixed on him, Rubashov, but on a point some distance in back of him.

Ivanov again repeated, somewhat more quietly, the names of their former friends. "I knew them just as well as you," he continued. "Now you'll kindly have to give me the right to be as convinced that all of *you* would run the revolution into the ground as you are of the opposite view. That is what matters; the methods reveal themselves through logical deduction. We can't afford to get involved with splitting hairs and legal she-nanigans. Did you ever do that?"

Rubashov said nothing.

"So it's all a matter of seeing," Ivanov continued, "that you get assigned to category T: in other words, a public trial. You know what criteria are used to select the cases chosen for public trials. I have to demonstrate to those above me that a trial in your case is justified. That's why I need the report with the partial confession. If you choose to play the hero and convince people that absolutely nothing can be started with you, then you'll be finished based solely on the statements made by X. If you make a partial confession, there will be grounds for a thorough investigation. At that point I would force the confrontation; we would contradict the most flagrant points of the accusation and confess to a clearly limited set of facts. Even then we're looking at a minimum of twenty years—which means one or two years, followed by an amnesty, and in five years you'll be back making policy. Now be so kind as to consider the matter calmly before you answer."

"I've already considered," said Rubashov. "I decline your proposal. Speaking purely logically, you may be right. But I've had enough of this logic. I'm tired, I don't want to play anymore. Now be so kind as to have me taken back to my cell."

"As you wish," said Ivanov. "I didn't expect that you'd agree right away either. Such conversations usually take a while to take effect. You have fourteen days. Ask to see me again once you have considered, or else send me a written declaration. I don't really doubt that you'll send it."

Rubashov stood up; Ivanov did likewise—once again half a head taller than Rubashov. He pressed a button next to his desk. They waited in silence for someone to come fetch Rubashov, then Ivanov said:

"A few months ago, in your last article, you wrote, 'The coming decade will decide the fate of the world in our historical epoch.' Don't you want to be around while that decision is being made?"

He smiled down ironically at Rubashov. Steps approached in the corridor; the door was opened. Two uniformed officials entered and saluted. Rubashov passed between them without saying a word and began marching back to his cell. The corridors were now dead; from a few cells he could hear muffled snoring that sounded like groaning, and the whole building was filled with the same pale yellow electric light.

THE SECOND INTERROGATION

When the existence of the Church is threatened, she is released from the commandments of morality. With unity as the end, the use of every means is sanctified, even deceit, treachery, violence, usury, prison, and death. Because order serves the good of the community, the individual must be sacrificed for the common good.

Ludwig von Pastor, *History of the Popes,*
from the Close of the Middle Ages, after
Dietrich von Nieheim in *De modis uniendiae*
reformandi ecclesiam, 1410

I.

From the Diary of N. S. Rubashov

Day 5 of Imprisonment

... *Whoever proves right in the end must first be and do wrong. But it is only after the fact that we learn who was right to begin with. In the meantime we act on credit, in the hope of being absolved by history.*

They say that Number One always keeps a copy of Machiavelli's The Prince *by his bedside. He's right to do so: since then, nothing of note has been written about the ethics of statesmanship. We were the first to replace the nineteenth-century liberal ethos of "fair play" with the revolutionary morals of the twentieth century. And we, too, were right to do so: the idea of a revolution following the rules of a tennis match is absurd. Politics can be fair when history pauses to catch its breath, but at critical turning points there is no other standard than the old proposition that the end justifies the means. We were the ones who introduced neo-Machiavellianism into this century; the others, the counterrevolutionary dictators, offered crude imitations. Our neo-Machiavellianism was on behalf of cosmopolitan reason—that was our greatness; theirs is in the name of a limited, nationalistic romanticism—that is their anachronism. Therefore in the end we will be absolved by history, and they will not* ...

For the time being, though, we think and act on credit. And because we have jettisoned all the norms and conventions of tennis-court morality, our only guideline is logic. We live with the terrible necessity of carrying our thoughts and actions through to their conclusion. We are sailing without ballast, so that every turn of the wheel is a matter of life and death.

Recently our leading agronomist, B., was shot along with thirty others because he favored nitrogen-based fertilizers to those heavy in potassium. Number One is convinced that potassium is superior; therefore B. and the thirty others had to be liquidated as wreckers. Where agriculture is centralized by the state, the question of nitrogen or potassium carries enormous weight; it can decide the outcome of the next war. If Number One is correct, history will absolve him, and the execution of the thirty-one will have been a trivial matter. If he is wrong . . .

This is all that matters: who is objectively correct. The tennis-court moralists agonize over a completely different question: whether or not B. was subjectively acting in good faith when he recommended nitrogen. If he was not, then according to their moral code he may be shot, even if it later turns out that nitrogen was the correct choice. If he was acting in good faith, then he must be acquitted and allowed to continue advocating for nitrogen, even if it brings ruin to the country . . .

Naturally this is absolute folly. (At least in periods where there's no time for experimenting and urgent decisions are required; in periods of rest it is different.) For our part we were never concerned with the question of subjective sincerity. Whoever is wrong must pay; whoever is right will be absolved. That is the law of historical credit, and the law to which we adhered.

History has taught us that it must be served more frequently with lies than with the truth, because its human material is by nature sluggish: before every new stage of development the people must first be led through the wilderness for forty years— driven on with threats and enticements, with false frights and feigned consolation, so that they do not stop to rest and entertain themselves with the worship of golden calves.

We learned history more thoroughly than the others. What separates us from everyone else is our consistency. We know that history does not care about morality and that it lets crimes go unpunished, but every error has repercussions and exacts revenge unto the seventh generation. For that reason we focus all our efforts on eliminating mistakes before they take root. Never before in history was so much power over the future of mankind concentrated in so few minds as in our revolution. Every wrong idea we acted on became a crime against future generations. Therefore we had to punish wrong ideas the way we punish other crimes: with death. People considered us fanatics, because we were so consistent, because we carried our thoughts and actions to their logical conclusions. People compared us to the Inquisition, because like them we always felt the full burden of responsibility for a hereafter, a future that transcended the individual. Like the great inquisitors we attempted to root out evil not only by prosecuting deeds; we delved into the thoughts themselves. We refused to acknowledge any private sphere, not even in the innermost space within the skull. Our lives were constrained by our own logic, by the need to think things through to the end. Because our thinking was shackled to chains of cause and effect, our feelings were constantly short-circuited. As a result we now must burn one another at the stake.

I have thought and acted as I had to. I was one of us: I have destroyed people who were close to me and given power to others whom I did not love; I took the place that history put before me; I have used up the credit that it extended; if I am right, I will have no cause for regret; if I am wrong, then I will pay.

But how can we decide in the present who will be proven right in the future? We practice the prophet's craft without his gift. We replace clairvoyance with logical deduction, but despite a common point of departure this has led to divergent results. The evidence was contradictory and in the end our justification was a question of faith—the axiomatic faith in the correctness of our own deductions. That is the crucial point. We have thrown all ballast overboard and are secured by a single anchor chain—the belief in ourselves. Geometry is the purest attainment of human reason, yet Euclid's postulates cannot be proven. And whoever does not believe them will see everything he's built come crashing down.

Number One believes in himself: tough, sluggish, dark, unwavering. He has the thickest anchor chain of all of us. My own has become a little worse for wear in these last years: at the end of the day it is a question of physical constitution . . .

The fact is: I no longer believe in my own infallibility. Therefore I am lost.

2.

The day after the first interrogation, Examining Magistrate Ivanov was sitting in the prison officers' canteen with his colleague Gletkin; they had just finished their supper. Ivanov was tired; he had propped his prosthetic leg on a nearby chair and undone the collar of his uniform. He filled their glasses with the cheap wine from the canteen and quietly wondered about Gletkin, who sat upright in his starched uniform, which creaked and crackled every time he moved. The younger officer hadn't even taken off his pistol belt, though he was bound to be as tired as Ivanov. As Gletkin drank, the conspicuous scar on his shaven skull turned slightly red. Three other officers were in the canteen, sitting at a distant table; two were playing chess while the third looked on.

"What's happening with Rubashov?" asked Gletkin.

"He's pretty worn out," replied Ivanov. "But he's still the old logician. Which is why he'll give in."

"I don't think so," said Gletkin.

"He will," said Ivanov. "Once he's thought everything through to its logical conclusion he will capitulate. The important thing for now is to leave him alone and make sure he isn't disturbed. I've let him have paper, pencils, and cigarettes to speed up his thinking."

"I think that's wrong," said Gletkin.

"You don't like him," said Ivanov. "You had a quarrel with him a few days ago, didn't you?"

Gletkin recalled Rubashov's sitting on his cot and exposing his sock full of holes as he pulled on his shoe. "That's immaterial," he said. "The person is immaterial. I consider the method wrong. This way he will never swallow his pride and give in."

"If Rubashov capitulates," said Ivanov, "it won't be out of cowardice, but because it's logical. Harsh methods won't work on him. He's made of a substance that gets tougher the more you hammer it."

"That's just talk," said Gletkin. "People capable of withstanding every degree of physical pressure don't exist. I've never seen one yet. Experience teaches us that the human nervous system's power of resistance is limited by nature."

"I wouldn't want to fall into your hands," said Ivanov, smiling, but with a trace of discomfort. "Incidentally you're the living contradiction of your theory."

He smiled and glanced at the scar on Gletkin's skull. The story was well-known: during the civil war Gletkin had fallen into enemy hands and they had fastened a glowing candlewick to his shaven skull to obtain certain information. When his own people retook the position hours later they found him unconscious. The wick had burned to the end; Gletkin had kept silent.

He looked at Ivanov with expressionless eyes. "That's also talk," he said. "The only reason I didn't give in was because I was unconscious. If I had stayed conscious one more minute I would have talked. It's a question of individual constitution."

He carefully drained his glass; his cuffs crackled when he placed it back on the table. "Back then when I came to, I first thought that I *had* talked. I didn't realize that I hadn't until the two noncommissioned officers who were freed at the same time assured me otherwise. That's why I was awarded the medal. It's a question of constitution; everything else is myth and legend."

Ivanov drank as well. He had already consumed a good amount of the cheap wine. He shrugged his shoulders.

"How long have you had your famous theory about human constitution? After all, these methods didn't exist in the first years. Back then we were full of illusions—doing away with the theory of punishment and retribution, building sanatoria with flower gardens for asocial elements. All a pipe dream."

"I don't think so," said Gletkin. "You are a cynic. In a hundred years we'll have all of that. But we have to get there first. The quicker the better. The only illusion was believing that the time had already come. When I was transferred here I was also living under this delusion. Most of us were—the entire apparatus all the way up to the top. We wanted to start right in with the flower gardens. That was a mistake. In a hundred years we'll be able to appeal to an inmate's common sense and communal spirit. Today we have to focus on his constitution and break him morally as well as physically whenever necessary."

Ivanov wondered whether Gletkin had drunk too much. But judging from his calm and expressionless look he realized that wasn't the case. Ivanov smiled vaguely in his direction. "In a word," he said, "I am the cynic and you are the moralist."

Gletkin was silent. He sat stiffly on his chair, in his starched uniform; his pistol belt smelled of fresh leather.

"Several years ago," said Gletkin after a while, "a small peasant farmer was brought to me for interrogation. It was out in the provinces, still during the time of the flower garden theory, as you put it. Everything proceeded very politely. The farmer had buried his grain; it was the beginning of the collectivization program. I followed the prescribed etiquette very exactly. I explained to him in a friendly way that we needed the grain to feed the growing population in the city and to export in order to develop our industry, so he should tell me where he'd hidden it. When they led him into my room the man had expected to be beaten and lowered his head. I knew the type; I come from the country myself. When instead of beating him I started talking to him and trying to persuade him, all the while addressing him politely as 'citizen,' he thought I was a moron. I could tell from the way he looked at me. I spent half an hour trying to convince him. He didn't open his mouth, just alternated between picking his nose and his ear. I kept on talking even though I could tell he considered the whole thing one big joke and wasn't listening at all. He was deaf to any and all explanations. His mind was clogged with centuries of stupidity—patriarchal, feudal earwax. I stuck to the protocol; it didn't even cross my mind that there might be other methods . . .

"Back then I had twenty to thirty cases like that every day. My colleagues did as well. The revolution was in danger of being ruined by these fat little farmers. The workers were undernourished; whole districts of poor peasants were suffering from typhus; we had no hard currency for building our military industry and every month we expected to be attacked. These men had two million in gold stuffed in their woolen socks, and half the harvest lay buried in the earth. And during the interrogations we addressed them politely as 'citizen' while they blinked at us with their dumb-clever eyes, thought the whole thing a joke, and picked their noses.

"My third interrogation with the farmer took place at two a.m.; I had worked straight through for eighteen hours. They had woken him up; he was drugged with sleep and scared and gave himself away. From then on I mostly called people in at night . . . One time a woman complained that she'd been made to stand outside my room the entire night. Her legs were shaking and she was physically exhausted; she fell asleep in the middle of the interrogation. I woke her up; she continued to talk, with a drowsy-slurred voice, without really knowing what she was saying, and then fell back asleep. I woke her up again and she confessed everything and signed the statement without reading it, just so I would let her sleep. Her husband had hidden two machine guns in the hayloft and talked the peasants in his village into burning their grain because the Antichrist had appeared to him in a dream. The fact that the woman had to spend the whole night on her feet was just an oversight on the part of my sergeant; from then on I encouraged that kind of oversight. Sometimes we kept hard cases standing in one spot for up to forty-eight hours; after that the earwax was gone and it was possible to talk to them . . ."

The two chess players in the far corner of the room reset their pieces for a new round. The third person had left their table to go to bed. Ivanov studied Gletkin, who was speaking as indifferently and impassively as ever.

"My colleagues had similar experiences. It was the only way to get results. We followed the protocol; no one laid a finger on the arrestees. But we didn't prevent them from accidentally witnessing their fellow prisoners getting shot. The effect was partly psychological and partly physical. The regulations prescribed showers and baths for reasons of hygiene. But the heating and hot water didn't function well during the winter, due to problems of industrial development. Prison personnel determined how long prisoners were allowed to bathe. Then again there were times when the heating and hot water functioned all too well—that was also up to the personnel. They were old comrades, there was no need to give them a long list of instructions, they understood what was at stake: nothing less than the survival of the revolution."

"Enough," said Ivanov.

"You asked how I developed my theory and I'm telling you," said Gletkin. "The main thing is to keep focused on what logic dictates in the name of development, otherwise you wind up becoming a cynic like yourself. It's getting late and I have to go."

Ivanov finished his glass and straightened out his prosthetic leg on the neighboring chair; the rheumatic pain in his stump had returned. He was annoyed at himself for starting the conversation.

Gletkin paid. Then, after the waiter had left, he asked as he was getting up:

"So what about Rubashov?"

"I've told you what I think," said Ivanov. "We ought to leave him alone."

Gletkin stood up. His boots creaked. He was standing in front of the chair where Ivanov's leg was resting. "I do not doubt his earlier merits and achievements," he said. "Today he has become harmful, just like my fat peasant back then—only more dangerous."

Ivanov looked up into Gletkin's expressionless eyes.

"I've given him fourteen days to think things over," he said. "Until then the man is to be left alone."

Ivanov had said this in an official voice to his subordinate. Gletkin saluted and left the canteen with squeaky steps.

Ivanov stayed seated. He drank one more glass, lit a cigarette, and blew the smoke out in front of him. After a while he stood up and hobbled over to the two officers to watch their game of chess.

3.

After his first interrogation, Rubashov's living conditions miraculously improved. The very next morning the old warder brought him paper, a pencil, soap, and a small towel. At the same time he issued Rubashov prison vouchers equivalent to his cash and let him know that he now had the right to obtain tobacco and additional food from the canteen.

Rubashov asked him to bring cigarettes and some food. The old man was just as sullen and monosyllabic as before, but he shuffled up promptly with the goods Rubashov had ordered. Rubashov briefly thought of asking to see a doctor from outside, to which he was entitled as a pretrial detainee, but then forgot about it. His tooth wasn't hurting, and after he had washed up and eaten something his body felt refreshed.

The yard had been swept clean of the snow, and the prisoners had resumed their group exercise walks—evidently stopped on account of the snow—with the exception of Harelip and his companion, who had been let out for ten minutes each day, perhaps because of special doctor's orders. Every time he entered or left the yard, Harelip had glanced up at Rubashov's window, a gesture too precise to be mistaken for coincidence.

When Rubashov wasn't working on his notes or pacing up and down the cell, he stood by the window, his forehead pressed against the pane, and watched the prisoners as they exercised. They were let out twelve at a time and circled the yard in pairs set ten paces apart. Four uniformed guards watched to make sure the walkers didn't speak to each other; they were stationed in the center of the yard, forming the axis of a kind of carousel that moved with a slow, even rotation for exactly twenty minutes. After that the prisoners were led back inside, still in pairs, through a door off to the right. Almost at the same time a new group was marched into the yard, and the carousel resumed its monotonous rotation, until the next shift.

During the first days of his confinement Rubashov had looked for familiar faces but not found any. That was reassuring; at the moment he didn't want any connection with the world outside, nothing to distract him from the matter at hand. His task was to think everything through to its logical conclusion and come to terms with past and future, with the living and the dead. He had ten days left of the time Ivanov had granted him.

He could only focus his thoughts by writing them down, but the act of writing was exhausting; at most he could force himself to do it for one or two hours. The rest of the time his mind was working on its own.

Rubashov had always thought he had a fairly accurate picture of himself. As he did not acknowledge moral judgments, he had no illusions concerning the phenomenon known as the first-person singular. He also freely admitted, without shame or emotion, to having impulses that most people were reluctant to put into words. Now, when he stood with his forehead pressed against the window or suddenly stopped on the third black tile from the window, he had a surprising experience. He discovered that a conversation with himself was not a monologue at all: it was a specific kind of dialogue between a partner who does not speak and another who addresses him—against all grammatical rules—as "I" instead of "you," just to gain his confidence and sound out his intentions. But the silent partner still says nothing, resists any observation, and even refuses to be located in time and place.

But now there were times when Rubashov thought that this otherwise-silent partner was starting to speak, without being addressed and with no clear cause; the voice seemed completely alien, and Rubashov listened to it with genuine amazement, checking to make sure it was his lips that were moving. There was nothing mystical or mysterious; the whole experience was very concrete and matter-of-fact, and these observations gradually convinced Rubashov that the first-person singular had a very tangible component that had kept silent throughout the years and had now begun to speak.

This discovery occupied Rubashov far more intensely than the details of his conversation with Ivanov. In his mind the matter was settled: he wasn't going to accept Ivanov's proposal; he was no longer going to play the game. As a result he was sure he had a limited amount of time left to live, and this conviction was the real basis for his reflections.

Rubashov wasted no thought on the ridiculous fiction about attempting to assassinate Number One; he was far more focused on Ivanov. Ivanov had claimed their roles could easily have been reversed, and he was undoubtedly right. He and Ivanov were practically twins, at least in terms of their development; they may not have come from the same ovum, but they were nourished from the same umbilical cord, from the same convictions; the same intensive party milieu had etched and formed their character in their crucial years; they had the same morals and the same philosophy, they thought in the same terms. The roles could just as easily have been reversed. Then he, Rubashov, would have been sitting behind the desk and Ivanov in front, and there he would presumably have advanced the same arguments that Ivanov had; the rules of the game were well established and only the details were allowed to vary.

Rubashov had succumbed yet again to his old compulsion of thinking through the mind of the other; he was sitting in Ivanov's place and seeing himself through Ivanov's eyes—the accused man on the opposite chair, just as he had once sat opposite Richard and Little Löwy. He saw a Rubashov who had been downgraded and demoted, a shadow of the former regimental comrade, and he understood the mix of tenderness and disdain Ivanov had been showing him. During the interrogation he had wondered repeatedly whether Ivanov's concern for him was genuine or feigned, whether Ivanov was setting a trap or truly wanted to show him a way out. Now, as he stepped into Ivanov's shoes, he understood that Ivanov was honest—as much or as little as he, Rubashov, had been toward Richard or Little Löwy . . .

These reflections, too, were a kind of soliloquy—albeit one that followed the old familiar form between "you" and "you." The newly discovered, true addressee of his inner speeches did not take part: that self's existence was confined to a grammatical abstraction. No direct questions or logical ruminations could induce that inner partner to speak, and when he did express himself it was for no apparent reason. His utterances always came unexpectedly, and—strangely—always accompanied by severe pain in the afflicted tooth. And his inner world seemed to consist of random parts as varied and unconnected as the pietà, Little Löwy's cats, the melody of "Come, Sweet Death," and a particular sentence that Orlova had said in a particular situation. That inner self's physical expressions were just as disjointed: for instance, the compulsion to rub his glasses on his sleeve, the impulse to touch the bright spot on the wall in Ivanov's room, the uncontrollable movement of his lips as they muttered phrases such as "I will pay," and the twilit daydreams of past episodes in Rubashov's life.

As he wandered around his cell, Rubashov concentrated

hard on this newly discovered entity, which he had dubbed "the grammatical fiction"—in keeping with the party tendency to shy away from using the first-person singular. He probably had only a few weeks left, and he felt an urgent need to come to terms with this new thing, to think it through to the end. But the grammatical fiction seemed to inhabit a realm that began precisely where thinking-through-to-the-end stopped. It was evidently in its nature to elude ordered thought, only to pounce later on, unexpectedly, as in an ambush, with daydreams and toothache. And so Rubashov passed the seventh day of his arrest—the second after being interrogated—almost exclusively in reliving one period of his existence, namely his relationship with Orlova, who had since been shot.

Against his intent, Rubashov had slipped back into day-dreaming, although afterward he couldn't say exactly when, any more than people can pinpoint the exact moment when they fall asleep. On the morning of that seventh day he had worked on his notes, had then probably stood up to stretch his legs, but it wasn't until he heard the key rattling in the door to the cell that he realized it was already noon, that he had spent hours marching up and down the cell, that he had draped the blanket over his shoulders because he was shivering with cold at regular intervals—probably also for hours—and that his nerve was throbbing all the way from the tooth into his temple. He spooned the soup out of his bowl, which the trusties had filled with their ladles, and resumed his wandering. The warder, who looked in on him from time to time through the spy hole, saw that he had hunched his shoulders because they were shivering and that his lips were moving. The memory was so intense it was like reliving what had happened; Rubashov felt himself breathing the air of his former office in the trade delegation, which was saturated with the distinctive scent of Orlova's shapely, large, and languid body; he saw her white blouse, and the curve of her neck as she bent over the shorthand pad, following his movements through the room with her round eyes whenever he paused between sentences. She always wore white blouses, with little embroidered flowers on the upturned collar, just as Rubashov's sisters had worn at home, and always wore the same cheap earrings that stuck out a little from her cheeks when she bent over the shorthand pad. Her languid, passive manner was ideal for taking dictation and had a tremendously calming effect on Rubashov's nerves when he was overworked. He had assumed his new post as leader of the trade delegation in B. immediately after the incident with Little Löwy and had thrown himself headlong into the work; he was grateful that headquarters had offered him this bureaucratic assignment. It was extremely rare that leading figures from the Internationale were given diplomatic posts within the government; Number One probably had something special in mind for him, because otherwise the two hierarchies were kept strictly separate, were not allowed to have any contact with each other, and frequently followed contradictory policies; only when viewed from the higher spheres around Number One were these apparent contradictions reconciled and the connections clear.

Rubashov needed some time to get used to his new way of living; he was amused to have a diplomatic passport that wasn't forged and was made out in his own name, that he had to take part in receptions wearing formal dress, that policemen stood at attention in front of him, and that the inconspicuously clothed men in black bowlers that he occasionally spotted following him did so out of thoughtful care for his safety.

At first he found the atmosphere in the offices of the trade mission, which was attached to the embassy, a little alienating. He understood that he was operating in the bourgeois world and that he had to play along, but it seemed to him that people were playing along a little too well, so that it was sometimes hard to tell appearance from reality. When the first secretary of the embassy pointed out that Rubashov needed to make some changes in his dress as well as in his personal lifestyle—before the revolution the same man had counterfeited money on behalf of the party—he did not do so in a comradely humorous manner but rather in such a carefully tactful tone it was embarrassing, and Rubashov was annoyed. His own staff consisted of twelve people, each of whom had a specific rank: there were first and second assistants, first and second accountants, secretaries and auxiliary secretaries. Rubashov felt the whole group viewed him as a combination of national hero and highwayman. They treated him with exaggerated respect and condescending forbearance. When the first secretary needed to discuss a document, he took visible pains to speak in the simplest possible terms, the way people talk to children or savages. The person who annoyed him the least was his private secretary, Orlova. He just didn't understand why along with her nice, simple skirts and blouses she insisted on wearing ridiculously high heels.

It was almost a month before Rubashov said anything personal to her. He was tired of dictating and of pacing up and down, and he suddenly noticed how quiet it was in the room. "Tell me, Citizen Orlova, why don't you ever say anything?" he asked as he settled into the comfortable armchair behind his desk.

"If you'd like," she answered with her sleepy voice, "I can always repeat the last word of each sentence."

Day after day she sat on the chair in front of the desk, in her embroidered blouse, her shapely, heavy bust tilted over the shorthand pad, with her head lowered and her earrings dangling alongside her cheeks. The only bothersome thing about her were the high heels, but she never crossed her legs the way most of the women Rubashov knew did. Because he always paced during dictation he usually saw her from the back or from the side, and what stuck most in his mind was the curved arch of her neck, which was hairless and unshaven; her white skin was stretched lightly over her cervical vertebrae, just above the embroidered flowers on the white edge of her blouse.

In his youth Rubashov hadn't been involved with many

women; they were almost always comrades, and each affair had almost always begun with a long discussion, either in his room or hers, until it was too late for whoever was the guest to go home.

Another fourteen days passed after that initial failed attempt to start a conversation. At first Orlova really did repeat the last word of each sentence, in her sleepy voice, but then she gave that up, and once again whenever Rubashov paused, the room was quiet and saturated with the distinctive, sisterly scent of her body. One afternoon Rubashov surprised himself when he stopped behind her chair, placed his hands lightly on her shoulders, and asked—with not a trace of huskiness in his voice—if she wanted to go out that evening with him. She didn't flinch; her shoulders stayed still under his touch; she nodded without saying a word and without turning her head. Rubashov was not very practiced at making lighthearted jokes, but he couldn't keep from saying to her later that same night—addressing her with the polite form they always used—"You know, you really don't need to act like you're still taking dictation." The familiar line of her warm, ample bosom stood out in the twilight of the bedroom as though it had always belonged there. Only now her earrings lay flat on the pillow. Her eyes had the same expression as always when in reply she uttered the sentence that would no more leave his memory than the smell of seaweed in the harbor or the folded hands of the pietà:

"You will always be able to do whatever you want with me."

"And why is that?" asked Rubashov, amazed, and somewhat shyly.

She didn't answer further. Probably she was already asleep. In her sleep she breathed as quietly as when she was awake; Rubashov had never even noticed her breathing. He had also never seen her with closed eyes, which made her face seem strange to him; it was far more expressive with closed eyes than with open ones. The dark shadows under her arms were also new to him, as was the fact that she slept with her chin pointed stiffly up, like a dead person, instead of lowered to her breast as in the office. But the light, sisterly fragrance of her body seemed familiar to him even in her sleep.

On the next day and on all the days that followed, she again sat bent over her desk in her white blouse; on the next night and on all the nights that followed, the brighter silhouette of her breasts stood out against the dark curtain in the bedroom. During the day and in the night Rubashov lived enveloped by the scent of her large, languid body. Her behavior at work remained unchanged; her voice and the expression in her eyes were the same as before, never hinting at or alluding to anything. Now and then, when he grew tired during dictation, Rubashov would stand behind her chair and rest his hands on her shoulders; he did not speak and her warm shoulders did not move beneath her blouse; then he would find the phrase he was looking for, resume his pacing, and go on dictating.

Occasionally he would add a sarcastic comment to what he was dictating; then she would stop writing, pencil in hand, and wait for him to finish, but she never smiled at his sarcastic remarks, and Rubashov never found out what she thought about them. Only once, when Rubashov made a particularly daring political joke referring to certain habits of Number One, did she blurt out in her sleepy voice: "You shouldn't say that kind of thing in front of other people; in general you ought to be a little more careful . . ." Nevertheless he occasionally felt compelled to express his heretical views, especially when instructions and circulars came "from above."

Preparations were under way for the second large trial conducted against members of the opposition. The atmosphere in the embassy had grown strangely thin. Overnight, photographs and portraits disappeared from the walls; in all the years they had hung there no one had looked at them, but now the bright patches were very conspicuous. The employees only spoke to one another on official business, with a studied, conspiratorial politeness. At meals in the embassy canteen, if conversations were unavoidable, they used semiofficial, wooden expressions that seemed grotesque and even a little uncanny given the informal atmosphere, as though between the saltshaker and the mustard jar people were trumpeting lines lifted from the latest party editorials. It also happened very often that someone would protest a presumably wrong interpretation of what he had just said, and with a distraught "I didn't say that" or "I didn't mean that" would call on his neighbors to back him up. The whole thing struck Rubashov as a bizarrely serious puppet theater, where roles were divvied up among marionettes that were controlled by wires and recited officially approved texts. Only Orlova showed no change in her quiet, languid manner.

The portraits on the wall weren't the only things to disappear; the library, too, was thinned out, as specific books and brochures vanished from the shelves. This was done discreetly, usually on the day following a new directive from above. During dictation Rubashov ventured some sarcastic remarks about this, too, which Orlova absorbed without comment. Almost all the writings on foreign trade and matters of currency disappeared from the shelves—their author, the people's commissar for finance, had just been arrested. Other writings that were removed included nearly all specialist presentations from the party congresses, most books and reference works on history and the background of the revolution, all the legal and philosophical works of living authors, brochures on population policy and birth control, manuals on the structure of the workers and peasants' army, treatises on trade unions and the right to strike in the people's state, in general nearly all theoretical research on issues of state that were more than two years old, and finally the volumes that had appeared to date of the *Encyclopedia of the Academy of Sciences*, which was slated to be replaced by a revised edition.

Meanwhile new books also arrived: classics of social science were published with new footnotes and commentary, old historical works were supplanted by new ones, and memoirs written by the deceased leaders of the revolution were replaced with new memoirs by the same deceased leaders. One time Rubashov joked to Orlova that the only thing left was to take daily newspapers from years gone by and print new and improved editions.

Meanwhile, a few weeks earlier a circular "from above" had called for the appointment of a librarian who would be politically responsible for the content of the embassy library. This post was assigned to Orlova. At the time Rubashov had mumbled something about "kindergarten" and at first he considered the whole thing ridiculous—until one evening during the official weekly meeting of the embassy party cell, when Orlova was sharply attacked from several directions at once. Three or four speakers, including the first secretary, stood up one after the other and voiced their criticism that the library was not only missing the most important and influential speeches of Number One but was also still full of oppositional writings. In particular, the books of politicians who had since been exposed and eradicated as spies, traitors, and foreign agents could until recently still be found in conspicuous places on the shelves, so that it was hard to rule out a definite intention. The speakers spoke without passion, with sharp-edged objectivity and in carefully calculated phrases; once again it sounded like they were reciting key phrases from a prescribed text. All the speeches ended with the conclusion that the prime duty of the party was to be vigilant, to denounce failings without mercy, and that whoever neglected this duty was an accomplice to the wreckers. When called to make a statement, Orlova said with her usual equanimity that any bad intention was far from her mind and that she had followed all the instructions in the circulars. As she spoke, however, in her deep, somewhat husky voice, she let her eyes rest for a long time on Rubashov, which she otherwise never did in the presence of others. The session ended with the decision to issue Orlova a "serious warning."

Rubashov, who knew all too well the recent methods used

in the movement, was concerned. He surmised that something against Orlova was already in the works, and for the first time in his political career he felt defenseless, because there was nothing concrete for him to fight against.

The air in the embassy grew even thinner. Rubashov stopped making his personal commentaries during dictation and as a result felt a peculiar sense of guilt. Seemingly nothing changed in his relationship to Orlova, but this odd sensation of guilt, which was solely due to feeling that he could no longer make witty comments during dictation, had the result that he also no longer stopped in back of her chair to rest his hands on her shoulders the way he had been doing. The next week Orlova stayed away from his room one night and didn't come on the following nights either. It took Rubashov three days to ask her for the reason. She said something in her sleepy voice about being indisposed, and Rubashov didn't press the matter. She never came again, with one exception.

That was three weeks after the evening meeting; fourteen days after she had stopped visiting him. Her behavior was scarcely different from before; still, Rubashov felt the whole evening that she was waiting for him to say something decisive. But he didn't. He only said that he was glad she was back, and that he was overworked and tired, which was also true. During the night he noticed repeatedly that she wasn't sleeping, that she was staring into the darkness with her open, round eyes. He couldn't shake the painful feeling of guilt, and the annoying toothache came back. That was her last visit.

The next morning, before Orlova reported to his office to receive dictation, the first secretary informed Rubashov in a tone that was meant to sound confidential that Orlova's brother and sister-in-law had been arrested "over there." Orlova's brother was married to a foreigner; both were accused of committing high treason on behalf of the foreign power in question, and on behalf of the internal opposition.

A few minutes later Orlova came in for dictation. She took up her usual position in front of the desk, dressed in her embroidered blouse, silent, her upper body tilted forward. Rubashov paced up and down behind her back, all the while focused on her curved neck, with the skin lightly stretched across the vertebrae. He couldn't take his eyes off this patch of skin and his discomfort verged on physical nausea. All he could think of was that the accused had been executed "over there" with a bullet to the back of the neck.

At the next evening session of the party cell, Orlova was removed from the position of librarian at the request of the first secretary, without commentary or discussion, on account of her "political unreliability." Rubashov, who was suffering from a nearly unbearable toothache, had excused himself and was not in attendance. A few days later Orlova was recalled to the homeland together with one other employee. Her former colleagues never mentioned her name, but in the remaining months that Rubashov spent at the embassy before he, too, was recalled, the sisterly scent of her large, languid body clung to the wallpaper of his office, and never evaporated.

4.

CORMADES, LET'S BRAVELY MARCH ONWARD . . .

Beginning with the morning of the tenth day after Rubashov's arrest, his new neighbor to the right in cell 406 kept tapping out the same verse, always with the same misspelling—"cormades" instead of "comrades." Rubashov had tried repeatedly to start a conversation with him. While Rubashov tapped, the newcomer would listen quietly, but the only replies were disjointed rows of letters and in the end the same mangled line: "Cormades, let's bravely march onward."

They had brought him in during the night. Rubashov was woken up but all he could hear were muffled sounds from cell 406 and the closing of the door. The next morning 406 started tapping immediately after the first bugle blast: CORMADES, LET'S

BRAVELY MARCH ONWARD. He tapped quickly and dexterously, with near-perfect technique, so that Rubashov assumed the misspelling and the nonsensical content of his other messages must be due to psychological causes and not technical ones. In all likelihood the man was mentally disturbed.

After breakfast the young officer in 402 tapped in for a conversation. A kind of friendship had developed between him and Rubashov. The officer with the monocle and the twirled moustache must have been terribly bored, because he was grateful to Rubashov for every scrap of conversation. Five or six times a day he would start tapping and meekly beg:

WON'T YOU TALK WITH ME FOR JUST A BIT . . .

Rubashov was seldom in the mood for that; besides, he didn't know what they might talk about. 402 usually told jokes he'd heard back in the officers' casino: the punch lines were usually followed by an awkward silence. The jokes were stale and smacked of old-fashioned, patriarchal ribaldry; when he had finished tapping Number 402 probably stared at the silent, whitewashed wall, hopelessly waiting for a roar of laughter. Now and then, out of sympathy and politeness, Rubashov used his pince-nez to tap HA-HA as loudly as he could, as a substitute for laughing. Then there was no stopping Number 402; he would mimic a laughing fit by pounding against the wall with his boots and fists, HA-HA-HA-HA! In between poundings he would pause for a few seconds to check if Rubashov was doing the same. If Rubashov was quiet he would tap a reproach: YOU DIDN'T LAUGH ALONG . . . And if Rubashov did tap HA-HA a few times 402 would respond with: WE HAD A RIPPING GOOD TIME.

Now and then he would berate Rubashov. Sometimes, when he didn't receive an answer, he would tap out entire soldier songs, down to the last stanza. It happened that while Rubashov was wandering through his cell lost in a daydream or deep in some complicated and intense thought process, he would suddenly start humming the refrain of an old marching song his ear had registered from the tapping without his noticing.

Nevertheless 402 was also useful. He had been locked up for more than two years; he knew the institution, was in contact with several neighbors, found out each bit of gossip, and in general seemed to know everything that was going on in the building.

One day after the new man had been brought in, the officer once again tapped in for "a visit." Rubashov asked if he knew who his neighbor in 406 was. To which 402 answered:

RIP VAN WINKLE.

Number 402 enjoyed expressing himself in riddles, to heighten the suspense of the conversation. Rubashov recalled his schooling and the legend about the villager who fell asleep for twenty years and couldn't find his way in the newly changed world.

HAS HE LOST HIS MEMORY? asked Rubashov.

Evidently pleased at having achieved the intended effect, 402 now related what he knew about the case. Number 406 had once been a lecturer in sociology in a small country in southeastern Europe, who at the end of the war—in other words, some twenty years earlier—had taken part in one of the revolutionary upheavals that had flared up then in various European cities. A commune was declared and led a romantic existence that lasted no more than a few weeks, only to come to the usual bloody end. The leaders of the revolution had been amateurs, but the repression was carried out by expert means; Number 406, whom the commune had given the illustrious title of "secretary for popular enlightenment," was sentenced to death by hanging. He waited a year to be executed, but the sentence was commuted to life in prison, where he spent twenty years.

For twenty years he was locked up, mostly in solitary confinement, having no contact with the outside world and no newspapers. He was forgotten; the penal system in that country was still somewhat paternalistic. Then suddenly a month ago he was amnestied—hence Rip van Winkle, finding himself in the world once again after twenty years of sleep and darkness. As soon as he was released he made his way here to this country, to the land of his dreams. Fourteen days after his arrival he was arrested. Perhaps after twenty years of silence he was too talkative. Perhaps he told people, during the days and nights he spent in solitary confinement, how he had imagined life would look here. Perhaps he asked for the addresses of old friends, the heroes from anno Domini 1917, without realizing they had all become traitors and spies. Perhaps he laid a wreath on the wrong grave or wanted to visit his esteemed neighbor, Comrade Rubashov. Now he was probably racking his brain trying to decide what was better: two decades of dreams on a straw tick in a dark cell, or two weeks of reality in broad daylight. Perhaps he was no longer in his right mind. So that was the story of Rip van Winkle . . .

◇

Some time after Number 402 had tapped out his lengthy report, Rip van Winkle again made contact: CORMADES, LET'S BRAVELY MARCH ONWARD. He repeated the mangled line five or six times and then was silent.

Rubashov lay down on the cot and closed his eyes. The grammatical fiction reappeared; it didn't speak in words but in a vague, agonizing sensation, which if translated into language might say: "For that, too, you must pay, for that, too, you share the guilt—because you acted while he was dreaming."

◇

That same afternoon Rubashov was taken to the barber to be shaved.

This time the procession consisted of only the old warder and a soldier; the old man shuffled two steps ahead, the soldier walked two steps behind Rubashov. They passed cell number 406, but there was no name posted. This time only one of the two prisoners assigned to run the barbershop was present; evidently Rubashov was not meant to have contact with too many people.

He sat down in the armchair. The facility was relatively clean; there was even a mirror. Rubashov removed his pince-nez and glanced at himself in the mirror; he couldn't discern any change in his face, apart from the stubble on his cheeks.

The barber worked quietly, quickly, and precisely. The door to the room stayed open; the warder had shuffled away; the soldier stood leaning against the door, overseeing the procedure. The lukewarm soap on his face felt pleasant, and Rubashov was somewhat tempted to mourn the comforts of life. He would have gladly chatted with the barber, whose broad, open face made a likeable impression—Rubashov thought he looked more like a locksmith or electrician—but the warder had warned him when they left the cell that this was forbidden, and Rubashov didn't want to cause the man any trouble. Once he was all lathered up, the barber made a few strokes with the razor and asked if the blade wasn't scratching, ending his question with "Citizen Rubashov."

It was the first sentence that had been spoken since they entered the room, and it acquired a strange significance despite the matter-of-fact tone. Then the silence returned; the soldier at the door lit a cigarette; the barber trimmed Rubashov's hair and pointed beard with quick, precise movements. As he stood bent over Rubashov, he exchanged a quick glance with him and in the same second shoved two fingers under Rubashov's collar, to more easily trim his neck hair; afterward, when the barber withdrew his fingers, Rubashov felt a small paper ball scratching his neck. Shortly after that the procedure was over, and the soldier and the warder escorted Rubashov back to his cell. He sat down on his cot, fixed his eyes on the spy hole to make sure he wasn't being watched, removed the paper from under his collar, smoothed it out, and read it. The message consisted of a single sentence, evidently scribbled in great haste:

"They've all chosen to spit on themselves—but you should die in silence."

Rubashov tossed the note in the bucket and resumed his

pacing. It was the first message he had received from outside. Back when he was imprisoned in the enemy country, he had frequently received smuggled messages telling him to raise his voice in the courtroom, so that his cry of indignation would resound throughout the world. Were there also moments in history when it was the revolutionary's duty to keep silent? Were there turning points in history that demanded only one thing of him, when the only correct action was to die and keep silent?

Rubashov's thoughts were interrupted by Number 402, who had started tapping as soon as Rubashov was back in his cell: 402 couldn't withstand his own curiosity and wanted to know where Rubashov had been taken.

FOR A SHAVE, Rubashov explained.

I ALREADY FEARED THE WORST, responded 402, with feeling.

AFTER YOU, Rubashov tapped back.

As always, 402 was a grateful audience.

HA-HA, he answered. TREMENDOUS CHAPS, YOU LOT.

Strangely this cheap compliment filled Rubashov with a kind of satisfaction. He envied 402 for belonging to a caste with a rigid code of honor regarding life and death. That was something one could cling to. For people like himself there was no manual; everything had to be thought out to the end.

Even for dying there was no proper etiquette. What was more honorable, to die in silence or to spit on oneself in public and thereby further the cause? He had sacrificed Orlova because his own existence was objectively worth more for the revolution. That had been the deciding argument his friends had used to convince him at the time: namely, that the duty of saving himself for later was more important than the mandates of bourgeois morality. For people like himself, who had once dug into the very bedrock, who had carved out a new channel for history, there was no other duty than to stand at one's post, ready and willing. "You can do with me whatever you want," Orlova had said, and he did do everything with her he wanted—so now should he treat himself more sparingly? "The coming decade will decide the fate of the world in our historical epoch," Ivanov had quoted Rubashov's own words to him. So was he supposed to slip away before that happened—out of private disgust, private fatigue, private vanity—to exit the stage with a romantic gesture? And what if Number One turned out to be right after all—the horrendous thing about Number One was that he might be right—that here, in the middle of the filth and blood and lies, the grand foundation of the future was being laid, in spite of everything? History was a master builder devoid of morals and had nearly always mixed its mortar with lies, blood, and excrement.

Die in silence—that was easy to say . . . Rubashov suddenly stopped on the third tile from the window: he had caught himself repeating the words "die in silence" several times out loud, in an ironic, sneering tone, as though to emphasize their full absurdity.

And now he realized that his decision to refuse Ivanov's offer wasn't nearly as firm as he had imagined. Now, after the fact, he even doubted whether he had ever believed he would decline the offer and exit the stage in silence.

5.

Rubashov's living conditions continued to improve. On the morning of the eleventh day following his arrest he was taken for his first walk in the yard.

The old warder came for him right after breakfast, accompanied by the same soldier who had joined the expedition to the barber. The warder informed Rubashov sullenly that as of today he was authorized to walk in the yard for twenty minutes "in consideration of your health." Rubashov was assigned to the first "carousel," which took its exercise immediately after breakfast. The warder then reeled off the regulations: all conversation with other prisoners was forbidden during the exercise, as were all hand signals and written communications; it was also forbidden to step out of place; any failure to observe the rules would result in immediate revocation of exercise privileges; severe violations would be punished with up to four weeks of confinement in a darkened cell. Then the old warder shut Rubashov's cell door from the outside, and the three men set off down the corridor. After a few steps the warder stopped again and opened the door of Number 406.

Rubashov, who had stayed next to the soldier some distance away from the door, glimpsed the inside of the neighboring cell and the legs of Rip van Winkle, who was lying on his cot. He wore black buttoned shoes and checkered suit pants that were frayed at the bottom but otherwise looked meticulously neat and clean. The warder rattled off the regulations; the checkered pant legs swung down off the cot, somewhat uncertainly; and a little old man stood blinking in the doorway. His face was covered with gray stubble; along with the checkered pants he wore a black vest with a metal watch chain and a black cloth jacket. He paused in the door and measured Rubashov with earnest curiosity, then gave him a short, friendly nod, and the four men set off. Rubashov had expected to see a mentally disturbed person, but now he changed his mind. Other than a constant nervous twitching of his eyebrows, which may have come from all the years spent in darkness, Rip van Winkle's eyes were clear and exuded an almost childlike friendliness. He walked with some difficulty but took short, determined steps, and from time to time stole a quick glance at Rubashov. When they climbed down a staircase, the old prisoner suddenly stumbled and likely would have fallen if the soldier hadn't grabbed his arm just in time. Rip van Winkle muttered a few words Rubashov didn't understand, because they were spoken too quietly, and which were undoubtedly meant to express a polite thank-you; the soldier responded with a stupid grin. Then they passed through an open grilled door into the yard, where the other walkers were already assembled in pairs. From the center of the yard, where the guards on watch were standing, came two short whistles, and the carousel slowly began to move.

The sky was clear, a rare pale blue, and the air was permeated with the pungent, crystalline smell of the snow. Rubashov hadn't brought his blanket and was shivering; Rip van Winkle had slung a tatty gray blanket over his shoulders, which the warder had handed him when they stepped into the yard—it covered him down to the knees, like a bell. He walked slowly alongside Rubashov, with short, determined steps, occasionally blinking at the bright blue sky overhead. Rubashov figured out which window belonged to his own cell; it was dark and dirty like all the others, so nothing could be seen behind it. For a while he observed the window at Number 402, but there, too, all he saw was the blank, barred windowpane. It seemed that Number 402 was not let out of his cell—not for exercise, nor to have his hair cut, nor to be interrogated; Rubashov had never heard him being taken out of the cell at all.

They walked in silence, slowly circling the yard. Rip van Winkle's lips were moving under the gray stubble of his beard, though this was barely noticeable; he was mumbling something Rubashov couldn't make out at first. Then he realized that the old man was quietly and incessantly humming the melody of "Comrades, let's bravely march onward." Rip van Winkle might not be crazy, but being imprisoned for seven thousand days and nights had probably left him a little peculiar. Rubashov watched him from the side and tried to imagine what it meant to be cut off from the world for two decades. Twenty years ago there had been no radios and just a few, strangely shaped automobiles, and the names of the current leaders of state had been unknown. No one had foreseen the new mass movements, the great political earthquakes, the twisting paths, the excruciating and confusing stages that the revolutionary state had to pass through—back then people thought the gates to utopia were open and humanity was standing on the threshold of a dazzling future . . .

Rubashov had to admit he didn't have enough imagination to fully envision his neighbor's internal state, despite his long practice in the art of "thinking through the mind of others." When it came to Ivanov, Number One, or even the monocled officer next door, he could do this without effort, but with Rip van Winkle he could not. He observed his neighbor from the side; the old man had just turned his head toward Rubashov and smiled; he gripped his gray blanket with both hands, keeping it tightly wrapped around his shoulders as he walked with his small, resolute steps and hummed the melody to "Comrades, let's bravely march onward" so quietly it was hard to hear.

Back inside, the old man again turned around in the door of his cell and nodded to Rubashov, and suddenly his blinking eyes had a very different expression, full of fear and desperation. Rubashov had the impression that the man wanted to call out to him, but the warder quickly locked the door to his cell. Once Rubashov was shut back inside his own cell he went straight to the wall separating him from Number 406, but Rip van Winkle was silent and did not answer his tapping.

Number 402, on the other hand, who had watched them from his window, wanted to hear every detail about the walk in the yard; he was bursting with curiosity, and Rubashov had to describe the smell of the air, whether it was cold or merely cool, whether he had met other prisoners in the corridor, and whether he might have been able to exchange a few words with Rip van Winkle after all. Rubashov patiently answered every question. He felt privileged compared to Number 402, who was never taken out to exercise, and he felt pity for the man—almost even a twinge of remorse.

◇

The next day and the one after that Rubashov was taken out for a walk, always at the same time, just after breakfast had been doled out; Rip van Winkle remained his partner in the carousel. They walked slowly alongside each other in a circle, each with his blanket wrapped around his shoulders, neither speaking—Rubashov sunk in thought, now and then carefully observing the other prisoners and the windows of the building through his pince-nez; the old man with his increasingly long stubble and his childlike, tender smile singing his eternal song.

On those first two days they didn't exchange a word, although Rubashov had noticed that the guards didn't take the speaking ban all too seriously, and that the other pairs spoke together almost all the time, only they kept their gaze fixed straight ahead and barely moved their lips when they spoke—a jailhouse technique Rubashov knew well.

On the third day Rubashov took his notepad and pencil and stuck the pad in the right outside pocket of his jacket. Some ten minutes into their walk the old man happened to notice it since the pad was sticking out a bit, and his eyes lit up. He stole a glance at the guards in the center of the carousel, who were speaking excitedly with one another and didn't seem interested in the prisoners; then with one quick move he grabbed both notepad and pencil out of Rubashov's pocket and began writing something under the cover of his bell blanket. He was soon finished, tore off the page and pressed it into Rubashov's hand, but held on to the pad and pencil and resumed writing. Rubashov made sure the guards weren't paying attention and looked at the paper. There was no text, just a drawing—a remarkably precise sketch of the country they were in, showing the most important cities, mountains, and rivers, with a flag in the middle that bore the official symbol of the revolution, large and clear.

After half a turn of the carousel, Number 406 tore off another page and thrust it into Rubashov's hand. It was an identical drawing, done in exactly the same way, of the homeland of the revolution. Number 406 looked at him and smiled as he waited for the effect. Rubashov was a little flustered and mumbled something meant to express his appreciation. The old man nodded and winked.

"I can also do it with my eyes closed," he said. Rubashov

nodded. "You don't believe me," said the old man, smiling. "But I practiced it for twenty years."

He looked quickly at the guards, closed his eyes, and began drawing a new page under his bell blanket, without changing his gait. He kept his eyes tightly shut and his white-stubbled chin jutting forward as he walked, like a blind man. Rubashov turned to look at the guards; he was afraid Number 406 might trip or drop out of line. But after half a turn the drawing was finished, a little more shaky than the previous ones, but just as exact, only the symbol in the flag in the middle of the country had come out a little too large.

"Now do you believe me?" whispered Number 406 with a happy smile. Rubashov nodded. Just then the old man's face darkened, and Rubashov recognized the same fear that the man showed each time he was being locked back up in his cell.

"It's no use," he whispered to Rubashov. "They put me on the wrong train."

"How's that?" asked Rubashov.

Rip van Winkle smiled at him gently and sadly. "When I was leaving they took me to the wrong station," he said, "and they think I didn't notice. Don't tell anyone that I know," he whispered, and winked slyly in the direction of the guards.

Rubashov nodded. Just then the whistle blew that sounded the end of the walk.

As they entered the building they had another moment when they weren't observed. Number 406's eyes were once again clear and friendly:

"Perhaps the same thing happened to you?" he asked Rubashov sympathetically.

Rubashov nodded.

"Never lose hope—we'll make it there yet one day . . . ," said Rip van Winkle, pointing to the crumpled map in Rubashov's hand.

Then he shoved notepad and pencil back in Rubashov's pocket. As he climbed the stairs he was already humming his eternal song.

6.

Three days before the deadline set by Ivanov, while the evening soup was being dispensed, Rubashov sensed that something unusual was in the air. He couldn't say exactly why: the meal was delivered according to the usual routine, the melancholy melody signaling the end of the day was sounded punctually at the prescribed time—nevertheless Rubashov felt a tension in the air. Perhaps one of the soup trusties had looked at him differently, a shade more meaningfully than usual, or perhaps the old warder's voice had had a particular undertone. Rubashov couldn't decide, but he was incapable of working; he felt the tension in his nerves the way a rheumatic feels the approaching storm.

After the second bugle sounded he peered out into the corridor; as always, the electric bulbs, darkened by accumulated dead flies, had insufficient power, and burned with only half their intensity, spilling their dreary light across the tile floors. But today the silence of the corridor seemed more absolute and hopeless than ever. Rubashov lay down on his cot, then got back up, forced himself to write a few lines, stubbed out his cigarette and lit a new one. He looked down into the yard; the thawing snow was dirty and soft, the sky was overcast, and the sentry posted on the outer wall paced off his hundred steps, shouldering his rifle and bayonet. Rubashov again looked through the spy hole: stillness, desolation, and electric light.

Against his custom, and in spite of the late hour, Rubashov began a conversation with Number 402. ARE YOU SLEEPING? he tapped.

For a while there was nothing and as Rubashov waited, he was embarrassed that he actually felt disappointed. Then came the answer, more quietly and slowly than was 402's usual style:

NO—YOU FEEL IT TOO?

FEEL—WHAT? asked Rubashov. His breathing was heavy; he had lain down on the cot and was tapping with his pince-nez.

Again it took 402 a while to answer. Then he tapped so quietly it sounded as though he wanted to speak with an especially soft voice:

IT'S BETTER IF YOU SLEEP.

Rubashov lay still on his cot and was ashamed that Number 402 could suddenly talk down to him like that. He lay on his back in the dark and looked at the pince-nez he was holding in his half-raised hand beside the wall. The silence in the corridor was so thick he felt it rushing in his ears. Suddenly the ticking in the wall resumed:

STRANGE—THAT YOU SENSED IT RIGHT AWAY . . .

SENSED WHAT? TELL ME! Rubashov tapped, and sat back up on the cot.

Number 402 seemed to reflect for a moment. After a short hesitation he tapped lightly:

POLITICAL DIFFERENCES ARE BEING SETTLED TONIGHT . . .

Rubashov understood. He sat leaning against the wall, in the dark, and waited for more. But Number 402 didn't say anything else. After a while Rubashov tapped:

EXECUTIONS?

YES, answered 402 laconically.

HOW DO YOU KNOW? asked Rubashov.

FROM HARELIP.

AT WHAT TIME? asked Rubashov.

I DON'T KNOW. Then, after a pause: SOON.

DO YOU KNOW NAMES? asked Rubashov.

NO, answered 402. But after another pause he added:

YOUR KIND. POLITICAL DIFFERENCES.

Rubashov lay back down and waited. After a while he put on his pince-nez, then he lay quietly on his cot for a little longer, his arms folded under his neck. Not a sound was to be heard from outside. Every movement in the building was stifled, frozen in the darkness.

Rubashov had never attended an execution—apart from what was nearly his own, but that had been long ago, in the middle of the civil war. He couldn't actually imagine how they might take place under routine, regulated conditions. He was vaguely aware that the shootings happened at night, in the basement, and that the offender was killed with a shot to the back of the head, but he didn't know the exact details. The revolutionary movement did not imbue death with any mystery; it had no romantic character. It was a logical consequence, a factor used in calculations, relatively abstract. It was seldom spoken about, and the words "shooting" and "execution" were hardly ever used: the usual expression was "physical liquidation"—which connoted the cessation of political activity and nothing else. The act of dying was in itself a technical detail of no interest; as a factor of logical calculation, death had forfeited any intimate, physical character.

Rubashov peered through his pince-nez into the darkness. Was the procedure already under way or had it not yet started? He had taken off his socks and shoes; his naked feet at the other end of the blanket were poking up toward the ceiling, white against the darkness. The stillness became even more unnatural. It was not the calming absence of sound: it was a silence that swallowed and stifled every sound, a taut silence that vibrated like a tightened drum skin. Rubashov looked at his naked feet and slowly wiggled his toes. What he saw looked grotesque, uncanny—as though the white feet had a life of their own. He had seldom been so intensely aware of his body; he felt the lukewarm touch of the blanket on his legs and the pressure of his palms beneath his neck. Where did the physical liquidation take place? He had a vague notion that it happened down below, beneath the stairs that led down from the barbershop. He could smell the leather of Gletkin's pistol belt and hear the creak of his stiff uniform. What did he say to his victims beforehand? "Stand with your face against the wall"? Did he address them less politely, with the familiar "you"? Or did he say: "Don't be afraid, it won't hurt"? Perhaps he shot without warning, while walking, from behind—except the victim kept turning around.

Perhaps he hid his pistol in his sleeve the way the dentist hides his forceps. Perhaps other people were there as well. How did they react? Did the man fall forward or backward? Did he call out? Perhaps they had to put a second bullet in him as a coup de grâce.

Rubashov smoked and studied his toes. It was so quiet he could hear the crinkling of the burning cigarette paper. He took a deep draw. *Nonsense*, he told himself. Rubbish, cheap literature, lurid fantasy. The truth was he had never believed in the physical aspect of "physical liquidation." Death was an abstraction, especially one's own. In all likelihood this case was all already over and done with, and what's over and done with has no reality.

Everything was dark and quiet, and Number 402 had stopped tapping.

He wished that someone outside would scream to break the unnatural stillness. He sniffled and realized that for a long time he'd felt Orlova's scent in his nostrils. The cigarettes, too, had her smell; she had kept a leather case in her purse, and all the cigarettes inside it had smelled like the powder she used, like her body. It was still quiet. Only the cot moaned quietly whenever he moved.

Rubashov was just about to get up and light another cigarette when the wall next to him began to tick. THEY'RE COMING, it said.

Rubashov listened. All he could hear was the hammering in his arteries. He waited. The silence grew more charged, more tense. He took his pince-nez and tapped:

I DON'T HEAR ANYTHING . . .

For a long time Number 402 didn't answer. Suddenly he tapped, long and hard:

NUMBER 380. PASS IT ON.

Rubashov quickly sat up. He understood: Number 380's neighbors, the inmates of cells 382 through 402, formed an acoustic courier service through the silence and darkness and had passed the news across eleven cells. Helplessly confined within their four walls, this was their way to show their solidarity. Rubashov jumped up from his cot; stepped quietly over to the other wall on his bare feet, next to the bucket; and tapped to Number 406:

ATTENTION. NUMBER 380 WILL NOW BE SHOT. PASS IT ON.

He listened. The bucket stank; its odor had dispelled Orlova's scent. There was no answer. Rubashov stepped quickly back to his cot. This time he didn't tap with the pince-nez but with his knuckle:

WHO IS 380?

Again there was no answer. Rubashov understood that 402 was doing the same thing he had done, shuttling between the walls of his cell to pass along the news. In each of the eleven cells to his left, the inmates were scurrying just as quietly, on bare feet, back and forth between the walls. Now Number 402 was back and tapped:

THEY ARE READING HIS SENTENCE. PASS IT ON.

Rubashov repeated his question:

WHO IS 380?

But Number 402 was already gone. It was pointless to pass the news to Rip van Winkle; nevertheless Rubashov tapped on the wall near the bucket and delivered his message; he was driven by a dark sense of duty, a feeling that the chain should not be broken. The proximity of the bucket made him nauseous. He stole back to his cot and waited. From outside there still was not the slightest sound—only the wall started ticking once again:

HE'S SHOUTING FOR HELP.

HE'S SHOUTING FOR HELP, Rubashov tapped to Number 406. He listened. Nothing. Rubashov was afraid he would throw up the next time he came close to the bucket.

THEY'RE BRINGING HIM. HE'S SHOUTING AND LASHING OUT. PASS IT ON . . . , tapped 402.

WHAT'S HIS NAME? Rubashov tapped quickly, before 402 could finish his sentence. This time he received an answer:

BOGROV. OPPOSITION. PASS IT ON.

Rubashov's legs suddenly felt heavy. As he made his way to the wall by the bucket he felt his knee starting to give. He leaned against the wall, then tapped to the feebleminded old man:

VLADIMIR BOGROV, FORMER SAILOR ON THE BATTLESHIP PO-TEMKIN, COMMANDER OF THE EASTERN FLEET, BEARER OF THE ORDER OF THE RED BANNER, IS BEING LED TO EXECUTION.

He wiped the sweat from his brow, vomited hastily into the bucket, and finished his message:

. . . PASS IT ON.

He couldn't recall exactly what Bogrov looked like, but he could see the outline of his hulking figure, the helplessly dangling arm, the freckles on his broad, flat face with the slightly upturned nose. After 1905 they had both been banished and had shared a room. Rubashov had taught him to read and write, and the basics of historical thinking; since then no matter where Rubashov happened to be, every six months Bogrov would send him a handwritten letter, which always ended with the same words: "Your comrade loyal to the grave, Bogrov."

THEY'RE COMING OUR WAY, tapped 402, hastily and so loud that Rubashov, who was still leaning against the wall next to the bucket, could hear it all the way across the cell . . . GO TO YOUR SPY HOLE. DRUM. PASS IT ON.

Rubashov stiffened. He tapped the message to Number 406: TO THE SPY HOLE. DRUM. PASS IT ON. He moved quietly through the darkness to the cell door and waited. In the corridor the dreary electric light was burning as always. And as always, it was quiet.

A few seconds later he heard the ticking on his wall: NOW.

Down the corridor came a quiet, choked sound of muffled drumming. No tapping or pounding; the men who formed the acoustic chain from cells 382 to 402 were now standing behind their doors as an honor guard, and their drumming was deceptively similar to a solemn muffled drumroll carried from a distance by the wind. Rubashov stood with his eye pressed to the spy hole and joined the chorus by beating rhythmically against the concrete door with both hands. To his amazement the muted wave continued off to the right, past Number 406 and beyond; Rip van Winkle must have understood after all and was drumming together with the rest. At the same time, from off to the left, still well beyond his field of vision, he heard the grating of an iron gate being slid open on its tracks. The drumming to the left grew a notch louder; Rubashov realized they had opened the iron door that separated the isolation unit from the regular cells. A key ring jangled—they were again closing the gate—and right away he could hear dragging and scuffing sounds advancing along the tiled floor of the corridor. The drumming from the left now came in a constant, muffled crescendo. Rubashov's field of vision, from cells 401 through 407, was still empty. The dragging, scuffing, and rasping on the tiles quickly came closer; now Rubashov could also hear groaning and a childlike whimper. The steps quickened; the drumming to the left fell off a bit and began to swell on the right.

Rubashov drummed. He had lost his sense of time and place; he only heard the dull toomm-toomm of jungle drums—perhaps they were apes standing in their cages behind the doors, beating their chests and drumming . . . Rubashov pressed his eye to the spy hole, bobbing rhythmically up and down on his toes as he drummed. He could still see nothing except the pallid yellow light of the electric lamps in the corridor, and the concrete doors of cells 401 through 407, but he heard the drumming grow louder and the rasping and whimpering come closer. Suddenly some half-dark forms slid into view: they had arrived. Rubashov stopped drumming and stared. And then they were gone.

Rubashov couldn't say exactly what he saw in those few seconds, neither while he was experiencing it nor later on. Two half-lit figures had marched past, two men in uniform, tall and blurred, dragging a third figure by the armpits. The figure in the middle dangled from their arms like a puppet, inert but stiff, with his body stretched out lengthwise, his face turned to the floor, and his stomach bulging downward. His legs were trailing behind; it was the caps of his shoes skidding across the stone tiles that had produced the rasping noise Rubashov had heard from a distance. Whitish hanks of hair hung across his face, which was dripping with sweat; spit was trickling out of his wide-open mouth and dribbling down his chin. After they had dragged him off to the right and out of Rubashov's field of vision, the groaning and whimpering gradually faded away; there was only a distant echo consisting of three plaintive, sustained vowels: u-a-o. But before they turned the corner at the end of the corridor across from the barbershop, Bogrov bellowed out loud twice in a row, and Rubashov now heard not just the vowels but the whole word: it was his name, he heard it clearly—Ru-ba-shov.

Then all at once it was still. The electric lights burned as always, and as always, the corridor was dead. Only from the wall to Number 406 came the ticking: CORMADES, LET'S BRAVELY MARCH ONWARD.

◇

Rubashov lay back down on his cot, without knowing how he got there. He still had the toomm-toomm of the drumroll in his ear, but now the silence was genuine, empty, and without tension. Number 402 was probably already asleep. Bogrov, or what was left of him, was probably already dead.

"Rubashov—Rubashov . . . !" That final cry with every nuance of its inflection was forever pressed into his acoustic memory. The visual image was less clear. It was still hard for him to recognize Bogrov in the wax-doll figure that for those few seconds had slid across his field of view, with the wet face and the stiff, skidding legs. It wasn't until later that he remembered the white hair. What had they put him through before this? What had they done to the onetime seaman, the later fleet commander, that he would whimper like a child? Had Orlova whimpered like that when they dragged her down the corridor?

Rubashov sat up and leaned his forehead against the wall behind which Number 402 was sleeping; he was afraid he'd have to throw up again. Up until now he had never imagined Orlova's death in this kind of detail. Up until now it had been an abstract process, one that had left him with a heavy feeling of unease, but until now he hadn't doubted the logical correctness of his action, judged from the standpoint of revolutionary morality. Now, amid the nausea that was churning his stomach and causing his cot to shake and making his forehead break out in a cold sweat, his past way of thinking seemed like a mental disease. Now, after the fact, Bogrov's whimpering, which was also Orlova's, rendered all such logical calculation meaningless. Until now Orlova had been a factor in the calculation, relatively insignificant compared to what was at stake.

But the equation no longer added up. The image of Orlova's legs dragging across the floor in her high heels upended the mathematical balance. The insignificant factor grew into something beyond measure, into something absolute; Bogrov's whimpering, the unhuman sound of his voice that had called out Rubashov's name, and the muffled toomm-toomm of the drumming all resounded in his ears, stifling the thin voice of logical calculation, silencing it the way the breaking surf smothers the burbling of a drowning man.

Rubashov was so exhausted he fell asleep sitting up, his head propped against the wall, his pince-nez perched in front of his closed eyes.

7.

Rubashov moaned in his sleep; the dream of his first arrest had returned: his hand dangling limply from the cot twitched as it sought to catch the sleeve of his robe. In his sleep he waited for the pistol butt to finally strike him, but it never did.

Instead he woke up, startled by the sudden electric light in his cell. A figure was standing by his cot and looking at him. Rubashov hadn't slept more than a quarter hour, but he always needed a few minutes to shake himself out of the arrest dream. As his eyes blinked in the harsh light, his mind quickly started working through the familiar hypotheses, as though he were performing some unconscious ritual—although this time it took more effort: he was in a cell, but not in the land of the enemy—that was just his dream. So he was free—but the color portrait of Number One was missing over his bed, and over there was the bucket. Besides, Ivanov was standing over his cot and blowing cigarette smoke in his face. Was that also a dream? No, Ivanov was real, the bucket was real, he was in a friendly country, but it had become an enemy country, and Ivanov, who had been his friend, was now his enemy as well. Orlova's whimpering wasn't a dream either. But it wasn't Orlova, it was Bogrov whom they had dragged past his cell like a wax doll, Comrade Bogrov, loyal to the grave, and he had called out Rubashov's name, and that wasn't a dream either. Orlova though had said: "You can do with me whatever you want."

"Feeling sick?" asked Ivanov.

Rubashov squinted at him, blinded by the light. "Hand me my robe," he said.

Ivanov looked at him closely. The right half of Rubashov's face was very swollen. "Do you want some brandy?" he asked. Without waiting for an answer he hobbled over to the spy hole and shouted something down the corridor. Rubashov squinted after him. He still couldn't shake the stupor. He was awake, but his sight, hearing, and thinking were all in a mist. "Did they arrest you, too?" he asked.

"No, my friend," Ivanov said calmly. "I just came to visit. I think you have a fever."

"Give me a cigarette," said Rubashov. He took a few deep drags, and his eyesight grew clearer. He lay back down, smoked, and stared at the ceiling. The cell door was open; a warder brought a bottle of brandy and a glass. This time it wasn't the old man, but a skinny youth in uniform with steel-rimmed glasses. He saluted Ivanov with an exaggerated posture, handed him the bottle and glass, and locked the door from the outside. They heard his steps moving away in the corridor. Ivanov sat down on the edge of Rubashov's cot and poured a full glass. "Drink," he said. Rubashov drained the glass. The fog in his head dissipated, and all the events and persons—his first and second arrests, Orlova, Bogrov, Ivanov—arranged themselves properly in time and space.

"Are you in pain?" asked Ivanov.

"No," said Rubashov. The only thing he still didn't understand was what Ivanov was doing in his cell.

"Your cheek is badly swollen. It looks like you have a fever, too."

Rubashov stood up from the cot, peered through the spy hole into the empty corridor, and paced up and down the cell a few times, waiting for his head to clear completely. Then he stood in front of Ivanov, who was patiently blowing smoke rings.

"What are you doing here?" he asked.

"I want to talk with you," said Ivanov. "Lie down and have another brandy."

Rubashov squinted at him through his pince-nez. "Up to now," he said, "I was tempted to believe you were acting in good faith. Now I see that you are a swine. Go away."

Ivanov didn't move. "Be so kind as to justify your allegation," he said.

Rubashov leaned with his back against the wall of Number 406 and looked down at Ivanov sitting on the cot. Ivanov met his gaze and calmly went on smoking.

"Point one," said Rubashov. "You know of my friendship with Bogrov. So you make sure that Bogrov—or whatever you and your people left of him—is led past my cell on his last journey, as a warning. And just to make sure I don't miss the show, Bogrov's execution is discreetly announced in advance, trusting that my neighbors will tap the news through, which they do. Another subtle directorial twist was letting Bogrov know that I'm also being held here—and this just before he was led away—with the assumption that Bogrov will audibly react to this last shock, which he does. Naturally the whole thing is calculated to push me over the edge into a state of depression. Then, in this blackest hour, Comrade Ivanov shows up as a savior, with a bottle of brandy. A great warm brotherly scene ensues, we fall into each other's arms, swap old war stories, and in passing I sign a statement before drifting into a gentle sleep; Comrade Ivanov tiptoes away, statement in hand, and advances his career . . . Now, would you be so good as to leave."

Ivanov didn't move. He blew smoke into the air and smiled, revealing his gold teeth. "Do you really think I'm that primitive?" he asked. "Or rather: do you think I'm such a poor psychologist?"

Rubashov shrugged his shoulders. "Your tricks disgust me," he said. "I can't exactly throw you out. If there's still just a spark of the old Ivanov in you, then go now and leave me alone. You have no idea how much the lot of you disgust me."

Ivanov picked the glass up off the floor, poured himself some brandy, and drank it. "I propose the following deal," he said. "Let me speak uninterrupted for five minutes and listen with a clear head to what I have to say. If afterward you still insist I should leave then I'll go."

"I'm listening," said Rubashov. He leaned against the wall, facing Ivanov, and looked at his watch.

"First," said Ivanov, "to rule out any doubt: Bogrov has indeed been shot. Second: he was in prison for several months and was tortured for several days toward the end. If you say in your public trial that I told you this, or even if you tap it through to Number 402, I am done for. We'll get to why we did that to Bogrov later. Third: it was indeed intentional that he be led past your cell and that he was told of your presence. Fourth: what you call a disgusting trick, and what I call bad staging, is not my doing but was directed by my colleague Gletkin, against my express instructions."

He paused. Rubashov stood against the wall and said nothing.

"I would never have made this mistake," Ivanov continued, "and not out of some gentle-hearted concern, but because it runs counter to my tactics and my knowledge of your psychology. You've recently displayed a host of Tolstoyan impulses—morals, humanistic sentimentality, and so on. Besides, the business with Orlova still weighs on you. The scene with Bogrov was only bound to intensify your depression as well as your moralistic tendencies—that was predictable; only a psychological bungler like Gletkin could make such a mistake. By the way, for ten days now Gletkin has been pestering me to use 'hard methods' on you. First of all, he doesn't like you because you showed him the holes in your socks; second, he's used to dealing with peasants . . . So much for Bogrov. Of course I ordered the brandy, because when I came in you were half out of your senses. I have no interest in getting you drunk. I have no interest in subjecting you to psychological shocks. That would just push you further toward this exalted sense of morality. On the contrary, I need you sober and logical. My only concern is that you think your case through, soberly and logically. Because once you've thought it through to the end, then, and only then, will you give in . . ."

Rubashov gave a sarcastic shrug, but before he could say anything Ivanov continued:

"I realize you're convinced you won't capitulate. But just answer this one question: if you could persuade yourself of the logical correctness and objective expedience of capitulating, would you do it?"

Rubashov didn't answer right away. He had a hollow sensation that the conversation had taken a turn he should not have allowed. The five minutes were over, and he hadn't thrown Ivanov out of the cell. That in itself, it seemed to him, was a betrayal of Bogrov and Orlova—as well as of Richard and Little Löwy . . .

"Go," he said to Ivanov. "There's no use. Go . . ." Only now did he realize he was no longer leaning against the wall but had for some time been pacing up and down the cell while Ivanov stayed sitting on the cot.

Ivanov leaned forward a little. "I can tell from your tone," he said, "that you recognize your mistake concerning my role with Bogrov. So why do you want me to leave? Why aren't you answering my earlier question?" He leaned forward even more, fixed his wry gaze squarely on Rubashov, and then said, slowly, emphasizing every word: "*Because you are afraid of me.* Because my way of thinking and debating is the same as yours and you are afraid of the echo in your own head. Any minute you're going to call out '*Apage Satanus!*'—'Begone, Satan . . .' "

Rubashov didn't answer. He paced up and down in front of the window, which meant turning either his back or his side to Ivanov. He felt helpless and incapable of arguing clearly. Moreover his feeling of guilt—what Ivanov called his "exalted sense of morality"—couldn't be expressed in terms of logical argument: it corresponded to the realm of the grammatical fiction, which eluded all discussions and debates. At the same time it was true that every sentence Ivanov uttered set off an echo inside him. He felt he should never have allowed this conversation. Now it seemed to him that he was on a smooth and slippery slope, inexorably sliding further and further down.

"*Apage Satanus!*" Ivanov repeated, pouring himself another glass. "Earlier the temptation was of the flesh, now it takes the form of pure reason. Values change. I'd like to write a passion play where God and the devil are fighting over the soul of Saint Rubashov. After a sinful life he has turned toward God—a god with the double chin of industrial liberalism and Salvation Army–style goodwill, whose epiphanies come from the lead articles of British commerce reports. Satan, on the other hand, is skinny, austere, and a fanatic when it comes to logic. He reads Machiavelli, Ignatius of Loyola, Marx, and Hegel; he is cold and has no pity for humanity, but does this out of a kind of mathematical compassion. And he is forever damned to do what he loathes the most: become a butcher in order to stamp out butchery, sacrifice lambs so lambs will no longer be sacrificed, whip people so they will learn not to let themselves be whipped, eradicate all his moral impulses in the name of a higher moral, and court humanity's hatred because he loves humanity so—abstractly and geometrically. *Apage Satanus!* Comrade Rubashov prefers to become a martyr. The editorial columnists in the West, who despised him while he was alive, will beatify him after he is dead. He has discovered his conscience, and a conscience is as useless for the revolution as a fat belly and a double chin. His conscience gnaws away at his brain like a cancer, until the gray matter is completely corroded. Satan is beaten and retreats. Except you have to imagine his departure correctly. Don't just think that he snarls and spits fire. He shrugs his shoulders, he is gaunt and resigned, he's seen so many souls grow weak and slink away from his ranks with pathetic excuses . . ."

Ivanov stopped speaking and poured himself another glass. Rubashov paced up and down by the window. After a while he said:

"Why did you kill Bogrov?"

"Why? Because of the submarines," said Ivanov. "The problem of tonnage—an old debate, I'm sure you're familiar with how it started.

"Bogrov was in favor of constructing larger submarines with a greater cruising radius. The party line is for small submarines with a lesser cruising radius. For the same money you can build three times more small submarines than large ones. Both sides had technical arguments. The expert journals were scribbled full of calculations and algebraic formulas. But in reality it was about something else. Large submarines point to an eventual war of aggression and world revolution. Small submarines mean protecting the coast, defending the country, temporarily relinquishing the idea of spreading the revolution. That's the position of Number One and the leadership. Bogrov had a strong following in the admiralty and among the officers of the old guard. It wasn't enough to remove him; he had to be discredited as well. A trial was planned to expose those who advocated for larger tonnage as saboteurs and traitors. We had already brought a few lesser engineers to the point where they were ready to testify against themselves, admit that they'd been in the service of a foreign power, etc. But Bogrov refused to play along. All the way to the end he spoke out for larger boats and world revolution. He was twenty years out of date. He refused to realize that the times were against us, that Europe was undergoing a period of reaction, that we were in a historical trough and had to lie low until the next crest. Nothing was to be gained with a public trial—he would have just driven the country mad. There was no choice but to liquidate him administratively. Wouldn't you have acted the same way in our place . . . ?"

Rubashov didn't answer. He interrupted his wandering near the window and again leaned against the wall separating him from Number 406, next to the bucket. A noxious odor rose from the bucket; he took off his pince-nez and looked at Ivanov with red-rimmed, haunted eyes:

"You didn't hear him whimpering," he said very quietly.

Ivanov lit a new cigarette with the stub of the old one; the stench from the bucket was beginning to bother him as well.

"No," he said, "I didn't. But I have heard and seen similar things. What of it?"

Rubashov said nothing. Trying to explain was pointless. Again he heard the whimpering and the muffled drumming, like an echo. That was something that couldn't be conveyed. Just like the geometric curve of Orlova's breast with its warm, tapered tip. None of it could be conveyed at all. "Die in silence" was what was written on the note he had received at the barber's.

"What of it?" Ivanov repeated. He stretched his leg in the direction of the bucket and waited. Since Rubashov didn't answer, he went on:

"If I had just a spark of pity for you," he said, "I would leave you alone now. But I don't have a spark of pity. I drink, and for a while I was shooting morphine, but up to now pity is one vice I've been able to stay away from. All it takes is one dose of pity mixed with humanism and you're lost. You know how members of our race are pathologically inclined to weep and wail, especially over their own fate. Our greatest poets drank that poison and that was what led to their ruin. Until the age of forty or fifty they were revolutionaries—then they became intoxicated, addicted to pity, and the world proclaimed them saints. You seem to have the same ambition and you're convinced your case is unique, that no one else has ever gone through the same process . . ." Ivanov had raised his voice a little and blew out a cloud of smoke. "Guard against such ecstatic feelings," he said. "We should all guard against the feeling of uniqueness—it is poisonous. Every bottle of liquor contains a measurable quantity of ecstasy. Unfortunately only a very few—especially among our countrymen—realize that ecstasies produced by tolerance and suffering are just as cheap as chemically induced ones. Back then, when I woke up from the anesthetic and discovered that my body suddenly stopped at my right knee, I experienced a kind of absolute ecstasy of unhappiness. Do you remember how you lectured me?" He poured a new glass and drained it.

"What I'm getting at," he continued, "is this: we're not allowed to view the world as some kind of metaphysical brothel of sentimentality. That is the first ethical commandment for our kind. For our kind pity, conscience, disgust, despair, and wallowing in atonement are hideous debaucheries with a transcendental, brothel-like allure. To sit down and let yourself be hypnotized by your own navel, to roll your eyes and humbly bare your neck for Gletkin's revolver—that's an easy way out. The greatest temptation for our kind is to renounce violence, do penance, come to peace with oneself. Most great revolutionaries succumbed to this temptation, from Spartacus to Danton and Dostoevsky—that's the classic form of betrayal of the cause.

God's temptations were always more dangerous to mankind than Satan's. As long as the world is ruled by chaos, God is an anachronism and every compromise with our own conscience is treacherous. Whenever that damned inner voice starts to speak you have to shut your ears . . ."

He reached behind him for the bottle and filled another glass. Rubashov noticed that the bottle was already half-empty. *It seems like you were in need of a little consolation yourself,* he thought.

"Objectively speaking," Ivanov went on, "the greatest criminals in history were not the Neros or Fouchés, but rather the Gandhis and Tolstoys. Gandhi's inner voice has done more to hold back the liberation of India than British guns. Selling oneself for thirty pieces of silver is an honest business, but whoever sells himself to his own conscience and his inner voice is giving up humanity for lost. History is by definition immoral: history has no conscience. Trying to steer it by the maxims of a Sunday sermon means leaving everything the way it is and putting a spoke in the wheel of progress. You know that as well as I do. You know what's at stake here, and here you come to me with talk about Bogrov whimpering . . ."

He finished his glass, poured another, and added:

". . . Or with pangs of conscience about your plump Orlova."

Rubashov knew from experience that Ivanov could hold his liquor, and this time was no exception—at most his speech was a little livelier than usual. *You really were in need of consolation,* thought Rubashov again, *perhaps even more than I was.* He sat on his narrow stool across from Ivanov and listened to him. None of it was new to him; for years he had stood for the same point of view, with the same or similar words. The difference today was that back then those inner processes that Ivanov was describing with such disdain had been mere abstractions; since then, however, he had experienced the grammatical fiction as a physical reality, on his own body. Still—were these irrational processes more worthy of endorsement just because he had made their personal acquaintance? And did the mystical "intoxication" become less worthy of combating just because he had succumbed to its influence? A year ago, when his public statement had sent Orlova to her death, Rubashov had not had sufficient imagination to picture exactly how that took place. Would he act differently today, just because he was now familiar with the details? Either it had been right or it had been wrong to sacrifice Richard, Orlova, and Little Löwy, but what did Richard's stuttering, the shape of Orlova's breast, or Bogrov's whimpering have to do with the objective rightness or wrongness of the measure taken?

Rubashov again started pacing up and down the cell, this time without turning his back to Ivanov. He felt that everything he had experienced, everything he had thought since his arrest, had been merely a prelude, and that all his deliberations had reached a dead end, that he had come to the threshold of Ivanov's "metaphysical brothel"—and now had to start all over again. But how much time did he have left? He stopped, took the glass out of Ivanov's hand, and drank the brandy down all at once. Ivanov studied him.

"Now I'm starting to like you better," he said with a fleeting smile. "Monologues in the form of a dialogue are a useful device. I hope I've done a decent job playing devil's advocate. Too bad that the opposing party isn't represented. But that's one of his tricks, not allowing himself to be drawn into a proper debate, along with pouncing on a person when he's helpless and alone, and staging his appearance for the most lurid effect, with burning bushes and cloud-topped mountains—and preferably when you're fast asleep. No, when it comes to methods, the Great Moralist is a bit theatrical and not very fair . . ."

Rubashov was no longer listening to him. As he paced up and down he wondered whether today, if Orlova were still alive, he would act the same way he had back then, whether he would again sacrifice her. This problem fascinated him; it seemed to contain the solution to all other questions. He stopped in front of Ivanov and asked him abruptly:

"Have you ever actually read *Crime and Punishment*?"

Ivanov smiled at him ironically. "I knew you'd come to that sooner or later. *Crime and Punishment* . . . You really are on the verge of turning infantile or senile . . ."

"Hold on, just wait a minute," said Rubashov, his pacing more animated. "That's all beside the point, but now we're getting closer. As far as I remember, it deals with the question of whether the student Raskolnikov had the right to kill the old woman. He is young and talented, looking at a new lease on life; she is old and of no use whatsoever to the world. But the equation doesn't add up. First of all the circumstances are such that he's forced to kill another person as well—and those are exactly the unforeseeable and illogical consequences of every seemingly simple and logical practical deed. And second, the equation doesn't add up because Raskolnikov discovers that two times two does not equal four if the arithmetic involves living beings . . ."

"So," said Ivanov. "If you want to hear my opinion, every copy of that book ought to be burned. Think where it all leads, if we take this nebulous humanistic philosophy literally. If we stick to the proposition that the individual is sacrosanct and must be respected as such, and that arithmetic should not be done with human beings, that would mean that the battalion commander would no longer have the right to sacrifice a patrol in order to save a regiment. That would mean that we couldn't sacrifice fools like Bogrov and should simply accept the fact that in two years our coastal cities will be blown to pieces . . ."

Rubashov shook his head impatiently: "Your examples all refer to war and exceptional circumstances."

"Since the invention of the steam engine," replied Ivanov, "the world has been in a permanent state of exception; wars and revolutions are just the visible manifestation. Your Raskolnikov is clearly a fool and a criminal, not because of his logic in killing the old woman, but because he's acting in his own individual interest. The principle that the end justifies the means is and remains the only useful standard of political morality; everything else is cheap literature, vague prattle that slips between your fingers. But the principle only holds true when the action serves a useful collective purpose and not merely an individual goal. If Raskolnikov had dispatched the old woman on assignment from the party, for instance to enrich a strike fund or enable an illegal print shop, then the calculation would add up, and the novel, with its misleading presentation of the problem, would never have been written, to the benefit of humanity."

Rubashov didn't answer. As before, he was fascinated with the problem of whether, after the experiences of the recent months and days, he would still send Orlova to her death. He wasn't sure. Logically everything Ivanov was saying was correct, but the invisible "opposing party" was silent, its existence revealed only through a dull feeling of unease. Here, too, Ivanov was probably right in saying that the tactics employed—refusing to be drawn into discussion and pouncing on people in defenseless moments—put the "opponent" in a thoroughly dubious light . . .

"I'm against mixing ideologies," Ivanov continued. "There are only two concepts of human ethics and they are polar opposites. One is Christian-humanitarian and declares that the individual is sacred and maintains that no calculations may be done with blood. The other is based on the principle that the collective goal justifies the means, and this not only allows but requires that the individual be subordinated to the collective in every way, including as a guinea pig or sacrificial lamb. We can call the first concept anti-vivisectional morality, and the second vivisectional morality. The dilettantes and sugarcoaters have always tried to mix the two concepts, but in practice they are irreconcilable. The first time anyone in a position of power and responsibility is faced with a decision, he immediately realizes he must make a choice, and the dreadful thing is that he is impelled to choose the second alternative. Do you know a single historical example since Christianity was first espoused as a state religion that any government pursued a genuinely Christian policy? You won't find one. In a crisis—and politics is one permanent crisis—those in power could always declare a state of emergency to justify exceptional measures. For as long as there have been nations and classes, they live in a state of mutual self-defense, which constantly forces them to postpone their humanist program to some 'later date' . . ."

Rubashov looked out the window. The thawed snow had again frozen over; the uneven surface was full of sparkling, yellow-white crystals. The sentry paced back and forth on the wall, his rifle shouldered. The sky was clear and moonless; over the machine-gun tower shimmered the Milky Way.

Rubashov shrugged his shoulders. "Granted," he said, "that humanism and politics, respect for the individual and social progress, are tragically irreconcilable. Granted, that Gandhi is a catastrophe for India. Granted, that chastity in the choice of means leads to political impotence. Granted, that the rules of 'fair play' can be used in tennis but not to make history. When it comes to the negative, we are in agreement. But look where such strict compliance with the alternative has led us, and where it is taking us . . ."

"Well," asked Ivanov slowly, "where?"

Rubashov paced up and down. "The history of revolutions is hardly uplifting reading for a Sunday afternoon, but no one's ever made such a mess of things as we have."

Ivanov smiled. "That may be," he said, pleased. "Until now all revolutions were made by moralizing dilettantes; they were always well-intentioned, and were invariably ruined by their dilettantism. We are the first to be consistent."

"So consistent," said Rubashov, "that in the interest of a just distribution of land we purposely let some five million large and middle landowners die of starvation. So consistent that in order to free people from the shackles of capitalist wage labor, we sent some ten million people to forced labor in the Arctic and the taiga, in conditions akin to those of the ancient galley slaves. So consistent that in the name of removing differences of opinion we recognize only one argument: death, whether it is a question of submarine tonnage or fertilizer or which party line should be pursued in Indo-China. Our engineers labor under the constant fear that one mistaken calculation could send them to prison or to the gallows; our administrative officials mercilessly destroy their subordinates because they know they must account for their actions and otherwise will be destroyed themselves; our writers carry out their debates on stylistic matters through denunciations to the secret police, because the Expressionists consider the naturalist style counterrevolutionary and vice versa. In the name of coming generations we have consistently forced such monstrous deprivations on those living in the present that their average life expectancy has been reduced by a quarter. In order to defend the existence of the revolutionary country, we have consistently embraced exceptional measures and passed provisional laws that contradict the goals of the revolution in every way. The living conditions of the masses are worse than they were before the revolution; the working conditions are harsher, the discipline less humane, the drudgery of piecework worse than in colonial countries with indigenous coolies. We have lowered the age limit for the death penalty to twelve years, our sexual laws are more antiquated than England's, the deification of our leader more grotesque than that of the jumping jack with the little moustache. Our newspapers and schools breed chauvinism, militarism, dogmatism, conformism, and empty-headedness. The power and arbitrariness of the regime is unchecked and unmatched in history, with freedom of the press, freedom of opinion, freedom of movement so utterly stamped out as though there had never been a Declaration of the Rights of Man. We have constructed the largest police state in history, the most gigantic stool-pigeon apparatus, the most sophisticated scientific system of physical and psychological torture. We lash the groaning masses of the country with knouts, driving them toward some theoretical future happiness that only we can see. Our generation's strength is spent, it wore itself out in the revolution, it has been bled dry; it is now nothing but a groaning, deadened mass of sacrificial flesh . . . Those are the consequences of our consistency. You called it vivisectional morality. Sometimes it seems to me that the experimenters have flayed the test person alive and left him facing history with exposed tissue, muscles, and tendons."

"Well, and!?" Ivanov called out, pleased. "Don't you think that's great? Has history ever seen anything greater? We tear the old skin off humanity and make a new one. That's not for people with weak nerves, but I remember a time when it filled you with enthusiasm. Tell me, what's made you change so much, that you're suddenly playing the coy old virgin?"

Rubashov wanted to say: "Because since then I've heard Bogrov whimpering," but he knew that this answer wouldn't make any sense. Instead he answered:

"To stick with the same image: I look at the battered body of this generation, but I don't see anything of the new skin. We thought we could manipulate history like a physical experiment. The difference is that experiments in physics can be repeated a thousand times, but experiments in history only once. Danton and Saint-Just can be sent to the guillotine one time only, and even if it later turns out that larger submarines may have been the right choice after all, nothing will bring Comrade Bogrov back to life."

"So what's the conclusion?" asked Ivanov. "Should we just sit still because we can never completely foresee the consequences and therefore all actions are evil? We vouch for every deed with our own heads; that's all that anyone can demand of us. The other side isn't so particular. They think every old fool of a general has the right to experiment with thousands of living bodies, and if he makes a mistake the worst that can happen is that he's forced to retire. The reactionary and counterrevolutionary forces never have any scruples or ethical dilemmas. Imagine a Sulla, a Galliffet, or a Kolchak reading *Crime and Punishment*.

Odd birds like you only nest in the trees of the revolution. The others have it easier . . ."

He looked at his watch. The window now showed a dirty gray; the newspaper covering the broken pane billowed and rustled in the morning breeze. On the outer wall the sentry was still counting off his hundred paces.

"For a man of your past," Ivanov continued, "this sudden reluctance to experiment really strikes me as a bit naïve. Every year a few million people perish in completely senseless ways from epidemics and natural disasters. So why should we shy away from sacrificing a few hundred thousand for the most sensible experiment in history? Not to mention the legions that die a miserable death in the coal mines, the mercury mines, the rice paddies and cotton plantations from starvation and tuberculosis. Nobody sheds a tear for them, no one asks why or what for, but when we shoot a few thousand genuinely harmful wreckers, humanists all across the globe start foaming at the mouth. Yes, we took the parasitic portion of the peasantry and annihilated them and let them die of starvation. It was an enormous, one-time surgical operation, but in the good old days before the revolution just as many people died whenever there was a drought—except without any point or goal. Every year anywhere from hundreds of thousands to a million people die in China when the Yellow River floods. Nature is unstinting in its pointless experiments with people, so why shouldn't people have the right to conduct a purposeful experiment on themselves?"

He paused; Rubashov didn't reply. Ivanov continued:

"Have you ever read a brochure from the anti-vivisection movement? It's all very unsettling and heartbreaking, and when you read how a poor dachshund that's had his liver cut out whimpers and licks the hands of his tormentors, you feel the same kind of nausea you felt tonight. But if those people had their way, then today we wouldn't have any serum against cholera, typhus, or diphtheria . . ."

He finished the bottle, yawned, stretched, and stood up. He hobbled to the window next to Rubashov and looked out.

"It's getting light," he said. "Don't be a fool, Rubashov. What I've been arguing is nothing new to you—it's pretty basic wisdom. Your nerves were shot, but now it's over." He stood at the window next to Rubashov, his arm draped over Rubashov's shoulder, his voice sounding almost soft. "Now go and get some sleep, you old warhorse; tomorrow your time is up, and we both need our wits about us to compile the statement. Don't shrug your shoulders—you're already halfway convinced that you'll sign. It would be intellectual cowardice to refuse. And you wouldn't be the first to become a martyr out of intellectual cowardice."

Rubashov peered out at the gray light. The sentry on the wall was just making an about-face. Over the machine-gun tower the sky was bright gray, with a slight tinge of red. "I'll think about it," Rubashov said after a while.

When the door clanged shut behind Ivanov, he knew that with this sentence he had already half capitulated. He threw himself on his cot, exhausted and in a strange way relieved. He felt hollow on the inside, sapped, and at the same time he felt a burden had been lifted. Bogrov's whimpering had lost some of its sharpness in his acoustical memory. Who could call it betrayal if one was loyal to the living instead of the dead?

◇

While Rubashov slept calmly and dreamlessly—his toothache had also subsided—Ivanov paid another visit to Gletkin on his way to his room. Gletkin was sitting at his desk, in his full uniform, working through some files. For years he'd made a habit of working through the night three or four times a week. When Ivanov entered his room, Gletkin stood at attention.

"It's all right now," said Ivanov, "he'll sign tomorrow. But I had my work cut out for me, fixing your stupidity."

Gletkin didn't answer; he stood erect in front of his desk.

Ivanov, who remembered the sharp words he'd had with Glet-kin before he visited Rubashov in his cell, and who knew that Gletkin wasn't one to quickly forget a reprimand, shrugged his shoulders and blew smoke into Gletkin's face. "Don't be a fool," he said. "You all continue to suffer from your private emotions. You'd be even more stubborn in his place."

"I'm not a weakling like him," said Gletkin.

"Just an idiot," said Ivanov. "And for that answer you should be shot before him."

He hobbled to the door and shut it from the outside.

Gletkin sat back down at his desk. He didn't believe Iva-nov would be successful and at the same time he was afraid of him. Ivanov's last sentence had felt like a threat, and with Ivanov it was never clear what was said in jest and what was serious. Perhaps he didn't know himself—like all those intel-lectual cynics . . .

Gletkin shrugged his shoulders, straightened the collar of his uniform and his crinkling cuffs, and continued working through his heap of files.

THE THIRD INTERROGATION

And yet if it be sometimes necessary to conceal facts with words, then it should be done in such manner that it shall not appear; or should it be observed, then a defense should be promptly ready.

Niccolò Machiavelli, "Confidential Instructions" to Raffaello Girolami (trans. C. Detmold)

But let your communication be, Yea, yea; Nay, nay: for whatsoever is more than these cometh of evil.

Matthew 5:37

I.

From the Diary of N. S. Rubashov

Day 16 of Imprisonment

. . . Vladimir Bogrov has fallen out of the swing. One hundred fifty years ago, on the day the Bastille was stormed, the European swing once again lurched into motion after a long period of inertia, with a vigorous push away from tyranny toward what seemed an unstoppable climb into the blue sky of freedom. The ascent into the spheres of liberalism and democracy lasted a hundred years. But lo and behold, it gradually began to lose speed as it came closer to the apex, the turning point of its trajectory; then, after a brief stasis, it started moving backward, in an increasingly rapid descent. And with the same vigor as before, it carried its passengers away from freedom and back to tyranny. Whoever kept staring at the sky instead of hanging on to the swing grew dizzy and tumbled out.

Whoever wishes to avoid getting dizzy must try to grasp the laws of motion governing the swing. Because what we are facing is clearly a pendulum swing of history, from absolutism to democracy, from democracy to absolute dictatorship.

The degree of individual freedom a nation is able to attain and retain depends on the degree of its political maturity. The pendulum swing described above suggests that the political maturity of the masses does not follow the same constantly rising curve of a maturing individual, but is subject to more complicated laws.

The political maturity of the masses depends on their ability to discern their own interest, which presupposes a knowledge of the process of production and the distribution of goods. A nation's ability to govern itself democratically is consequently determined by how well it understands the structure and functioning of the social body as a whole.

However, every technical advance leads to a further complication of the economic framework, to new factors, new connections that the masses are at first unable to comprehend. And so every leap of technical progress brings with it a relative intellectual regression of the masses, a decline in their political maturity. At times it may take decades or even generations before the collective consciousness gradually catches up to the changed order and regains the capacity to govern itself that it had formerly possessed at a lower stage of civilization. The political maturity of the masses can therefore not be measured in absolute numbers, but always only relatively: namely in relation to the developmental stage of any given civilization.

When the balance between mass consciousness and objective reality is achieved, then democracy will inevitably prevail, by either peaceful or violent means, until the next, nearly always volatile leap of progress—for example, the invention of gunpowder or the mechanized loom—again places the masses in a condition of relative immaturity and makes it possible or necessary for the establishment of a new authoritarian regime.

The process is best compared to a ship being lifted through a series of locks. At the beginning of each stage, the ship is at a relatively low level, from which it is slowly raised until it is even with the next lock—but this glorious stage is of short duration, as it now faces a new set of levels, which again can be attained only slowly and gradually. The sides of the chamber represent the objective state of technological advancement, the mastery of natural forces; the water level in the chamber symbolizes the political maturity of the masses. Any attempt to measure this as an absolute height above sea level would be pointless; what is measured instead is the relative range of levels in each lock.

The invention of the steam engine brought a period of rapid

objective progress, and as a consequence, a period of equally rapid subjective political regression. The industrial era is still historically young, the gap still very great between its enormously complicated economic structure and the intellectual awareness of the masses. It is therefore understandable that the relative political maturity of people in the first half of the twentieth century is less than it was two hundred years BC or at the conclusion of the feudal period.

The historical mistake of socialist theory was to believe that mass consciousness rises at a constant and consistent rate. This explains its helplessness in the face of the recent pendulum swings of history, and the ideological self-emasculation of the people. We believed that aligning the worldview of the masses to the changed reality was a simple process, the course of which we measured in years, whereas history teaches that a measure of centuries would be more appropriate. Intellectually, the nations of Europe are still far from having digested the consequences of the invention of the steam engine. The capitalist system will perish before the masses have fully understood it.

As far as the fatherland of the revolution is concerned, its masses are subjected to the same laws of thought as elsewhere. They have reached the next higher lock, but they are still at the lowest point in the new chamber. The new economic system is even more incomprehensible to them than the old one it replaced. The arduous and painful climb begins anew. It will probably take several generations before the people are able to mentally master what they themselves accomplished in the revolution.

Until then a democratic form of government is not possible, and the measure of individual freedom that can be granted is less than in other countries. Until then our leadership is forced to rule in a vacuum. By classic liberal standards this is not a pleasant state of affairs. The terror, the falsehood, and the general debasement that are so evident are merely the visible and inevitable expression of the causal connection described above.

Woe to the fools and aesthetes who ask only the how but not the why. Woe, too, to the opposition in periods of relative immaturity such as this.

In periods of political maturity it is the task and function of the opposition to appeal to the masses. In periods of relative immaturity only demagogues manage to invoke the "higher reason" of the people. In such situations the opposition has only two ways open: either wresting power with a surprise strike, without being able to count on the support of the masses, or allowing itself to fall off the swing in silent despair—the way of "die in silence."

There is yet a third way, one that is no less consistent and that we have developed into a system: repudiating one's own beliefs, when there is no real prospect of helping them gain ascendance. Because social utility is the only moral criterion we recognize, it is obviously more moral to publicly forswear one's convictions, so as to remain active, than to carry on a futile quixotic struggle.

Questions of subjective vanity; prejudices, such as exist elsewhere against certain forms of self-abasement; private feelings such as exhaustion, disgust, and shame; temptations such as that of martyrdom and the yearning to become silent and lay one's head to rest—must be pulled up by the roots.

2.

Rubashov had started writing his thoughts on the "swing" immediately after the morning bugle call on the day following Bogrov's execution and Ivanov's visit. When they brought breakfast he drank a sip of coffee, then let the rest grow cold while he went on working. His handwriting, which in recent days had become somewhat limp and disjointed, once again became more contained, more disciplined: the letters grew smaller, the sweeping loops gave way to sharp angles. He noticed this himself when he read through what he had written.

At eleven a.m. they came as usual to take him for exercise, so he had to interrupt his work. Once in the yard he was paired not with Rip van Winkle, but with a thin peasant wearing birch-bark shoes. Rip van Winkle was nowhere to be seen; only now did Rubashov recall that he hadn't heard the usual "Cormades, let's bravely march onward" at breakfast. Evidently the old man had been shipped off, heaven only knew where to—a poor old moth from the previous year who had miraculously but need-lessly outlived his appointed time, only to appear at the wrong moment, flutter about blindly for a while, and then crumble to dust in some corner.

At first the peasant plodded alongside Rubashov in silence, examining him from the side. After they completed their first turn around the yard he cleared his throat a few times, and after one more he said:

"I come from province D. Have you ever been there, sir?"

Rubashov said he hadn't—D. was a remote province in the east of which he had only a vague notion.

"It's a long way to go," said the peasant. "You have to ride on camels to get there. Are you also a political, sir?"

Rubashov said he was. The soles of the birch-bark shoes were half torn off, and the man's toes stuck out as he walked on the firmly trampled snow. He had a thin neck and nodded when he spoke, as though he were reciting responses from a litany.

"I'm a political as well," he said. "A reactionary. They say that all reactionaries get sent away for ten years. Do you think they're going to send me away for ten years, sir?"

He nodded again as he eyed the guards in the middle of the yard, who were huddled in a small circle, stamping their feet and not paying attention to the prisoners.

"What did you do?"

"I revealed myself to be a reactionary when they were going to stick the children with needles," said the peasant. "Every year the government sends a commission to us. Two years ago they sent manuals for us to read and lots of pictures of themselves.

Last year they sent a thresher and brushes for scrubbing your teeth. This year they sent little glass tubes with needles at the end, for pricking the children. There was a woman dressed in men's clothes; she wanted to prick each of the children one at a time. When they tried to come inside our house my wife and I barricaded the door and that's how we revealed we were reactionaries. Afterward we burned all the manuals and the pictures and broke the threshing machine and then they came for us a month later."

Rubashov mumbled something and thought about the next installment of his discourse on self-government. He remembered reading about some aboriginal tribes in New Guinea that were intellectually no more evolved than the peasant next to him, but who nevertheless lived in complete social harmony, with remarkably developed democratic institutions. They simply didn't possess any industry . . . The peasant took Rubashov's silence for a sign of disapproval and withdrew even further into himself. His toes were frozen blue; as he plodded alongside Rubashov he sighed occasionally, resigned to his fate. A moment later the whistle signaled the end of the exercise. As soon as he was in his cell, Rubashov went back to his writing. He believed he had made a discovery with the "law of relative maturity" and wrote in a state of intense excitement. When they brought the midday meal he had just finished. He cleaned his bowl and stretched out on his cot, content.

He slept for over an hour, calmly and dreamlessly, and woke up refreshed. Number 402 had been tapping on the wall for a while; evidently he felt neglected. He asked about Rubashov's new partner in the exercise yard, but Rubashov interrupted him and tapped, clearly and concisely with his pince-nez, smiling as he did so:

I AM CAPITULATING.

He was curious to see the effect.

For a while there was nothing. 402 was suddenly mute. After a full minute the ticking resumed:

BETTER TO DIE.

Rubashov smiled. He tapped:

TO EACH HIS OWN.

Actually he had expected an outburst of rage. Instead the tapping sounded muted, as though resigned:

I WAS INCLINED TO THINK YOU WERE AN EXCEPTION. DON'T YOU HAVE EVEN A SPARK OF HONOR?

Rubashov lay on his back, holding his pince-nez. He felt a sensation of peace, a serene contentment. He tapped:

WE HAVE DIFFERENT CONCEPTS OF HONOR.

402 answered quickly and precisely:

THERE IS ONLY ONE KIND OF HONOR: TO LIVE AND DIE FOR ONE'S IDEALS.

Rubashov wrote back just as quickly.

HONOR MEANS BEING USEFUL WITHOUT VANITY.

402 replied, this time louder and more vehemently:

HONOR IS DECENCY—NOT UTILITY.

WHAT IS DECENCY? asked Rubashov, taking his time. The more casually he tapped, the more fierce the ticking in the wall.

SOMETHING YOUR KIND WILL NEVER UNDERSTAND, 402 replied. Rubashov shrugged his shoulders.

WE HAVE REPLACED DECENCY WITH LOGICAL CONSISTENCY, he tapped back.

Number 402 stopped answering.

◈

Before the evening meal was doled out, Rubashov reread what he had written. He made a few corrections and copied the entire text in the form of a letter addressed to the state prosecutor of the republic. He underscored the closing paragraphs describing the alternatives for oppositionists, and ended the document with a final sentence:

"For the above-cited reasons the undersigned, N. S. Rubashov, former member of the Central Committee, former people's commissar, former commander of the Second Division of the Revolutionary Army and bearer of the Revolutionary

Order for Bravery in the Face of the Enemy, has decided to sign his capitulation, to publicly acknowledge his mistakes, and to forswear his oppositional attitude."

3.

For two days Rubashov waited to be taken to the examining magistrate. He had imagined this would happen when the two weeks granted by Ivanov were over, on the day he had entrusted the document containing his capitulation to the old warder. But it seemed they were no longer in such a hurry to deal with him. Perhaps Ivanov was still studying the theory of "relative maturity," although it was more likely the document had already been passed on to the higher authorities.

Rubashov smiled at the thought of the consternation it must have caused among the theoreticians of the Central Committee. Before the revolution and also for a short time afterward, while the old leader was still alive, there had been no difference between "theoreticians" and "politicians." The tactic to be adopted in any given situation was derived directly from the theory, through open discussion; strategic measures during the civil war, the requisitioning of grain and the parceling out of land, the introduction of a new currency, the reorganization of the factories and the fixing of wages—every administrative ordinance represented an act of applied philosophy. Every one of the men with the numbered heads on the old photograph that had once decorated Ivanov's wallpaper knew more about economics, philosophy of law, and theories of government than the fusty professors holding chairs at European universities. The discussions at the congresses during the civil war had been on a level unmatched in history by any political body; they were like expert treatises from specialist journals—with the notable difference that the outcome of the discussion decided the life and well-being of millions, as well as the future of the revolution . . .

Now the old guard had been used up; the logic of history held that as the regime grew more stable, it also grew more rigid, and it now wished to prevent the tremendous, dynamic forces unleashed by the revolution against the external enemy from turning inward and imploding. The time of the philosophizing congresses was over; a bright spot on Ivanov's wall had replaced the old portraits; incendiary philosophy had given way to salutary sterility. The revolutionary theory had frozen into a dogmatic cult, with a simplified and easily understandable catechism, and at the top was Number One—the high priest celebrating a philosophical mass. Even the outward form of his speeches and essays resembled an infallible catechism; they were divided into questions and answers, and showed an admirable consistency in oversimplifying and vulgarizing true connections. Instinctively, Number One probably understood the law of relative maturity of the masses better than anyone else. Amateur tyrants had forced their subjects to act on command; Number One had taught them to think on command.

Rubashov smiled as he imagined what the party's present-day "theoreticians" would make of his letter. Under the current circumstances it represented the wildest heresy: the fathers of the doctrine, whose words were off-limits, were criticized; the real state of things was called by name; and the sacrosanct personage of Number One was subordinated to its proper place within an objective historical context. The hapless theoreticians of today, whose sole task was to dress up Number One's political leaps and abrupt changes of course as the latest philosophical revelations, were probably in fits. Now and then Number One himself enjoyed playing unusual jokes on his "theoreticians." Once he had demanded that the staff of experts in charge of the official party organ undertake an analysis of the American economic crisis. That took several months to complete; finally the results were published in a three-hundred-page special edition proving the validity of Number One's thesis delivered at the latest party congress, namely that the American business cycle was a pseudo-cycle, and that in reality the country was in an absolute economic crisis that could only be overcome by a successful revolution. On the same day this special edition appeared, Number One received an American journalist and flabbergasted him and the world with the lapidary sentence, uttered between puffs on his pipe:

"Your crisis is over, and business is up and running again."

That very night, the members of the collegium, aware of their imminent dismissal and possible arrest, composed letters in which they publicly acknowledged and regretted their "error in advancing counterrevolutionary theories and misleading analyses," and promised to improve. Only Isakovich, a contemporary of Rubashov and the only member of the editorial board who had belonged to the old guard, preferred to shoot himself. As it happened, those in the know maintained that Number One had launched the whole incident just to get rid of Isakovich, whom he suspected of oppositional leanings.

Rubashov considered the whole thing a grotesque spectacle. Essentially all the gibberish about "revolutionary philosophy" was merely a pretext for safeguarding the dictatorship, which represented a historical necessity no matter how disagreeable the manifestation. All the worse for those who took the theater seriously, who only saw the poor staging and not the rigging backstage. Earlier revolutionary politics had been conducted on a public soapbox; now it was done behind the scenes. That, too, was a logical conclusion derived from the "relative maturity" theory of the masses.

Rubashov longed to again be able to work in a quiet library with green lamps, as he once had, to ground his new theory in sound historical research. The most productive times for the development of revolutionary philosophy were always the periods of emigration, the forced rests between cycles of political activity. He paced up and down his cell, absorbed in the idea of spending the next years, politically neutralized, in a kind of inner emigration; surely his public recantation would give him a chance to catch his breath. He didn't care about the external form of his capitulation; they could have however many mea culpas and credos affirming Number One's policies as the only salvation they wanted. That was merely a matter of formal etiquette—a Byzantine ceremony that had gradually emerged from the need to drub every sentence into the masses through endless repetition and oversimplification: what was presented as right had to glitter like gold, and what was presented as wrong had to appear as black as pitch, while political confessions of faith and guilt were made to look colorful, like the gingerbread men sold at the fair.

Rubashov considered all these to be matters of appearance that 402 knew nothing about. His naïve concept of honor came from a different era. What is decency? A certain form of convention, a holdover rooted in the rules and traditions of knightly tournaments. The new formulation of honor was: to be useful without vanity and to the very end.

"Better to die than debase yourself," Number 402 had proclaimed, presumably twirling his moustache. That was the classic formula of personal vanity. 402 tapped his sentences with his monocle, Rubashov with his pince-nez—and therein lay the entire difference. Today the only thing Rubashov wished for was to be able to sit quietly in a library and develop his new ideas. The project would almost certainly take several years to complete and would probably result in a weighty tome. In all likelihood it would provide the first serviceable key to understanding the various forms of state throughout history, while instantly illuminating the pendulum swings of mass psychology, which this generation had experienced so starkly and which the classical theory of class struggle failed to explain . . .

Rubashov paced rapidly back and forth in his cell and smiled. Nothing else mattered as long as he was given time to develop his theory. His tooth no longer hurt; he felt fresh, adventurous, filled with an anxious impatience. Two days had passed since his nighttime conversation with Ivanov and his subsequent declaration, and he still hadn't received a reply. And suddenly time, which had passed so quickly during his first two weeks in prison, began to languish. The hours grew long, slowly disintegrating into minutes and seconds. He worked in spurts but invariably got stuck because he was lacking the historical documents; every new start fizzled out. He stood by the spy hole for fifteen minutes in the hope of seeing the uniformed guards who would take him to Ivanov, but the corridor was dead—only the electric lamps went on burning as always.

At times he hoped Ivanov himself would come and take his formal statement right there in the cell, which would be considerably more comfortable. Nor did he now have any objection to the brandy. He imagined the conversation in detail, their joint editing of the glib phrases of repentance, Ivanov's cynical jokes. Rubashov smiled as he walked up and down, impatiently checking his watch every ten minutes. Hadn't Ivanov promised to fetch him the very next day?

His impatience grew more and more feverish, so that by the third night after his conversation with Ivanov he could no longer sleep. He lay on his cot in the dark, tossing and turning, listening to the hushed, muffled noises in the building, and for the first time since his arrest he wished for the nearness of a female body. He tried breathing deeply and regularly, in order to fall asleep, but became increasingly agitated. He fought off the desire to start a conversation with Number 402, who had not communicated with him since their disagreement over "What is decency?"

Toward midnight, after he had lain in the dark for more than three hours without sleeping, staring at the newspaper covering the broken pane, he could no longer stand it and rapped his knuckles against the wall. He waited anxiously; the wall stayed silent. He tapped again and waited, feeling the heat of shame rising in his head. Still no answer from 402, but he was doubtless awake on the other side of the wall, passing the time by recalling past affairs; he had told Rubashov in plain terms that he could never fall asleep before two a.m. and that he had resorted to adolescent habits. "Any port in a storm" was how he put it. Nine out of ten inmates did the same—the politicals just like the others. Once, during the monarchy, when the movement was still in its romantic stage, the inmates of the most famous political prison had carried on a tapped debate on whether revolutionaries should remain chaste or not. The discussion had lasted several months, because the long theoretical discourses together with all the replies and rejoinders had to be tapped out to each inmate before everyone could be polled. The large majority voted against abstention, because it was "damaging to the health and absorbed more mental energy than the emergency measure imposed by the circumstances."

Rubashov lay on his back, staring into the darkness. His straw tick was flattened and thin and he could feel the wire mesh underneath. The woolen blanket was too warm and drew an unpleasant moisture from his skin, but if he tossed it off he began to shiver. He was already smoking his seventh or eighth cigarette in a row; the stubs lay scattered in a circle on the tiles beside his cot. Not the slightest sound could be heard; time seemed to stand still, as though it had dissolved in darkness and formlessness. Rubashov closed his eyes and imagined Orlova next to him, the familiar curve of her breast arching up against the darkness—forgetting that they had dragged her down the corridor as they had Bogrov. The silence grew so intense it seemed to whir and sway. What was 402 up to in the darkness, on the other side of the wall? What were the two thousand men doing who were walled in this concrete hive? The darkness swelled with their inaudible breath, their invisible dreams, their stifled gasps of fear, and their rutting breaths. If history was a mathematical calculation, then what was the weight of two thousand nightmares, the two-thousandfold pressure of their impotent desires? Now he could actually sense the sisterly fragrance of Orlova's limbs, his own body was covered with sweat under the woolen blanket, and in his half sleep he felt a sudden release that did not however bring any peace. At the same time, or so he thought, the cell door was wrenched open with a clatter.

Blinking into the harsh light that stung his eyes, he saw two uniformed guards he had never seen before step through the door. Both were wearing pistol belts. One of the two men stepped up to the cot; he was extremely tall, with a brutal face and a rasping voice that seemed to Rubashov exaggeratedly loud. He told Rubashov to get up and follow them, without saying where they were headed.

Rubashov groped under the blanket for his pince-nez, put it on, and stood up from the cot. He felt an oppressive weariness as he walked down the corridor alongside the giant, who was a whole head taller than Rubashov. The other guard trailed behind.

Rubashov automatically looked at his wristwatch; it was two a.m., so he must have had some sleep after all. They were walking toward the barbershop—the same route they had taken Bogrov. The second guard kept three paces behind Rubashov. Rubashov felt the urge to turn his head around and look at him like a physical itch in his neck, but he restrained himself. *In any case they can't just up and shoot someone just like that, with no ceremony whatsoever*, he thought, but was not completely convinced. Nor at the moment did he really care; he just had a burning desire for it all to be over with quickly. He tried to assess whether he sensed fear, but all he felt was a physical discomfort, caused by the frantic exertion required not to turn his head toward the man behind him.

They passed the barbershop and turned the corner, and the narrow flight of stairs loomed into view. Rubashov watched to see if the giant walking beside him would slow his pace; at the same time he observed himself: he still didn't sense any fear— just curiosity and uneasiness. Nevertheless once they were past the stair he was surprised to feel his knees suddenly start to go soft, and he had to brace up not to give himself away. At the same time he noticed he was reflexively rubbing his pince-nez on his sleeve; it seemed he had unwittingly taken it off before reaching the barbershop. *It's all a sham*, he thought. *Up above you pretend one thing but down below, from the stomach on down, you know what's what; in the final analysis Gletkin is right. If they beat me now I'll sign whatever they want, and then I'll retract it tomorrow . . .*

A few steps later he remembered his theory of relative maturity and the fact that he had already decided to capitulate and sign everything anyway. At once he felt an immense relief but wondered how he could have so completely forgotten all his decisions of the past days. The giant next to him stopped, opened a door, and stepped aside, revealing a room that was similar to Ivanov's but had an unpleasant glaring light that hurt Rubashov's eyes. And sitting behind the desk opposite the door was Gletkin.

Rubashov stepped inside, the guard closed the door, and Gletkin looked up from his stack of files. "Sit down," he said in the colorless, dry tone Rubashov recalled from their first encounter. He also recognized the broad scar on Gletkin's skull, though Gletkin's face was in shadow because the only light in the room—a tall, metallic standing lamp—was placed behind Gletkin's armchair. The unusually strong bulb emitted a harsh white light that blinded Rubashov, so that it took him a few seconds before he realized there was a third person—a secretary, who was sitting at a small table behind a screen, her back to the room.

Rubashov sat down in front of the desk across from Gletkin, on the only empty chair. It was uncomfortable and had no armrests.

"In the absence of Commissar Ivanov I have been assigned to conduct your interrogation," said Gletkin. The glare hurt Rubashov's eyes, and even if he looked off to the side the strong light hitting the corner of his eye was almost as aggravating; besides, it was embarrassing to have to speak with his head turned away.

"I prefer to be interrogated by Ivanov," said Rubashov.

"The choice of magistrate is determined by the authorities," said Gletkin. "You have the right to make a statement or to refuse. In your case a refusal would be tantamount to a retraction of your written statement from two days ago expressing your readiness to confess your guilt and would result in the immediate termination of the investigation. In that event I have been instructed to forward your case to the people's court for administrative adjudication."

Rubashov thought quickly. Evidently something had gone awry with Ivanov. Perhaps he had suddenly been sent on leave, or dismissed, or arrested—perhaps because someone had dredged up his earlier friendship with Rubashov, or perhaps because he was too facetious and superior and because his loyalty to Number One was based on perceptive logic and not blind faith. He was too superior, that was the old school—the new one was Gletkin and his methods . . . *Go in peace, Ivanov.* Rubashov had no time for sympathy; he had to think quickly, and the light made that difficult. He took off his pince-nez and blinked; he knew that without the pince-nez he looked naked and helpless and that Gletkin's expressionless eyes would register every feature of his face. If he said nothing, it would mean the end; now there was no going back, and the sooner everything was dealt with, the better. Gletkin was an odious character, but he embodied the new generation; the old had to either come to terms with the new one or be crushed by it, there was no alternative. For the first time in his life, Rubashov suddenly felt old. He had never given any thought to the fact that he was in the sixth decade of his life. He put on his pince-nez and tried to meet Gletkin's gaze, but the glare made his eyes run and he immediately took it back off.

"I am prepared to make a statement," he said, trying to fight the testiness in his voice. "But under the condition that you refrain from all your tricks. Turn off the light and save those methods for counterfeiters and counterrevolutionaries."

"You're not in a position to set conditions," said Gletkin with his calm voice. "I can't change the lighting in my room on your account. Moreover you don't seem to have a clear picture of your situation, especially considering that you yourself are accused of counterrevolutionary activities and have even confessed to the same in two public declarations made over the past few years. If you think you're going to get off so lightly this time, you are mistaken."

You swine, thought Rubashov, *you uniformed piece of dung . . .* He turned red. He could feel it and knew that Gletkin saw it as well. How old could this Gletkin be? Thirty-six or -seven at most; he had probably experienced the civil war as an adolescent, and the revolution as a boy. He belonged to the generation that had started thinking after the deluge. They had no traditions, no memory that connected them to the old, sunken world. It was a generation born without an umbilical cord. And they were right. The umbilical cord needed to be torn off; the last tether to the old vain concepts of honor, to the phony decency of that old world, needed to be broken. Honor meant being useful without vanity, without sparing oneself, to the very end.

Rubashov gradually calmed down inside. Holding his pince-nez in his hand, he turned his face to Gletkin. Since he had to close his eyes to do that, he felt even more naked, but that no longer bothered him. Behind his closed eyelids the light shimmered as a reddish brightness; he had never had such an intense feeling of loneliness.

"I will do everything to be of use to the party," he said. The hoarseness had vanished from his voice; he continued to keep his eyes closed. "I request that you spell out the specific points of the accusation. This has not been done previously."

Rubashov heard rather than saw through his squinting eyes a short, strong movement ripple through Gletkin's stiff figure: his cuffs crackled on the armrests; his breathing grew a bit deeper; it was as though his entire body had relaxed for a moment.

Rubashov guessed that Gletkin was experiencing one of the biggest triumphs of his existence. To bring down a Rubashov meant the beginning of a great career, while just a minute earlier everything had been hanging in the balance—with Ivanov's fate serving as a warning before his very eyes.

Rubashov suddenly realized that he had just as much power over this Gletkin as Gletkin had over him. *I have you by the throat, my boy*, he thought with an ironic smirk; *we're holding each other by the throat, and if I fall backward out of the swing I'm taking you with me.* For a moment Rubashov toyed with this thought, while Gletkin, once more stiff and methodical, searched through his files, but then Rubashov discarded the idea and slowly closed his sore eyes. One had to burn out the last vestige of vanity, and what was suicide but an inverted form of vanity? Naturally Gletkin believed it was his tricks and not Ivanov's arguments that had brought Rubashov to capitulate; he had probably even managed to convince his superiors of that and so bring about Ivanov's downfall. *You swine*, thought Rubashov, but this time without ire. *You logical swine in the uniform that* we *created, you creature from the jungle of this new epoch now beginning. You have no idea what's at play here, but if you did you would be of no use to us . . .*

Rubashov noticed that the light had turned brighter by a degree—he knew there were mechanisms to increase or decrease the glare of such lamps during interrogation. He was forced to turn his head away completely and dry his eyes, which were filling with tears. *You brute*, he thought, almost tenderly, *a whole generation of brutes like you is exactly what we need . . .*

Gletkin had begun reading the indictment. His monotone voice sounded even more irritating than before; Rubashov listened with his head averted and his eyes closed. He was resolved to view his "confession" as a formality, as a ridiculous and necessary comedy whose convoluted sense was clear only to the people in the know backstage; nevertheless, the absurdity of what Gletkin was reading here exceeded his expectations. Did

Gletkin truly believe that he, Rubashov, had forged these child-ish conspiracies? That for years his sole aspiration had been to tear down the building whose foundation he himself had laid, together with the old guard? And all the others, the men with the numbered heads, the heroes of Gletkin's childhood years—did Gletkin really believe they had all succumbed to some epidemic, that with one blow they had all turned venal and corrupt and wanted to undo the revolution? And with methods that these great theoreticians of political tactics appeared to have lifted from a cheap detective novel? How did this Neanderthal actually imagine his, Rubashov's, psychological makeup, as he sat across from him with closed eyes?

Gletkin read monotonously, with no expression, in the colorless, brittle voice of people who had learned to read as adults. He came to the part describing negotiations with a representative of a foreign power that he, Rubashov, had allegedly cultivated during his stay in B., with the goal of violently reinstating the old regime. The diplomat was named, also the day and place of the meeting. Rubashov now listened more closely. A paltry, insignificant scene flashed in his memory, one he had immediately forgotten and not thought of since. He quickly calculated the date; in all probability it could be correct. So that was what they intended to hang him by? Rubashov smiled and rubbed his watering eyes with his handkerchief.

Gletkin read on, unmoved, stiffly, and in a deadly monotone. Did he really believe the text he was reading? Was he unaware of its grotesque absurdity? Next he came to Rubashov's activities as head of the aluminum trust and read some statistics that showed severe disorganization in the too-hastily-constructed industry, and listed the number of workers who had suffered accidents at the workplace, as well as a series of planes that had crashed because of defective material. That was all due to Rubashov's devilish wrecking. The word "devilish" really did keep appearing in the text, amid technical phrases and columns of numbers. For a few seconds Rubashov considered the hypothesis that Gletkin had gone insane; the mixture of logic and absurdity in the document resembled the systematic delusion of a schizophrenic. But the indictment did not come from Gletkin; he was merely reading it out loud, and either actually believed it or at least considered it believable . . .

Rubashov turned his head to the stenographer in her half-lit corner. She was short and thin, and wore glasses. She calmly sharpened her pencils without even once turning her head in his direction. Evidently she, too, found the monstrosities that Gletkin was reading completely plausible. She was still on the young side, perhaps twenty-five or -six; she, too, had come into the world after the deluge. What did he, Rubashov, mean to this generation of modern Neanderthals? There he sat in the glaring spotlight, unable to keep his teary eyes open, as they read to him in their colorless voices and watched him with their colorless eyes, detached, as though he were an object on the dissection table.

Gletkin had reached the last paragraphs of the indictment. These contained the jewel in the crown: the planned attempt on the life of Number One. The mysterious X, whom Ivanov had mentioned during the first interrogation, reappeared. It turned out that X was the administrator of the government cafeteria, from which Number One had his famous cold lunch brought at noon on busy days. The cold lunch was something carefully nurtured by the office of propaganda as evidence of Number One's spartan style of living, and it was precisely by means of this cold lunch that the cafeteria administrator X was to prepare Number One's untimely end—all at Rubashov's instigation. Rubashov smiled with his eyes closed; when he next opened them Gletkin had stopped reading and was looking at him. After a few seconds of silence, Gletkin said in his indifferent intonation that made the words sound more like a statement than a question:

"You have heard the indictment and plead guilty."

Rubashov struggled to look him squarely in the face but

couldn't—once again he had to close his eyes. He had a caustic reply on the tip of his tongue, but instead stated so quietly that the skinny secretary recording the interview had to lean her head in to hear what he was saying:

"I plead guilty to not having correctly assessed the dire constraints imposed on the leadership and its policies, and thereby to having adopted an oppositional attitude. I plead guilty to having followed sentimental inclinations that were in conflict with the logic of history. I opened my ear to the whimpering of the sacrificed and so was deaf to the arguments that demanded their sacrifice. I plead guilty to having placed a higher value on the question of guilt versus innocence than on the question of utility versus detriment. Finally I plead guilty to having placed a higher value on the individual human than the concept of humankind . . ."

Rubashov paused and again attempted to open his eyes. He squinted, his head turned away from the light, in the direction of the corner with the secretary. She was just finishing taking down his sentences; he thought he detected an ironic smile on her angular profile.

"I acknowledge," Rubashov continued, "that my errors were ultimately bound to endanger the revolution. At critical turning points in history every oppositional stance carries the seed of a potential schism within the party and therefore the possibility of civil war. In periods when the masses are politically immature, tenderhearted humanist impulses and liberal democratic leanings spell suicide for the revolution. My oppositional stance manifested itself in calling for a liberal reform of the dictatorship, for a broad popular democracy, for an end to the terror and a loosening of the strict party governance—demands that are tempting on the surface but deadly in their consequences. I acknowledge that in the current historical situation such demands have an objectively harmful and therefore counterrevolutionary character . . ."

He paused again, since his throat had become dry and his

voice hoarse. All he heard was the scratching of the secretary's pencil. He lifted his head a little, keeping his eyes closed, and continued:

"In this sense, and in this sense alone, may you call me a counterrevolutionary. I have nothing to do with the absurd criminal accusations in the indictment."

"Are you finished?" asked Gletkin.

His voice sounded so brutal that Rubashov looked at him, astounded. Gletkin's harshly illuminated figure stood silhouetted behind the desk in his usual correct posture. Rubashov had long been searching for a simple characteristic to describe Gletkin: "punctilious brutality"—that was it.

"Your present statement is not new," Gletkin continued with his grating voice. "Already in both of your previous declarations of remorse, the most recent twelve months ago, and the first a year before that, you confessed publicly to your 'objectively counterrevolutionary attitude that was inimical to the people.' Each time you contritely asked the party to forgive you and vowed loyalty to the leadership. Now you want to try playing the same game with us for the third time. Your previous declaration is a sham. You confess your 'oppositional stance' but deny the actions that are the logical consequence of that stance. I told you before that this time you weren't going to get off so lightly."

Gletkin stopped as abruptly as he had begun. In the ensuing silence Rubashov could hear the electric lamp quietly humming behind the desk. At the same time the light grew a notch brighter.

"My previous declarations," said Rubashov quietly, "were tactical dodges. Surely you realize that a large number of oppositional politicians were able to continue their work in the party by making such declarations. This time it is something else . . ."

"So this time you are being honest?" asked Gletkin. He asked the question quickly, with no trace of irony.

"Yes," said Rubashov calmly.

"And back then you were lying?"

"If you say so," said Rubashov.

"To save your neck?"

"To be able to remain active."

"You can't be active without your neck. So to save your neck?"

"If you say so."

All Rubashov could hear in the brief spaces between Gletkin's rapid questions and his own answers was the scratching of the secretary's pencil and the humming of the lamp, which along with its white cascade of light emitted a constant heat that forced Rubashov to wipe the sweat from his forehead. He struggled hard to keep his sore eyes open, but the interludes where they were closed became longer and longer. He sensed a growing need to sleep, and when Gletkin allowed a few seconds to elapse after a quick series of questions, Rubashov observed with a kind of detached interest that his head was dropping slowly toward his chin. When Gletkin's next question jerked him back up, he had the feeling that he had slept but didn't know for how long.

"I repeat"—Gletkin's voice now sounded overly loud—"your previous declarations of remorse were therefore intended to deceive the party by concealing your true attitude in order to save your neck."

"I just admitted that," said Rubashov.

"And your public distancing from your former secretary Citizen Orlova, did that serve the same purpose?"

Rubashov nodded mutely. The pressure in his eye sockets radiated to every nerve in the right half of his face. Only now did he notice that his tooth had been hurting again for quite some time.

"Are you aware that Citizen Orlova repeatedly called upon you as a witness for her defense?"

"So I was informed," said Rubashov. The throbbing in his tooth intensified.

"Are you also aware that the declaration you issued at the

time, which you just described as a lie, was the deciding factor in sentencing Citizen Orlova to death?"

"So I was informed."

Rubashov felt the entire right half of his face cramping up. His head became increasingly heavy and hollow; it took effort not to let it fall on his chest. Gletkin's boorish voice droned in his ear:

"So it is possible that Citizen Orlova was innocent . . ."

"It is possible," said Rubashov with a last remnant of irony, which tasted of blood and bile on his tongue.

". . . and that she was executed on account of your false declaration that was meant to save your neck?"

"So it would seem," said Rubashov. *You scoundrel,* he thought with a limp, impotent rage, *of course what you say is the naked truth. I'd like to know which one of us is the bigger scoundrel. But he has me by the throat and I can't defend myself because falling out of the swing and taking him with me is not allowed. If he would only let me sleep. If he tortures me any longer I'll take everything back and not say anything—and then it will be over for both of us.*

". . . And after all that you still insist on being treated deferentially?" Gletkin's voice continued, still with the same brutal correctness. "You dare to deny these criminal activities? And on top of all that, you demand that we believe you?"

Rubashov gave up trying to keep his head up. Gletkin was perfectly right not to believe him. In fact he was starting to lose his own way in this labyrinth of dialectical feints and necessary lies, where being and appearance were blurred. The ultimate truth kept shrinking back, just one step out of reach, leaving nothing to grasp but the penultimate lie—a masquerade in the service of that truth. And what pitiful distortions and contortions this required! How could he convince Gletkin that this time he really was being honest and sincere, having arrived at the final stage? This constant need to persuade, to discuss, to argue his point— whereas all he really wanted was to sleep and fade away . . .

"I'm not demanding anything," said Rubashov, and with some effort turned his head in the direction of Gletkin's voice, "except to once again prove my devotion to the party."

"For you there is only one proof," came Gletkin's voice, "your complete confession. We've heard enough of your oppositional stance and your motives. What we demand is the full, public confession of your criminal activities, which were the inevitable consequence of this stance. The only way in which you can still serve the party is as a deterrent example—by showing on your own person where rebelling against the policy of the party inevitably leads."

Rubashov thought about Number One's cold meal. His inflamed facial nerve was now throbbing with full intensity, but the pain was no longer sharp and burning, rather it came in dull, numbing blows. He thought about Number One's cold meal, and his cramped facial muscles contracted into a grimace.

"But I can't confess what I didn't do," he said with a slight quiver in his voice.

"No," said Gletkin's voice, "of course you can't." And for the first time Rubashov thought he heard something like mockery in that voice.

◇

From that point on Rubashov's later recollections of the interrogation were somewhat blurry. After the sentence "No, of course you can't"—he could still hear Gletkin's peculiar intonation—there was a gap in his memory, though he couldn't say for how long. Afterward he sensed he must have dozed off, as he had a vague recollection of a wonderfully pleasant dream. This had probably lasted only a few seconds—a loose, timeless series of images of bright landscapes alive with animals and people, with the familiar poplars that had lined the drive onto his father's estate and a particular white cloud formation he had once observed hovering above these poplars.

The next thing he remembered was the presence of a new

person in the room and Gletkin's jarring voice—Gletkin must have leaned across the desk, over Rubashov's head:

"I ask that you concentrate your attention on the interrogation. Do you recognize this person?"

Rubashov nodded. He had recognized Harelip right away, despite the missing raincoat he otherwise always wore wrapped around his hunched shoulders as he walked around the yard, visibly freezing. A series of numbers flashed in his memory: 2-3; 1-1; 4-2; 1-5; 3-1 . . . "Harelip sends greetings." What was it that had prompted 402 to pass along the message?

"Where do you know him from?"

Rubashov had a hard time speaking; he couldn't get rid of the bile on his parched tongue.

"I've seen him several times through my window, exercising in the yard."

"And you didn't know him previously?"

Harelip stood a few steps away beside the door, diagonally behind Rubashov's chair, fully lit by the lamp. His generally yellowish face was now chalk white, his nose waxen and pointed; his split upper lip with the fleshy red bulge in the middle quivered above his bared teeth, and his hands dangled limply by his knees; Rubashov, who had now turned his back to the lamp, saw him as clearly as if he were in a spotlight onstage. A new series of taps ran through his mind: 4-4; 3-4; 4-2 . . . "tortured yesterday." And almost at once a memory wafted into his brain, a wisp he couldn't retain—the memory of having one time seen the original living version of this human wreck, long before he set foot in cell number 404.

"I can't say exactly," was his hesitant answer to Gletkin's question. "Now that I see him close up, I have the feeling I must have met him somewhere before."

Even before he finished the sentence Rubashov sensed it would have been better not to say it at all. His optical nerve was pounding his head with dull blows. He wished intensely that Gletkin would give him a few minutes to collect himself.

Gletkin's manner of spitting out his questions in quick sequence without a break called to mind a bird of prey hacking away at his quarry with his beak.

"Where did you last meet this man? After all, you are known for having an excellent memory."

Rubashov was silent. He scoured his memory but could not place the apparition with the constantly trembling lips standing in the spotlight. Harelip ran his tongue across the red bulge on his upper lip but otherwise made no move, while his gaze strayed from Rubashov to Gletkin and back to Rubashov.

The stenographer had stopped writing; the only sounds were the even humming of the lamp and the crackling of Gletkin's starched cuffs as he leaned forward and propped his arms on the armrests before asking the next question:

"You refuse to answer the question?"

"I don't remember," said Rubashov.

"Fine," said Gletkin. He leaned a bit further forward and turned his entire torso to face Harelip.

"Help Citizen Rubashov with his memory. Where did you last meet him?"

If anything, Harelip's face blanched even whiter. His eyes rested for a few seconds on the secretary, whose presence he was apparently only now registering, but then strayed again, as though they were fleeing somewhere and searching for a place to rest. Once again he ran his tongue over his lips and then said hastily, in one breath:

"Citizen Rubashov solicited me to physically liquidate the leader of the party by use of poison."

At first the only thing that struck Rubashov was the deep and melodic voice that rose so unexpectedly from the interior of this human wreck—evidently the only part of the man that had remained intact, in eerie contrast to his appearance. It was only after a few seconds that Rubashov grasped the content of what he had said. Rubashov had expected something of the sort and had sensed the danger as soon as Harelip was brought in, but now he was astounded by the sheer grotesqueness of the accusation. And right away he heard Gletkin's voice behind him—because he was still facing Harelip—this time sounding vexed, even a bit anxious:

"I didn't ask you about that yet. I asked where you last met Citizen Rubashov."

Mistake, thought Rubashov. *He shouldn't have called attention to the wrong answer; I wouldn't have even noticed.* At that moment it seemed to him his head was completely clear, with an overly bright, feverish alertness. He searched for an image. *This witness is a mechanical organ*, he thought, *and Gletkin just inserted the wrong waltz.* Harelip's next answer sounded even more melodious and angelic:

"I met Citizen Rubashov after a reception at the trade mission in B. That is where he induced me to commit my terrorist act."

As he spoke, his haunted gaze suddenly settled on Rubashov and rested there. Rubashov put on his pince-nez and returned the gaze with intense curiosity. But he was unable to read any plea for forgiveness in the young man's eyes, only a brotherly trust and the mute reproach of a defenseless person who's been tortured. It was Rubashov who first turned away, confused.

Behind his back he heard Gletkin's voice, once more self-assured and correct:

"Can you remember the date of the meeting?"

"I can remember exactly," said Harelip with his unnaturally harmonious voice. "It was right after the celebration commemorating the twentieth anniversary of the revolution."

His gaze still lingered, naked and exposed, on Rubashov's eyes. A memory flickered in Rubashov's brain, first indistinct but increasingly sharper. He finally figured out who Harelip was, but instead of a sensational revelation he felt only a pained astonishment. He turned his head toward Gletkin and said, squinting in the light from the lamp:

"The date is correct. I didn't recognize the professor's son right away, because I only saw young Misha once—and that was before he went through your hands. You may congratulate yourselves on the result."

"You admit, then, to knowing him and to having met him on the day at the stated occasion?"

"I just told you," Rubashov said, tired. The sudden, exaggerated alertness from before had faded; once again he felt the need to sleep, and the dull hammering in his head resumed. "If you had told me right away that this had to do with the ill-fated professor, I would have recognized his son earlier."

"His full name was mentioned in the indictment," said Gletkin.

"Like the rest of the world, I only knew the professor by his nom de plume—Mikhail."

"That detail doesn't matter," said Gletkin. He again turned his upper body to face Harelip, as though he wanted to crush him by throwing his full weight across the gap between them. "Continue with your report. Explain how your meeting came about."

Another mistake, thought Rubashov, despite his sleepiness. *That detail does indeed matter. If I really had instigated this man to attempt this idiotic assassination, I would have surely remembered who he was at the first reference, whether he was named or not.* But Rubashov was too tired to explain all that, and besides, doing so would have meant once again having to face the lamp. This way he could turn his back to Gletkin.

While the two men discussed his identity and his father, Harelip stood in the white light, with his head lowered and his lip quivering. Rubashov thought about his old friend and comrade Mikhail K., the great historian of the revolution. In the famous photograph from the party congress, where everyone at the table had beards and little numbered circles over their heads like halos, Mikhail had sat just two seats to the left of the old leader. He had been the old man's collaborator on questions of philosophy of government and history, also his chess partner and possibly his only friend. After the death of the "Old Man," Mikhail—who had known him more intimately than other contemporaries—had been officially tasked with writing his biography. He labored on this for ten years, but the biography was never to appear. During that time the official narrative of the revolution had undergone strange twists and turns—the roles played by its leading actors had to be rewritten after the fact, and the performances reevaluated—but old Mikhail was thick skulled and didn't understand anything of the new era under Number One . . .

"I had accompanied my father," Harelip said in his unnaturally harmonious voice, "to a European conference for historians. On the way back we made a detour to B., where my father wanted to visit Citizen Rubashov, who was a friend of his . . ."

Rubashov listened with an odd mix of curiosity and melancholy. Up to that point everything was accurate: the old professor had traveled to him to unburden his heart, in part also to ask for advice. The evening they had spent together may have been the last bright spot in the old professor's life.

"We could only stay one day," Harelip continued, his gaze still fixed on Rubashov's face, as though he were looking to find some strength and encouragement there. "It happened to be the anniversary of the revolution, which is why I remember the date so well. All day and into the evening Citizen Rubashov was very busy with receptions and could only see my father briefly. But after the reception in the embassy was over, he waited for my father in his room. My father had allowed me to come along. Citizen Rubashov was a little tired; he was wearing a robe but welcomed us very cordially. He had set the table with cake, wine, and cognac. He embraced my father and greeted him with the words: 'Farewell feast of the last of the Mohicans' . . ."

Gletkin's voice grated behind Rubashov's back:

"Did you realize right then that it was Rubashov's aim to get you drunk so you would be more receptive to his intentions?"

Rubashov thought he saw a smile flit across Harelip's ravaged face—the first time he had seen anything that resembled the young Misha of that evening. But the expression vanished immediately; Harelip blinked and ran his tongue over his cleft lip.

"There was something suspicious that I sensed right away, but at the time I didn't realize the connection."

Poor dog, thought Rubashov, *what have they done to you . . .*

"Go on," said the voice of Gletkin.

It took Harelip a few seconds to collect himself after the interruption. In the meantime they heard the skinny stenographer sharpening her pencil.

"At first Rubashov and my father spent a good while talking about the old days. They hadn't seen each other for a long time. They spoke about the period before the revolution, about people of the older generation I knew only from hearsay, and about events during the civil war. They frequently made allusions that I couldn't follow and laughed at memories I didn't understand . . ."

"Was there a lot of drinking?" asked Gletkin.

Harelip squinted forlornly into the light. Only now did Rubashov notice that he was swaying slightly as he spoke, as if he had difficulty staying on his feet.

"I think they drank a fair amount," Harelip went on. "I never saw my father in such a good mood during his last years."

"That," Gletkin's voice sounded, "was three months before the discovery of your father's counterrevolutionary activity, which three months later led to his execution?"

Harelip licked his lips, gazed dully into the light, and was silent. Following a sudden impulse, Rubashov had turned to Gletkin, but he immediately had to shut his eyes since they were blinded by the light. Then he slowly turned back around and rubbed his pince-nez on his sleeve with his familiar gesture. The secretary's pencil scratched on the paper and went silent. Then Gletkin's voice sounded again:

"Were you already aware of your father's counterrevolutionary activities at the time?"

Harelip licked his lips.

"Yes," he said.

"And did you know that Rubashov shared your father's views?"

"Yes."

"Describe the main phases of the conversation, leaving out anything that isn't pertinent."

Harelip had now folded his hands behind his back and was leaning his shoulders against the wall.

"After a while my father and Rubashov came to the present day. They spoke disparagingly about the current state of affairs within the party and the methods of the leadership. Between themselves, Rubashov and my father referred to the leader of the party only as 'Number One.' Rubashov said that ever since Number One had sat down on the party with his broad bottom, the air beneath was no longer breathable. That was the reason he preferred to work abroad . . ."

Gletkin turned to Rubashov:

"That was shortly before your first declaration of loyalty to the policies and person of the party leader?"

Rubashov turned halfway into the light. "That would be about right," he said, tired.

"During the conversation, did Rubashov mention his intent to make such a declaration?" Gletkin asked Harelip.

"Yes. My father reproached Rubashov for that and said that Rubashov had disappointed him. Rubashov laughed and called my father an old fool and a Don Quixote. He said the main thing now was to hold out and wait for the right moment."

"What did he mean by 'wait for the right moment'?"

"The moment when the party's leader would be removed from his post."

Rubashov's smile did not escape Gletkin, who said dryly:

"These recollections seem to amuse you?"

"Perhaps," said Rubashov, once again shutting his eyes.

Gletkin straightened his crackling cuffs and continued with the interrogation:

"So Rubashov made reference to the time when the leader of the party should be removed from his post. In what manner was this event supposed to happen?"

"My father believed the day would come when a final straw would break the camel's back and the party would either depose him or force him to leave on his own, and that the opposition should propagate this idea."

"And Rubashov?"

"Rubashov laughed at my father and repeated that he was an old fool and a Don Quixote. Then he explained that Number One was not some random phenomenon, but the embodiment of a human condition defined by an absolute belief in his own person and in the exclusive validity of his convictions, from which he derived the moral strength for his absolute lack of scruples. Therefore he would never freely relinquish power and could only be removed by force. For the time being there could be no hope that the party would do this, since Number One held all the strings and had made the party bureaucrats his accomplices: they realized that they would either stand or fall with Number One."

Despite his sleepiness, Rubashov noticed how exactly the young man had noted his words. He himself didn't remember his exact wording, but he had no doubt it was all true. He observed the professor's son with renewed interest through his pince-nez.

Gletkin's jarring voice resumed:

"So with that, Rubashov emphasized and justified the inevitability of using force against 'Number One,' that is to say, the leader of the party?"

Harelip nodded without saying anything.

"And his arguments, reinforced by the generous consumption of alcoholic beverages, made a strong impression on you?"

Misha didn't answer right away. Then he said, somewhat more quietly than before:

"I had barely drunk anything. But everything he said made a deep impression on me."

Rubashov lowered his head. He began to feel a nagging suspicion that soon caused such an immediate, practically physical pain he forgot about everything else. Was it possible that this unfortunate young man really had drawn his own conclusions from his, Rubashov's, thoughts, so that what he was seeing here in this blinding glare was nothing but the consequence of his own logic made flesh?

Gletkin didn't let him finish his thought. His voice grated.

". . . And after this theoretical preparation he then urged you directly to perform the deed?"

Harelip squinted and said nothing.

Gletkin waited a few seconds for the answer. Even Rubashov involuntarily raised his head. More seconds passed in which nothing was heard except the electric thrum of the lamp, followed once again by Gletkin's voice, more correct and colorless than usual:

"Would you like us to jog your memory?"

Gletkin uttered this sentence with a pronounced casualness, but Harelip cringed as though he'd been whipped. He licked his lips, and his eyes flickered with an unrestrained, animal-like terror. Then once again came the harmonious, organlike voice:

"That did not happen on that same evening, but the next morning, during a private conversation between Citizen Rubashov and me."

Rubashov smiled. Postponing the alleged conversation to the next day was apparently a finesse of Gletkin's stage direction; the idea of old Mikhail sitting there while his son accepted the mission to poison the leader was too implausible even for Neanderthal psychology. Rubashov forgot the shock he had just suffered; he turned to Gletkin and asked, squinting into the light:

"According to procedure, do I have the right to ask questions during the confrontation?"

"You do have the right," said Gletkin.

Rubashov turned to face the young man. "As far as I remember," he said, looking at Misha through his pince-nez, "you had just finished studying at the university when you and your father came to visit me?"

Now that he was speaking to him directly for the first time, the same hopeful, pleading expression came to the man's face that Rubashov had noticed earlier. Misha nodded his head without saying a word.

"That's correct, then," said Rubashov. "If I further remember rightly, you were planning to work in the institute for historical research, under your father. Did you do that?"

"Yes," said Harelip. After a brief hesitation he added: "Until my father was arrested."

"I understand," said Rubashov. "That made it impossible for you to stay on in the institute, and you had to find a way to earn a living . . ." He paused, turned to Gletkin, and said slowly:

". . . from which it clearly follows that at the time of my meeting with the professor's son neither he nor I could foresee what he would be doing in the future, and so the idea of assigning him a mission to poison anyone is logically impossible."

The secretary's pencil suddenly stopped scratching on the paper. Without having to look, Rubashov knew that she had stopped recording and that she had turned her pointy mouse face to Gletkin, with a questioning gaze. Harelip, too, looked at Gletkin, as he licked his lip, but in his eyes there was no relief, just helplessness and fear, and Rubashov's momentary feeling of triumph evaporated; strangely, he had the sensation that he had committed an indiscretion, of having impertinently disturbed the course of a solemn ceremony. And indeed, the tone of Gletkin's reply was even cooler and more correct than usual.

"Are you finished with your questions?"

"For the time being," said Rubashov.

"No one claims that your instructions to the assassin were limited to the use of poison," said Gletkin calmly. "The assignment was a terrorist assassination, but the choice of means was left to the assassin. Is that correct?"

"Yes," answered Harelip with some relief in his voice.

Rubashov remembered that the indictment expressly referred to instigating an assassination by means of poison, but now the whole matter seemed beside the point. So, too, did the question of whether Misha had actually attempted the senseless deed or had only planned something similar, or whether he had memorized his confession completely or only partly—this was only of juristic interest and didn't alter Rubashov's guilt. The only thing that really mattered was that this wretched person was simply the embodiment of Rubashov's own logic. The roles had reversed themselves; now it wasn't Gletkin but Rubashov himself who was attempting to muddle the facts with sophistic quibbles. The accusation, which until now had seemed so grotesque and monstrous, was merely supplying the missing links in the logical chain, albeit in a crude and clumsy fashion.

Nevertheless, in one fundamental point Rubashov felt that he was being treated unjustly—but he was too exhausted to bring that up now . . .

"Do you have any further questions?" asked Gletkin.

Rubashov shook his head.

"You may go," Gletkin said to Harelip. He pressed a buzzer; a uniformed official stepped in and placed metal handcuffs on the young man. At the door, before he was led off, he turned again to look at Rubashov, the way he did after exercise in the courtyard. Rubashov felt the weight of his gaze like a heavy burden; he took off his pince-nez, rubbed it on his sleeve, and turned away. The hammering in his face resumed.

Once Harelip had gone he almost envied the young man. At least he could sleep now . . .

Gletkin's voice grated in his ear, correct and brutally crisp:

"Do you now admit that in its essential points the witness's confession is in accord with the facts?"

Once again Rubashov was forced to face the lamp. His ears were buzzing, and the light came flaming hot and red through the thin walls of his eyelids. Even so the phrase "in its essential points" did not escape him. That allowed Gletkin to bridge the rift in the indictment and created the possibility of correcting "instigating to poison" to "instigating to murder."

"In its essential points, yes . . ." said Rubashov.

Gletkin's cuffs crackled, and even the stenographer couldn't help shifting on her chair—indicating to Rubashov that he had only now spoken the decisive sentence, which sealed his admission of guilt. But what did these Neanderthals know what for him was truly decisive, what mattered most, what he considered truth, measured by his own standards?

"Does the light bother you?" Gletkin asked suddenly.

Rubashov smiled. Gletkin paid in cash. That was the Neanderthal psychology. Still, Rubashov felt a soothing relief when the glaring light was softened by a degree, as well as something akin to gratitude.

Now, if he squinted a little, he could even look Gletkin in the face. He again saw the broad red scar on his shaven head.

". . . except for one point that I consider essential," said Rubashov.

"Namely?" asked Gletkin, stiff and cold once more.

Of course now he thinks I mean the private conversation with the boy that never took place, thought Rubashov, *because that's what matters to* him—*dotting every i even if the dots look like blotches. Then again, he's probably right, from his point of view . . .*

"The main point I'm referring to," he said, "is this. In keeping with my beliefs at the time, I probably did mention the inevitability of using force. But by this I meant political action rather than individual assassinations."

"In other words, civil war?" said Gletkin.

"No, mass action," said Rubashov.

"Which, as you know yourself, necessarily leads to civil war. Is that the distinction that is so important to you?"

Rubashov said nothing. That was indeed the point that had seemed so important to him a moment earlier, but now that, too, didn't seem to matter. Indeed, if at the end of the day the organized opposition against the party bureaucracy and its monstrous apparatus could achieve victory only by means of civil war, how was that any better than slipping poison into Number One's cold lunch, since his disappearance could possibly bring about a quicker breakdown of the system and without such bloodshed? To what degree was political murder less honorable than mass action when it came to doing away with the leadership? It was likely that the boy had misunderstood him, but perhaps he was more logical in his misunderstanding than Rubashov himself?

Whoever enters into opposition against a dictatorship must accept civil war as a means. Whoever shies away from civil war must abandon opposition and accept the dictatorship.

These clear postulates, which he had written nearly a lifetime ago in a polemic against the "moderates," contained his own sentence. He felt incapable of debating with Gletkin any further. The awareness of his complete defeat filled him with something almost like relief; the obligation to continue the struggle, the burden of responsibility, had been lifted from him; the sleepiness from before came back. Now the hammering in his head was just a distant echo, and for a few seconds it seemed to him that it was not Gletkin he was facing behind the desk, but Number One, with the same look of knowing irony with which he had shaken his hand when they said goodbye after their last meeting. Then Rubashov remembered the inscription that had once marked the entrance to Errancis Cemetery, in which Saint-Just, Robespierre, and their sixteen beheaded comrades were buried. It consisted of two words:

Dormir enfin—"To sleep at last."

◇

From that point on Rubashov's recollection once again grew blurry. He must have fallen asleep for a second time during the interrogation, either for several minutes or a few seconds, but this time he did not remember any dream. Gletkin probably woke him to sign the statement. He took out his fountain pen and handed it to Rubashov. The pen felt warm from being in Gletkin's pocket, which Rubashov found unpleasant. The secretary was no longer recording the proceeding; the room was completely quiet. Even the lamp had stopped humming and now shed a normal, somewhat pallid light, since dawn was already beginning to show outside the window. As Rubashov signed the paper he still felt the relief and freedom from responsibility that he had experienced earlier, though he had forgotten the reason. He read the statement, half-asleep, in which he confessed to having instigated Misha to murder the leader of the party. For a few moments he had the feeling everything was a grotesque mistake, and felt an impulse to scratch out his signature and tear up the statement, but then it all came back; he rubbed his pince-nez on his sleeve and pushed the paper across the desk to Gletkin.

The next thing he remembered was the uniformed giant— the one who had brought him to Gletkin's room an immeasurably long time ago—once more escorting him down the corridor. The barbershop and the stair leading to the basement drifted by in his half-awake state, and through a mist he recalled his fears on the way there; he was a little surprised at himself and smiled vaguely. Then he heard the cell door clang shut behind him, and with a feeling of intense physical delight he sank lengthwise onto the cot, observed the gray light of dawn in the windowpanes and the familiar sight of the newspaper covering the missing pane, and instantly fell asleep.

When the cell door opened again, it was still not quite light outside; he couldn't have slept more than an hour. At first he thought they were bringing him breakfast, but instead of the old warder standing outside it was the same giant as before, and Rubashov realized that he had to go back to Gletkin, and that the interrogation was to resume. He went to the basin, splashed some cold water on his forehead and neck, put on his pince-nez, and once again set off down the corridors, past the barbershop and the stairs to the basement, with a slight stagger that he did not even notice.

4.

From that point on Rubashov's memory became increasingly foggy. All he could later remember were scraps of his dialogue with Gletkin that stretched over several days and nights, with short breaks lasting between one and two hours, which he passed more unconscious than asleep. Nor could he say exactly how many days and nights this lasted—probably about a week. Rubashov had heard of this method before, designed to wear down the accused by subjecting him to constant interrogation, usually performed by two or three examining magistrates working in shifts. What set Gletkin's approach apart was the fact that he never had anyone relieve him; in other words he demanded as much of himself as he did of Rubashov. In that way he deprived Rubashov of his last refuge: the pathos of being accused, the moral superiority of the victim.

Within forty-eight hours Rubashov had already lost all concept of day and night. When the gigantic guard jostled him awake after one or two hours of sleep, he could never tell if the gray light in the window was dusk or dawn. The corridor with the barbershop, the stairs to the basement, and the iron door was always uniformly lit with the pallid, yellowish light from the electric bulbs. If during the interrogation the window slowly grew brighter, until Gletkin finally turned off the lamp, it was morning. If it got darker and Gletkin turned the lamp on, it was evening.

If Rubashov grew hungry during the interrogation, Gletkin had tea and sandwiches brought in for him. But he seldom had any real appetite, only sudden fits of intense hunger, and the sight of the bread set before him made him nauseous. Gletkin never ate in his presence, and for some reason he didn't fully understand, Rubashov found it humiliating to ask for food. Everything that had to do with bodily functions became a source of humiliation in front of Gletkin, who never showed any sign of fatigue, never yawned, never smoked, seemed to neither eat nor drink, and always sat across from Rubashov in the same correct posture, in his starched uniform, with his crackling cuffs. The deepest humiliation for Rubashov was when he had to request permission to relieve himself. Gletkin would then have him led out by the guard on duty—usually the giant—who would wait for him outside the door to the toilet. Once Rubashov fell asleep behind the closed door, and from then on it was always left ajar.

During the interrogation, his condition alternated between complete apathy and an unnatural, almost crystalline alertness. Only once did he lose consciousness; he frequently felt on the verge of doing so, but each time a strange feeling of shame jerked him back at the last minute. He would light a cigarette and blink at the light, and the interrogation would continue.

In between times he was surprised that he could stand it all. But he knew that the popular estimation of the limits of physical resistance was far too low; most people had no idea how astonishingly resilient the human body is. He had heard of cases where the accused had been deprived of sleep for fifteen to twenty days and had nonetheless endured.

As he was signing the statement during the first interrogation with Gletkin, he had succumbed to the illusion that he had weathered the entire storm. With the second interrogation he realized that it was really only just beginning. The indictment contained seven points, and he had admitted only one. He thought he had already exhausted the feeling of defeat, but now he saw that there were as many degrees of powerlessness as there were of power, that defeat could elicit the same enormous and dizzying intensity as victory. Gletkin was forcing him down the ladder rung by rung.

Of course he could have had it easier. All he had to do was sign or deny everything all at once and he would have peace. A convoluted sense of duty prevented him from giving in to this temptation. Rubashov's life had been so devoted to a single absolute idea that he was barely familiar with the concept of temptation. Now it accompanied him through the indistinguishable days and nights, as he staggered past the barbershop and the basement staircase, in the white glare of Gletkin's lamp—the temptation that consisted of a single word, the word inscribed over the cemetery of the great ones defeated by history: "sleep."

This temptation was hard to resist, because it was so quiet, so peaceful, without cheap makeup, with neither siren tones nor carnal overtones. It was mute and did not argue or debate. All the arguments were on Gletkin's side; the temptation merely repeated the words from the note passed by the barber: "They've all chosen to spit on themselves—but you should die in silence." At times, in the moments of apathy between the flashes of clear alertness, this temptation would move Rubashov's lips from the inside, but Gletkin couldn't hear the words being formed. He merely cleared his throat and fixed his cuffs. And Rubashov, sleepy and confused, rubbed his pince-nez on his sleeve and nodded, because he had finally identified the temptation and recognized that silent partner he thought he had forgotten, and who had less business in this room than anyone—the grammatical fiction.

"So you deny," said Gletkin's voice, "having negotiated with the representatives of foreign powers on behalf of the opposition, in order to overthrow the current regime with their help? You dispute the charge that you were prepared to pay for their direct or indirect support of your plans with territorial concessions—in other words, by giving up extensive areas of the country?"

Yes, Rubashov disputed that, and Gletkin repeated to him the day and place of his conversation with the foreign diplomat—and Rubashov again recalled the brief, inconsequential scene that had surfaced in his memory when the indictment had been read out loud. In his sleepy, muddled state he looked at Gletkin and realized it was hopeless to try to explain it to him. The scene had taken place after a diplomatic breakfast in the embassy in B. Rubashov was sitting next to the corpulent Herr von Z., who was the deputy embassy counselor of the country where Rubashov had had his teeth bashed in a few months earlier. They had enjoyed an excellent conversation on the subject of a certain strain of guinea pig that had been cultivated with great success on both the Rubashovs' estate as well as the von Z.s'. In all probability their fathers had exchanged specimens.

"So what ever became of your father's guinea pigs?" asked Herr von Z.

"They were slaughtered and eaten during the revolution," said Rubashov.

"Ours are now being used as a fat substitute," said Herr von Z. sadly. He made no secret of his disdain for the new regime in his homeland; it was probably just by accident that he had not yet been removed from his post.

"You and I, sir, find ourselves in a similar situation," he said, clearly at ease, raising his liqueur glass to Rubashov. "Slated for extinction, that is. The time of raising guinea pigs is over; now it is the century of the plebeians."

"But I'm committed to the plebeians," Rubashov had answered with a smile.

"That's not what I meant," said Herr von Z. "At the end of the day I'm also in accord with the program of the little man with the black moustache, if only he wouldn't shriek so much. One is always only crucified in the name of one's own faith."

They sat there for a while, and when they said goodbye, after black coffee had been served, Herr von Z. said, "If you wish to make yet another revolution at home, Herr Rubashov, and depose your head shrieker, then take better care of the guinea pigs."

"That will hardly happen," Rubashov answered, and added: ". . . Although you evidently seem to take this possibility into account?"

"Indeed," replied Herr von Z., still in the same easy tone, "judging from the reports of the most recent trial, all sorts of things seem to be going on in your country."

"And in that extremely unlikely event," said Rubashov, "would you have any idea what your country might decide to do?"

Herr von Z. answered with unexpected precision, almost as though he had been waiting a long time for this question: "We would keep still. But that would come with a cost."

They were standing next to the table, which had been half cleared, coffee cups in hand. "And have your leaders agreed on a particular price?" asked Rubashov, sensing that the joking quality of his reply sounded somewhat forced.

"Certainly," answered Herr von Z., and named an area that was rich in grain and inhabited by a national minority. And then they said goodbye.

It had been years since Rubashov had thought of that encounter, or at least consciously recalled it. A silly palaver over liqueur and coffee—how could he show Gletkin how utterly insignificant it really was? He blinked sleepily at Gletkin sitting across the desk, stone-faced and expressionless as always. No, the idea of explaining to him about the guinea pigs was out of the question. This Gletkin understood nothing of guinea pigs. He had never drunk coffee with the Herr von Z.s of the world. Rubashov remembered how haltingly Gletkin had read the indictment, occasionally with the wrong intonation. He came from a proletarian background and had learned to read and write only as an adult. He would never understand how a conversation that began with guinea pigs could end heaven only knows where.

"So you admit that this conversation took place," stated Gletkin.

"It was completely insignificant," said Rubashov, tired, and immediately recognized that Gletkin had forced him one more rung down the ladder.

"As insignificant," said Gletkin, "as your purely theoretical explanations to Professor K.'s son concerning the necessity of removing the leader by force?"

Rubashov rubbed his pince-nez on his sleeve. Had the conversation really been as insignificant as he had tried to make himself believe? To be sure, he had neither "negotiated" nor made any agreements, nor did the easygoing Herr von Z. have the authority to enter into any. At most the whole thing could be construed as a "sounding," as it was called in diplomatic circles. But this sounding had been completely in line with his logic at that time, and moreover it corresponded to certain traditions within the party. Hadn't the old leader used the services of the general staff of that same country in order to return from banishment so he could lead the revolution to victory? And later had he not relinquished territories in the first peace treaty, as a price for the other power's keeping still? "The old man is sacrificing space to gain time," a witty friend of Rubashov's had remarked back then. The forgotten, "insignificant" conversation suddenly became so exactly ordered in a logical chain that Rubashov found it difficult to see it other than through the eyes of Gletkin—this same Gletkin who read so haltingly and ploddingly, and whose mind worked just as ploddingly and arrived at simple, easily grasped results, perhaps precisely because he understood nothing of guinea pigs . . . Where did Gletkin learn of this conversation, anyway? Either someone had been listening in, which given the circumstances was rather unlikely—or else the portly Herr von Z. had been acting as an agent provocateur, heaven only knew for what complicated motives. Similar things had happened often enough. They had set a trap for Rubashov—a trap constructed according to the primitive design of Gletkin and Number One—and he, the superior Rubashov, had promptly fallen in.

"If you are so precisely informed about the conversation with Herr von Z.," said Rubashov, "then you must also know that it was completely without consequence."

"Certainly," said Gletkin. "Thanks to the fact that we arrested you in time and have squashed the opposition. Had we failed to do this, then the consequences of the attempted high treason would have come to pass."

What could he say to that? That it would never have had any serious consequences, if only because he, Rubashov, was too old and spent to be able to follow through with the consistency that was the hallmark of party tradition, and as Gletkin would have done in his place? That the entire activity of the so-called opposition was nothing but senile, impotent prattle, because the generation of the old guard was just as spent as he was? Exhausted by decades of illegal struggle, corroded by the dampness of the prison walls where they had spent half their youth, mentally sapped by their internal conflict with the party, by the constant nervous strain in suppressing the physical fear that was never spoken of but that they had each had to cope with all alone for years, for decades? Exhausted from the years of emigration, the caustic acrimony of factional disputes and the unscrupulousness with which they were carried out; worn out from constant defeats and from the demoralizing effects of the final victory? Should he say that there had never been a truly determined, active opposition to the dictatorship of Number One, that everything had been mere talk, ineffective babble, children playing with fire, because this generation, the old guard, had given all that humans could give, because history had squeezed them to the very last drop, to the last calorie of their souls, so that they had but one thing to expect, like the dead in Errancis Cemetery: to sleep and wait for future generations to prove them right?

What was he supposed to say to this unmovable Neanderthal? That he was correct in everything except for one fundamental error, namely believing it was still the old Rubashov sitting across from him, whereas in reality he was speaking to that man's shadow? That the entire matter boiled down to punishing him not for deeds he had committed but for ones he had neglected to perform? "One is always only crucified in the name of one's own faith," had said the corpulent Herr von Z.

Before Rubashov signed the statement and was led back to his cell to lie on his cot, unconscious, until the next torment began, he asked Gletkin a question. The question did not pertain to the investigation, but Rubashov knew that each time he signed off on a further point of the indictment, Gletkin grew a notch more agreeable—Gletkin paid in cash. Rubashov's question concerned the fate of Ivanov.

"Citizen Ivanov is under arrest," said Gletkin.

"May one learn the reason?" asked Rubashov.

"Citizen Ivanov conducted the investigation against you in a negligent manner and in private conversations voiced cynical doubts as to the correctness of the indictment."

"What if he simply couldn't believe the accusation?" asked Rubashov. "Perhaps he had too high an opinion of me?"

"In that case," said Gletkin, "he was duty-bound to stop the investigation and officially present his view to the proper authorities concerning your innocence."

Was Gletkin making fun of him? He looked as correct and expressionless as ever.

◇

And after their next meeting, when Rubashov was once again holding Gletkin's warm fountain pen, ready to sign another statement—the stenographer had just left the room—he said to his interrogator:

"Permit me one more question."

As he spoke he looked at the broad scar on Gletkin's shaved head.

"I was told you are a proponent of certain drastic measures, the so-called hard method. Why have you never tried using direct physical pressure on me?"

"You mean physical torture," said Gletkin casually. "As you know, our penal code forbids this."

He paused a moment. Rubashov had just finished signing the statement. "Besides," he continued, "there is a certain constitutional type that will confess under pressure and then recant at the public trial. You belong to this tough type. The political usefulness of your testimony comes from its being voluntarily given."

It was the first time Gletkin had mentioned a public proceeding. But as he walked back down the corridor, following the giant with small, tired steps, it was not that perspective but the words "You belong to this tough type" that occupied his thoughts. Against his will this sentence filled him with a pleasant sense of satisfaction.

I'm growing senile and childish, he thought as he lay down on the cot. Even so, the pleasant feeling stayed with him as he fell asleep.

◇

Each time he signed a new statement after a tough debate and stretched out on his cot exhausted and nevertheless strangely satisfied, aware that he would again be awakened in one or at most two hours—each time Rubashov had but one wish: that Gletkin would let him sleep as long as he could, just once, to allow him to reflect. He knew this yearning would go unfulfilled until the struggle had been fought to the end, the last *i* dotted, and he also knew that every new encounter would end in a new defeat and that there was no possible doubt as to the final outcome. Why then was he still tormenting himself and letting himself be tormented, instead of breaking off the lost battle—simply not to be awakened anymore? The idea of death had long lost any transcendental character for him; it was filled with a warm, living, bodily content, the same as sleep. Yet still he felt driven by some strange, convoluted sense of duty to stay awake and continue fighting the lost battle to the end—even if this was merely tilting at windmills. Until the hour when Gletkin had forced him down the last rung of the ladder and the last rough splotch of the indictment had been transformed before his blinking eyes into the logical dot above the *i*. He had to follow this path to the end. Only then, when he stepped into the darkness with open eyes, would he have the right to sleep and no longer be awakened.

◇

During this almost uninterrupted chain of days and nights Gletkin, too, was undergoing a certain transformation. It was slight, but it did not escape Rubashov's feverish, glowing eyes. He maintained his stiff posture to the end, with his unmoved face and crackling cuffs, protected by the lamp behind his desk, but little by little the brutality of his voice abated, just as little by little he lowered the intensity of the lamp until it emitted an almost normal light. He never smiled, and Rubashov wondered whether the Neanderthals were even capable of smiling, nor was his voice supple enough to express nuances of feeling. But once, when Rubashov ran out of cigarettes after a dialogue lasting several hours, Gletkin, who himself did not smoke, took a pack out of his pocket and handed it across the table to Rubashov.

In one single matter Rubashov even managed to win a victory: that was the point of the indictment regarding his alleged wrecking activity in the aluminum trust. It was an accusation that did not carry much weight, considering the entire complex of crimes to which he had already confessed, but Rubashov fought against it as fiercely as he contested the major points. They spent nearly the entire night sitting opposite each other. Rubashov refuted all the incriminating testimonies and one-sided statistics point for point; in a voice slurred from exhaustion he recited numbers and dates that had miraculously appeared in his befuddled brain at the right moment, and Gletkin never managed to find a link from which he could derive the logical chain. They had long come to a tacit agreement that Gletkin, once he had succeeded in proving that the basic gist of the accusation was correct—even if this was nothing but a logical abstraction—had free rein to fill in the missing details, to dot the *is*. Without realizing it they had become used to this rule, and neither of them any longer differentiated between actions that Rubashov had actually performed and those that he was simply *bound to* have performed as a logical consequence of his convictions; gradually they had lost their perception of appearance and reality, logical fiction and actual fact. Occasionally, in his rare moments of clarity, Rubashov would suddenly become aware of this, and each time this happened he had the feeling of waking up from a peculiar state of intoxication; Gletkin on the other hand seemed not to pay it any conscious heed.

Toward morning, when Rubashov still had not given in to the charge of sabotaging the aluminum trust, Gletkin's voice took on an undertone of nervousness—just like at the beginning, when Harelip had produced the wrong answer. He turned the lamp up, which hadn't happened in a long time, but then, when he noticed Rubashov's ironic smile, he let it be. He posed a few questions that had no effect and then said, in conclusion:

"You categorically deny having committed acts of disorganization in the branch of industry entrusted to you—or even having planned the same?"

Rubashov nodded—with a sleepy curiosity as to what would then follow. Gletkin turned to the stenographer:

"Write: the examining magistrate recommends that this point of the indictment be dropped due to insufficient evidence."

Rubashov quickly lit a cigarette to hide the sign of childish triumph that overcame him. It was the first time he had scored a victory over Gletkin. To be sure, it was only a pitiful partial victory in a lost battle, but a victory nevertheless, and it had been many months, years—actually even decades—since he had had that feeling once so familiar to him . . . Gletkin took the protocol from the secretary and dismissed her, following the ritual that had recently developed between them.

When they were alone and Rubashov had risen from his chair to sign the statement, Gletkin said, as he handed Rubashov his pen:

"Experience teaches that industrial sabotage is the most effective means for the opposition to disrupt the government and generate ill will toward the regime. Why are you so insistent that you did not use or intend to use this means?"

"Because technically speaking it is absurd," said Rubashov. "And because this constant evoking of saboteurs as bogeymen creates a psychosis of denunciation I find repulsive." The sense of triumph he had gone so long without caused Rubashov to feel refreshed, and to speak more loudly.

"If you consider the sabotage employed by the opposition as a bogeyman, to what do you attribute the less-than-satisfactory conditions in our industry?"

"To substandard wages, slave-driving, and barbaric disciplinary measures," said Rubashov. "I know of several cases from my trust where workers were shot as saboteurs for small acts of carelessness that were due solely to overexhaustion. Whoever was late for his shift by just two minutes was dismissed and was given a black mark in his work permit that made it impossible to find employment elsewhere."

Gletkin looked at Rubashov with his usual expressionless eyes and asked in his usual expressionless tone:

"Were you given a pocket watch as a child?"

Rubashov looked at him, puzzled. The most striking feature of the Neanderthal was his lack of humor, or more precisely, the absolute absence of frivolity.

"Do you not want to answer my question?" asked Gletkin.

"Of course," said Rubashov, more and more astonished.

"How old were you when you were given the watch?"

"I don't know," said Rubashov, "eight or nine."

"I," said Gletkin in his usual correct voice, "was sixteen

years old when I learned that the hour was divided into minutes. In my village, when the peasants had to go into town they went to the train station at sunrise and slept in the waiting room until the train came, usually toward noon, but sometimes not until the evening or even the next morning. These are the same peasants that are working in our factories. My village, for example, now has the largest steel-rail factory in the world. The blast furnace has to be tapped to drain the slag. During the first year the foremen used to take a nap in between drainings, until eventually they were shot. In all other countries the peasants had one to two hundred years to get used to industrial precision, to dealing with machines. In ours they just had ten years. If we didn't dismiss and shoot them for every little thing, the whole country would have come to a standstill, and the peasants would simply have lain down in the machine room until grass started growing out of the chimneys and everything went back to the way it was before. Last year a politically moderate delegation of women came from Manchester in England to visit our factory. They were shown everything, and afterward they wrote indignant articles about how the textile workers in Manchester would never stand for such treatment. I once read that the textile industry in Manchester is two hundred years old. I also read how the workers were treated there two hundred years ago, when it started. You, Citizen Rubashov, have just put forward the same arguments as the women's delegation from Manchester. Of course you know better than these women. So it's amazing you would use the same arguments. But you have something in common with these women: you were given a pocket watch when you were just a child . . ."

Rubashov said nothing and looked at Gletkin with renewed interest. What was that? Was the Neanderthal opening his soul? But Gletkin sat stiffly on his chair, his eyes as expressionless as ever.

"You may be right about many things," Rubashov said at last. "But you provoked me. What use is it to be constantly

searching out scapegoats, when the real problems are fundamental, and rooted in the causes you just described so convinc-
ingly?"

"Experience teaches," said Gletkin, "that the masses need to
be given simple explanations for complicated connections that
are difficult to understand—explanations that are easily grasped.
From what I've learned of history I see that mankind has never
managed without scapegoats. I believe this has always been an
indispensable institution; your friend Ivanov taught me that its
origins lie in religion. As far as I remember he explained that the
word comes from a custom of the Israelites, who several times a
year would make a sacrifice to their god of a goat that had been
ritually burdened with their sins." Gletkin paused and adjusted
his cuffs. "Incidentally history also has examples of voluntary
scapegoats. When I was the same age you were when you were
given your watch, the priest taught me that Jesus Christ called
himself a lamb and took on all the sins of the world. I never
understood how it was supposed to lighten the fate of mankind
if someone declares he is letting himself be crucified in its name.
But for two thousand years people have considered this entirely
natural."

Rubashov looked at him. What was Gletkin getting at? What
was the point of this conversation? In what logical labyrinth
had his Neanderthal logic lost its way?

"Even so," said Rubashov, "it would be more suited to our
view to tell people the plain truth rather than populate the
world with saboteurs and devils."

"If the people in my village," said Gletkin, "were told that
they were sluggish and backward despite the revolution and the
factory, nothing would be attained. If they are told that they are
heroes of labor, more diligent and efficient than the Americans,
and that everything bad is solely due to the devils and saboteurs, then at least something can be achieved. What is true is
what serves mankind, and whatever harms it is a lie. The party's
primer of world history published for use in the adult night

schools makes a point of saying that during its first centuries, the Christian religion brought some measure of objective progress for humanity. No reasonable person is interested in whether Christ was lying or speaking the truth when he claimed he was the son of a god and a virgin. People said this was symbolic, but the peasants took it literally. We have the same right to invent useful symbols that the peasants take literally."

"Your logic," said Rubashov, "sometimes reminds me of Ivanov's."

"Citizen Ivanov," said Gletkin, "belonged like you to the old intelligentsia, so that in conversations with him I was able to acquire historical knowledge I never had due to inadequate schooling. The difference is that I take pains to think logically in the service of the party; Citizen Ivanov, however, was a cynic."

"Was?" asked Rubashov, taking off his pince-nez.

"Citizen Ivanov," said Gletkin, fixing his expressionless eyes on Rubashov, "was shot last night following an administrative proceeding."

◇

After this conversation Gletkin let Rubashov sleep for two full hours. On the way back to his cell Rubashov wondered why the news of Ivanov's death hadn't upset him more. At most it chased away whatever encouragement he had gained from his tiny victory, so that he quickly grew tired and sleepy again. Evidently he was in no condition to experience deeper emotions. Besides, even when they were talking he had felt ashamed of that vain sense of triumph. Gletkin's personality had gained such power over him that even his victories were transformed into defeats. The way he sat there, solid and expressionless, the brutal embodiment of the state that owed its existence to the Rubashovs and Ivanovs! Flesh from their flesh that had grown independent and lost all feeling. Hadn't Gletkin himself admitted that he was the spiritual heir of Ivanov and the "old intelligentsia"? Rubashov told himself for the hundredth time that Gletkin and the new Neanderthals were simply finishing the work of the generation with the numbered heads. The fact that the legacy of the old generation, their teachings, sounded so inhuman in the mouths of the new one also had to do with a change in climate, so to speak. When Ivanov put forward the same arguments, his voice resonated with the past, the memory of the sunken world. You can repudiate your childhood but not get rid of it. Ivanov had taken his with him to the end, which was why everything he said had that undertone of frivolous melancholy—and that was why Gletkin called him a cynic. The Gletkins of the world didn't have anything to rid themselves of; they didn't need to repudiate their past because they didn't have one. They were born without an umbilical cord, without frivolity, and without melancholy.

5.

Fragment from the Diary of N. S. Rubashov

. . . What gives those of us now exiting the stage the right to look down so condescendingly upon the Gletkins? The apes must have laughed among themselves at the sight of the first Neanderthal. The highly cultivated primates swung gracefully from branch to branch; the Neanderthal was earthbound and clumsy. The apes lived sated and peaceful lives, in playful serenity, or else caught fleas in philosophical contemplation; the Neanderthal lumbered darkly through the world, swinging his clubs. From their treetop perches, the apes looked down on him, amused; they performed acrobatics above his head and pelted him with nuts. Occasionally they were filled with dread; while they ate fruits and tender plants, daintily and gracefully, the Neanderthal devoured raw meat; he killed animals, even his own kind. He cut down trees that had stood forever, rolled rocks away from their hallowed ground, defied all the laws and traditions of the jungle. He was ungainly, cruel, un-animal-like—and

from the point of view of the highly cultivated apes, a barbaric
regression of history. To this day the last surviving chimpanzees
wrinkle their noses whenever a human passes by . . .

6.

Five or six days later Rubashov lost consciousness in the middle
of his interrogation. The discussion had arrived at the closing
point of the indictment, namely the question of Rubashov's motive for committing his acts. The accusation simply referred to
his "counterrevolutionary attitude" and mentioned in passing—
and as an obvious corollary—that he had been in the service of
a hostile foreign power. Rubashov was fighting his last battle
against this formulation. The discussion had already ground on
from the wee hours into midmorning when—at a completely
undramatic moment—Rubashov slid off his chair sideways and
collapsed onto the floor.

When he woke up a few minutes later, he saw above him
the small, fuzz-covered ostrich skull of the doctor, who was
splattering water on his face from a bottle and rubbing his temples. Rubashov could feel the doctor's breath, which smelled
of buttered bread and peppermint, and he threw up. The doctor cursed in his shrill voice and advised that Rubashov be
taken outside for some fresh air for a few minutes. Gletkin
had watched the scene with his expressionless eyes. He rang
and told the orderly to clean the carpet, then had Rubashov
escorted to his cell. A few minutes later the old warden took
him to walk in the yard.

At first Rubashov felt intoxicated by the fresh, sharp air. For
a few minutes he sensed his lungs taking in the oxygen like a
sweet, refreshing drink. The winter sun shone pale and clear; it
happened to be eleven a.m.—the same time he had been accus-
tomed to being taken outside, back before an immeasurably long
sequence of days and nights had merged into an indistinguish-

able blur. Why couldn't he simply live—breathe, walk through the snow, feel the pale warmth of the sun? The nightmare of Gletkin's room, the glare of the lamp, the crackling cuffs—why couldn't he just shake off this whole unnatural horror and go on living like others did?

Because it was his usual exercise hour, he had the thin peasant with the birch-bark shoes as his neighbor in the carousel. The man watched from the side as Rubashov walked beside him with slightly faltering steps, cleared his throat a few times, and then said, keeping an eye on the guards:

"It's been a long time since we saw you here, sir. You look sick, as though you won't last much longer. They say there's going to be a war soon."

Rubashov didn't say anything. He fought the temptation to pick up a handful of snow and press it into a ball. The parade moved around the yard. Twenty steps ahead of them another pair was stamping along the path between walls of snow—two men approximately the same height, in gray coats, with little clouds of steam in front of their mouths.

"It'll soon be time for seeding," said the peasant. "After the snow melts, the sheep go to the mountains. It takes them three days to get there. In the old days all the villages in the province sent their sheep on the same day. It started at sunrise; there were sheep everywhere on all the roads and in the fields, and on the first day the whole village trailed behind the herds. You probably never saw so many sheep in your life, sir, and so many dogs and so much dust. My God, that was a merry sight."

As he walked, Rubashov lifted his face into the sunlight; the sun was still pale, but it gave a lukewarm softness to the air above the snow. High over the machine-gun tower he watched the swooping and gliding antics of some birds. The peasant went on in his weepy voice:

"A day like today, when you can smell the thaw in the air, it really makes you tingle. Neither of us is going to last much longer, sir. They've stomped on us because we are reactionaries and because the old times when we were happy aren't supposed to come back."

"Were you all that happy, back then?" asked Rubashov, but the peasant merely mumbled something he couldn't understand, while his Adam's apple bobbed up and down his thin neck as though he were swallowing. Rubashov looked at him from the side and after a moment asked: "Have you read the Bible?"

The peasant nodded.

"Do you remember the passage," asked Rubashov, "where the people begin to cry out in the wilderness, 'Let us choose a captain, and let us return to the fleshpots of Egypt'?"

The peasant nodded eagerly but without understanding. Shortly afterward they were led back into the building.

The effect of the crisp air disappeared; the leaden sleepiness, the dizziness, and the nausea returned. At the entrance Rubashov bent down, picked up a handful of snow, and rubbed his forehead and burning eyes.

◇

He was not led back into his cell as he had hoped, but straight to Gletkin's room. Gletkin was sitting at his desk in the same position in which Rubashov had left him—how long ago was that? He looked as though he hadn't moved during Rubashov's absence. The curtains were pulled back; the lamp was burning; time stood still in this room like a stagnant pool that had no inflow and no outflow. As he returned to his seat across the desk from Gletkin, Rubashov noticed a wet stain on the carpet. He remembered his malaise. Evidently no more than an hour had passed since he had been helped out of the room.

"I trust you're feeling better," said Gletkin. "We had left off at the final question—the motive for your counterrevolutionary activity."

He adjusted his cuffs and looked somewhat surprised at Rubashov's right hand, which was resting on the back of the chair and which was still clutching a tiny clump of firmly pressed snow. Rubashov followed his gaze; he smiled, raised his hand, and held it in front of the lamp. They both watched as the snow in Rubashov's hand melted in the warmth of the bulb.

"The question of motive is the last one," said Gletkin. "Once you have signed that we will be finished with each other . . ."

The lamp was turned up and the glare was more piercing than it had been for some time. Rubashov was again forced to squint.

". . . and then you will have some peace."

Rubashov rubbed his temples, but the freshness from the snow had disappeared. Gletkin's last word, "peace," hovered in the silence. To rest, to sleep . . . Let us make a captain, and let us return into Egypt . . . He squinted through his pince-nez sharply at Gletkin.

"You know my motives as well as I do," he said. "You know that I acted neither because of a 'counterrevolutionary attitude' nor 'in the service of a foreign power.' What I thought, I thought, and what I did, I did, to the best of my knowledge and belief."

Gletkin had taken a stack of files out of the drawer. He leafed through them, pulled out a document, and read in his brittle, monotone voice:

". . . 'we were never concerned with the question of subjective sincerity. Whoever is wrong must pay; whoever is right will be absolved . . . That is the law to which we adhered . . .' That's what you wrote in your diary shortly after your arrest."

Rubashov sensed the familiar flickering behind his eyelids. The sentences he had thought and wrote acquired an oddly shameless character in Gletkin's mouth—as though a confession meant only for the ear of an invisible priest had been recorded on a phonograph and was now being played back, the voice hoarsely distorted.

Gletkin had taken a new paper from the file but read only one sentence out loud, his eyes fixed on Rubashov, as expressionless as always:

"'Honor means being useful without vanity, to the very end . . .'"

Rubashov tried to withstand his gaze.

"I don't see," he said, "what benefit the party gains by demanding that its members defile themselves publicly before the world and history. I have signed everything you've asked me to. I have confessed to having followed a false and objectively harmful political line. Isn't that enough for you?"

He put on his pince-nez, squinted helplessly past the light, and finished, hoarse and tired:

"After all—the name N. S. Rubashov is part of the party's history. By dragging it through the mud you are also defiling the history of the revolution."

Gletkin leafed through the files. "On that point I can also reply with a quote from your own writings. You wrote of 'the need to drub every sentence into the masses through endless repetition and oversimplification: what is presented as right has to glitter like gold, and what is presented as wrong has to appear as black as pitch, while political confessions of faith and guilt must be made to look colorful, like the gingerbread men sold at the fair . . .'"

After a moment's silence, Rubashov spoke:

"So that's what you're after. I'm supposed to play the bogeyman at your fair, howling and baring my teeth and sticking out my tongue—and all of my own free will. At least Danton and his friends were spared *that*."

Gletkin closed the file. He leaned forward and adjusted his cuffs:

"Your appearance at the trial will be the last service you can render the party."

Rubashov didn't answer. He kept his eyes closed and let the lamp shine on him like a drowsy person napping in the sun, but there was no escaping Gletkin's voice.

"Your Danton and the Committee of Public Safety," said the

voice, "were all genteel child's play compared to what we are after. I've read books about it. Those people wore wigs and declaimed their personal honor. Their only concern was to die with a beautiful gesture, without any consideration as to whether the gesture was useful or harmful."

Rubashov said nothing. His ears were buzzing; Gletkin's voice came from above him, it came from all sides, it pounded on his skull, and there was no escape.

"You know that for us everything is at stake," Gletkin continued. "For the first time in history a revolution was not only victorious but also maintained its ground. We have converted our country into a bastion of the future. It covers one-sixth of the earth and contains one-tenth of all mankind . . ."

Gletkin's voice now sounded behind Rubashov's back. Gletkin had stood up and was pacing up and down the room. That had never happened before. His boots creaked with every step; his stiff uniform crackled; a sour smell of leather and sweat filled the air.

"Once our revolution had attained its goal on one-sixth of the earth, we believed that the rest of the world would soon follow us. In its stead came a reactionary wave, which threatened to sweep us away as well. Within the party there were two currents of thought. One consisted of adventurers willing to risk everything to help the world revolution to victory outside the country. You belonged to that group. We recognized this direction as harmful and stamped it out."

Rubashov wanted to lift his head and say something. Gletkin's pacing thudded in his skull. He was too tired. He let himself sink back and did not open his eyes.

"The leader of the party," Gletkin's voice continued, "had a broader perspective and tougher tactics. He recognized that everything depended on holding the fort, withstanding and outlasting the period of global reaction. He recognized that it might take ten, twenty, or possibly fifty years until the world was ready for a new revolutionary wave. Until that time we would have to stand alone. Until then we had only one single duty: not to perish . . ."

Rubashov vaguely recalled a sentence that said: "It is the duty of the revolutionary to survive." Who had said that? He himself? Ivanov? In the name of this sentence he had sacrificed Orlova. And where had it led him?

". . . not to perish," Gletkin's voice echoed. "The bastion must be held at any price, any sacrifice. The leader of the party recognized this with unrivaled clarity and has acted accordingly, with absolute consistency. The politics of the Internationale had to be subordinated to the domestic policy of the revolutionary homeland. Whoever did not recognize this necessity had to be exterminated. Whole cadres of our best functionaries in Europe had to be physically liquidated. We did not shy away from shattering our own organizations abroad if it was in the interest of preserving the bastion. We did not shy away from working with the police of reactionary countries to suppress revolutionary movements that came at the wrong time for us. We did not shy away from betraying our friends and allying with our enemies in order to preserve the bastion. That was the task that world history had set for us, the bearers of the first victorious revolution. The shortsighted, the aesthetes, the moralists, did not understand this. But the leader of our movement recognized that everything boiled down to this one point: having the longer endurance in the face of history and making sure that the others perished but not us."

Gletkin interrupted his pacing. He stopped behind Rubashov's chair. The scar on his shaven skull glistened with sweat. He panted, ran his handkerchief over his skull, and seemed to be embarrassed that he had broken his reserve. He returned to his place behind the desk and straightened his cuffs. He lowered the light by a degree and continued in his usual expressionless voice:

"The line proposed by the party leadership was clearly defined and utterly consistent. Its tactics were determined by the principle that the end justifies the means—all means without exception. In the spirit of this principle the prosecutor will demand your head, Citizen Rubashov. The arguments put forth will of course be different. But in the background of this fairground performance, as you call it, you will know just as well as the prosecutor what is at stake—the restoration of party unity.

"Your faction, Citizen Rubashov, has been beaten and destroyed. You followed the policy of an adventurer, a policy that would lead the country to ruin. Your motives do not interest us. What we are interested in is the restoration of party unity, which has been threatened by your actions.

"You wanted to split the party, although you had to know that splitting the party would mean civil war. You know the dissatisfaction among our peasants. They haven't yet learned how to understand the sense of the sacrifice we have imposed on them. In case of war, which may be only months away, such an attitude can be disastrous. Today more than ever, all depends on the party being unified. It has to be as if made of one piece, filled with blind discipline and absolute trust. You and those in your faction, Citizen Rubashov, have caused a tear in the party fabric. If your regret is genuine you must help us repair this tear. I have already told you that this is the last service that the party will demand of you.

"Your task will be simple. You have already set it for yourself: gilding what is right and blackening what is wrong. Therefore your task is to make the opposition appear contemptible, to make clear to the masses that opposition is a crime and oppositionists are criminals. That is the simple language that the masses understand. If you start to speak of complicated motives you will only create new confusion in the masses. Your task, Citizen Rubashov, is to avoid awakening sympathy and compassion. Sympathy and compassion for the opposition are dangerous for the country.

"I hope, Comrade Rubashov, that you have understood the task the party is assigning you."

It was the first time since they had met that Gletkin had referred to Rubashov as "comrade." Rubashov quickly raised his head. He felt a hot wave rising inside him and was helpless against it. His chin quivered slightly as he put on his pince-nez:

"I understand."

Gletkin continued: "Note that the party does not offer you anything in return. We have brought some of the accused to submit by applying physical pressure. Others by promising to save their head—or the heads of their loved ones who were hostages in our hands. For you, Comrade Rubashov, there is no promise and no deal to be made."

"I understand," Rubashov repeated.

Gletkin leafed through the files.

"In your diary there is one passage that made an impression on me," he went on. "You wrote: 'I have thought and acted as I had to. If I am right, I will have no cause for regret; if I am wrong, then I will pay . . .' "

He looked up from the file and fixed his gaze squarely on Rubashov:

"You were wrong, and you will pay, Comrade Rubashov. The party promises you only one thing: after the victory, one day, when no harm can come of it, the material from the secret archives will be made public. Then the world will see what was behind this fairground performance—as you call it—that we had to stage according to the script of history . . ."

He hesitated a few seconds, straightened his cuffs, and closed, somewhat awkwardly, as the scar on his skull turned red:

". . . And then you and some of your friends from the older generation will not be denied the sympathy and compassion that you must forgo today."

As he spoke he handed Rubashov the statement along with his fountain pen. Rubashov stood up and said with a twisted smile:

"I always wondered what it looked like when Neanderthals turned sentimental. Now I know."

"I don't understand you," said Gletkin, who had also risen.

Rubashov signed the statement. When he lifted his head, his gaze fell on Number One's picture on the wall, and he again recognized the expression of knowing irony on Number One's face when they parted years ago—that melancholy cynicism, which stared down at humanity from every oil print of his ubiquitous portrait.

"It doesn't matter if you don't understand," said Rubashov. "There are some things that only the older generation, the Ivanovs and Rubashovs and your professor Mikhail, understood. That is over."

"I will give the order that you are not to be bothered anymore before the trial," said Gletkin after a brief pause, once again stiff and correct. Rubashov's smile irritated him. "Do you have any other special wish?"

"To sleep," said Rubashov. He stood in the open doorway, small, feeble, and unimposing with his pince-nez and pointed beard next to the uniformed giant, who received him outside.

"I will make sure your sleep is no longer disturbed."

After the door closed behind Rubashov, Gletkin went back to his desk. For a few seconds he sat quietly. Then he called his secretary.

The secretary took her usual place in the corner. "I congratulate you on your success, Comrade Gletkin," she said.

Gletkin turned the lamp down to its normal brightness.

"This here," he said, glancing at the lamp, "together with sleep deprivation and physical attrition. It's all a question of constitution."

THE GRAMMATICAL FICTION

Show not the goal.
But also show the path. So closely tangled
On earth are path and goal, that each with th' other
Their places ever change, and other paths forthwith
Another goal set up.

Ferdinand Lassalle, *Franz von Sickingen*
(trans. Daniel de Leon)

I.

"'Asked whether he acknowledges his guilt, the accused, Rubashov, answers with a clear "Yes" . . . To the further question of the state attorney, whether the accused had been in the service of the counterrevolution, he answers with a similar "Yes," this time a little more quietly . . .'"

The daughter of Vasily the caretaker read haltingly, pronouncing each syllable one at a time. She had spread out the newspaper on the table and was following the lines with her finger, while in between she fiddled with her floral headscarf.

"'When asked if he desires a counsel for his defense, the accused Rubashov states that he will waive this right, after which the court proceeds to read the indictment . . .'"

The caretaker Vasily was lying on his bed, his face turned to the wall. Vera Vasilyevna never knew whether the old man was listening to what she read or sleeping. At times he would mumble something to himself, but she had learned to ignore that. Every evening she read the entire newspaper out loud—for educational purposes—even when she had to attend a meeting of the party cell after work at the factory and didn't get home until late.

"'The indictment states that the accused Rubashov, in light of documentary and material evidence, as well as by his own confession in the preliminary examination, is guilty on all counts of the accusations against him. To the question of the presiding judge of whether he wishes to register any objections concerning the preliminary investigation, the accused declares he does not, and adds that his confession was voluntary and his remorse sincere regarding the crimes he committed against the people.'"

Vasily the caretaker did not move. Above his bed, squarely

over his head, hung the oil-print portrait of Number One. Next to the portrait was a rusty hook where the picture of Rubashov as partisan commander had hung until recently. Vasily's hand searched reflexively for a hole in the horsehair mattress, where he used to keep his greasy Bible hidden from his daughter, but shortly before Rubashov's arrest the daughter had found it and thrown it away, for educational purposes.

"'At the request of the prosecutor, the accused Rubashov proceeds to describe his passage from oppositionist to counterrevolutionary and traitor to the homeland of the revolution. Before the eagerly attentive courtroom he prefaces his account with the following words: "Citizen Judges, I wish to explain to you how I came to capitulate, before the examining magistrates and before yourselves, the representatives of our revolutionary justice. My story will prove to you how the slightest deviation from our party's line must inevitably degenerate into counterrevolutionary banditry. The logic behind our struggle pushed us deeper and deeper into the swamp. I wish to tell you about my path, so that the example of my downfall may serve to warn those who in this crucial hour may vacillate or harbor hidden doubts about the party leadership and the correctness of the party line. Covered with disgrace, cast down into the dust, soon to be cut off from my life, I wish to tell you of the sad progression of a traitor, so that it may serve the millions in our country as a lesson and a deterrent. . . ."'"

Vasily the caretaker had thrown himself onto the bed and buried his face in the mattress. The picture of the bearded partisan commander Rubashov was before his eyes, his little commander, who in the worst situations could curse so affably and amiably it delighted God and man alike. "Cast down into the dust, soon to be cut off from life . . ." Vasily groaned. The book was gone, but he knew many passages by heart.

"'At this point the state attorney interrupts with some further questions concerning the fate of the former secretary of the accused Rubashov, Citizen Orlova, who was executed for treasonous activities. It emerges that at that time the accused, Rubashov, cornered by the vigilant organs of the party, shifted blame onto the innocent Orlova in order to save his own skin and thus be able to continue his disgraceful activities. N. S. Rubashov confesses these monstrous crimes with a cynical and shameless candor. When the citizen prosecutor addresses him with the words: "Evidently you have lost all moral standards," the accused answers with a sarcastic smile, "Evidently." His behavior in the courtroom provokes repeated spontaneous outbursts of anger and scorn among those in attendance, which the presiding citizen judge quickly quiets down. Only once do these expressions of revolutionary justice give way to amused laughter, namely when the accused interrupts his depiction of his crimes with a request to pause the proceedings because he is suffering from "an unbearable toothache." In a telling gesture of how properly our revolutionary justice is handled, the presiding judge immediately grants this request and with a disdainful shrug of the shoulders declares a five-minute recess.' "

Vasily the caretaker lay on his back and thought about the time Rubashov had been saved from a German prison and escorted in triumph through the party assemblies, where he had stood at the dais, leaning on his crutches, beneath the red flags and banners, smiling as he rubbed his pince-nez on his sleeve and as the shouts and jubilation rang out in the hall on and on without stopping . . .

Then the soldiers of the governor took him into the common hall, and gathered unto him the whole band of soldiers, and put on him a scarlet robe, and they spit upon him, and took the reed, and smote him on the head, and they bowed the knee before him, and mocked him.

Old Vasily rolled back against the wall. He groped for the hole in the mattress but it was empty. The picture hook above his head was empty as well. When his daughter had taken Rubashov's picture off the wall and tossed it into the wastebasket, he had not resisted—because he was too old for the disgrace of going to prison.

His daughter had interrupted her reading and put the gas cooker on the table to boil water for tea. A pungent odor of kerosene filled the porter's lodgings. "Were you listening to what I read?" asked the daughter.

Vasily turned his head obediently. "I listened to everything very exactly," he said.

"Now you see," said Vera Vasilyevna, pumping kerosene into the hissing device. "He admits that he is a traitor. If it weren't true, he wouldn't say it himself. At the factory meeting we passed a resolution that everyone signed."

"As if you understand it all," Vasily sighed.

Vera Vasilyevna shot him a quick glance that caused Vasily to turn his head back to the wall. Whenever she looked at him like that, Vasily was reminded that he was in Vera Vasilyevna's way, because she wanted the porter's lodging all to herself. Three weeks earlier she had registered to be married to an assistant mechanic from the factory, but the couple didn't have an apartment; the young man shared a room with two colleagues and nowadays it often took several years to get an apartment from the housing trust.

The gas cooker was finally lit. Vera Vasilyevna put on the kettle with the sooty bottom.

"The cell secretary read us the resolution. It says we demand that traitors must be exterminated without mercy. Whoever shows them sympathy is a traitor himself and has to be reported," she recited with deliberate indifference. "The workers must be vigilant. We were each given a list to collect signatures for the resolution."

Vera Vasilyevna had taken a crumpled paper out of her blouse, which she smoothed out on the table. Vasily was now lying on his back, the rusty hook directly over his head. He peered at the paper next to the gas cooker. Then he quickly turned his head away.

And he said, I tell thee, Peter, the cock shall not crow this day, before that thou shalt thrice deny that thou knowest me.

The water in the kettle began to hum. Vasily made a sly face.

"And those who were in the civil war, do they have to sign as well?"

His daughter stood leaning over the teakettle with her floral headscarf. "No one has to," she said, giving the old man that same quick, peculiar look again. "Of course, everyone in the factory knows that he lived here in our building. After the meeting the cell secretary asked me if you'd been his friend up to the end and whether you had spoken with him much."

Vasily hitched himself upright on the mattress. The sudden exertion made him cough, and the veins on his thin, scrofulous neck swelled.

His daughter placed two glasses at the edge of the table and sprinkled a little tea leaf dust out of a bag into each. "What are you always muttering about?" she asked.

"Hand me the damn paper," said Vasily.

His daughter handed him the paper. "Should I read to you exactly what it says?"

"No," said the old man as he added his signature to the list. "I don't want to know. Now give me the tea."

His daughter handed him the glass. Vasily's lips moved; he mumbled something to himself as he sipped at the bright yellow fluid.

After they had drunk the tea, his daughter read more from the paper. The trial of the accused, N. S. Rubashov and M. M. Kieffer, was approaching its end. The recitation of the attempt to poison the leader of the party had sparked storms of outrage among the audience; there were repeated loud cries of "Shoot the mad dogs." When the prosecutor asked about the motives for his deeds, the accused Rubashov, who seemed to have broken down after the recess, explained in a tired, halting voice:

"I can only say that once we, the opposition, had resolved

to remove the government of the revolutionary homeland, we used methods we considered adequate to the task—methods that were as base and vile as the goal that we had set."

Vera Vasilyevna pushed her chair back. "That's disgusting," she said. "It makes me want to throw up, the way he's crawling on his belly."

She shoved away the paper and noisily began clearing off the gas cooker and the glasses. Vasily watched her. Emboldened by the hot tea, he sat up in his bed:

"Just don't think you understand it," he said. "God knows what he was thinking at the time. The party has taught you all to be clever and cunning, and people who are too clever have to stop being decent. And don't just shrug your shoulders," he went on, now angry. "These days the world is such that cleverness and decency are at loggerheads, and whoever holds with one has to give up the other. It's not good for people to over-think things. That's why it is written: 'Let your communication be, Yea, yea; Nay, nay: for whatsoever is more than these cometh of evil.' "

He collapsed back onto the mattress and turned his head away, so he wouldn't have to see what kind of face his daughter was making. It had been a long time since he had contradicted her so boldly. Who knew what that would lead to, if she wanted the place for herself and her husband. In this life you had to be sly—otherwise you might get sent to jail in your old age or else be forced to sleep under the bridge in the cold. No two ways about it: you had to either act cleverly or behave decently; it was impossible to do both at once.

"I'll read the ending now," the daughter announced.

The prosecutor had finished his examination of Rubashov. Afterward he again called on the accused Kieffer, who recapitulated in full his statements concerning the attempted poisoning . . . " 'Asked by the presiding citizen judge whether the accused Rubashov wishes to put questions to the accused Kieffer, as is his right according to the rules of the court, the accused Rubashov states that he waives this right. With that the evidentiary phase of the proceedings is closed and the session adjourned. Upon resumption of the proceedings the presiding judge gives the floor to the prosecutor . . .' "

Vasily didn't hear the speech for the prosecution. He had turned to the wall and fallen asleep. Later he didn't know how long he had slept, how often his daughter had refilled the lamp with kerosene, how often her index finger had reached the bottom of one column and glided up to a new one. He didn't wake up until the prosecutor was summarizing his speech and demanding the death penalty for the accused. Perhaps his daughter had changed her intonation toward the end, perhaps she had paused; in any case Vasily was again awake as the final, bold-type sentence of the prosecutor lingered:

"I demand that dogs gone mad should be shot—every one of them."

After that the accused were granted a last plea.

" '. . . The accused Kieffer appeals to the citizen judges and pleads for clemency in view of his young years. He once more admits the baseness of his crime and attempts to place the entire blame on the instigator Rubashov. In the process he lapses into an excited stutter, which triggers some merriment in the courtroom but is quickly suppressed by the presiding judge, who then gives the accused Rubashov the final word . . .' "

Here the newspaper reporter provided a vivid description of how the accused Rubashov "fervently scans the room and, finding not a single sympathetic face, sinks his head in desperation."

The speech of the accused Rubashov was short and reinforced the shameful impression his behavior in the court had elicited.

"Citizen Judge," proclaimed the accused Rubashov, "I speak here for the last time in my life. The opposition has been beaten and destroyed. If I ask myself today: 'What are you dying for?' I have no answer, only an absolute, black emptiness. There is nothing worth dying for, if that means dying without remorse, unreconciled with the party and the movement. Therefore now, on the threshold of my final hour, I kneel before the country, the masses, our whole people. The political charades and conspiratorial masquerades are over, with all their discussions and debates. We were shot dead long ago, in a political sense, well before the citizen state attorney demanded our heads. Woe to the vanquished whom history tramples into dust. Here before you, Citizen Judge, I have only one justification to offer: I did not take the easy way out. Vanity and the last vestiges of pride whispered to me: 'Die in silence,' or else die with a beautiful gesture, a moving swan song on my lips, baring my breast and throwing the gauntlet to my accusers. That would have been easier for an old rebel, but I overcame the temptation. With that my task is finished. I have paid; my account with history is settled. To ask you for mercy would be ridiculous. I am finished."

"'. . . After a brief deliberation the presiding judge pronounced the verdict. The Collegium of the Supreme Revolutionary Court sentenced all the accused to the maximum penalty: death by shooting, and confiscation of all personal property.'"

Vasily stared at the empty hook above his head and mumbled: "Thy will be done. Amen," and turned back toward the wall.

2.

So now it was over. Rubashov knew that before midnight he would cease to exist.

He wandered through his cell, where they had returned him after the uproar of the trial; six and a half steps to the window, six and a half steps back. When he stopped to listen, on the third black tile from the window, the silence came surging between the whitewashed walls as though from the depths of a well. He still couldn't fully grasp that it had become so quiet, both outside and within himself. But he knew for certain that nothing more could disturb this peace.

Looking back, he could even determine the moment in which this blessed tranquility had descended upon him, enveloping him completely. It had been during the trial, before he had spoken his final words. He thought he had burned the last remnants of egoism and vanity out of his consciousness, but in that moment, when his eyes scanned the faces of the onlookers and read nothing but scorn and indifference on all of them, he was overcome one last time by a hunger for just a scrap of sympathy, a shivering yearning to warm himself with his own words. The temptation tugged away at him to speak of his past, to rise up just once and tear the net in which Ivanov and Gletkin had entangled him, to cry out to his accusers like Danton: "They have laid hands on my whole life, may it now stand up and confront them . . ." Oh, he knew Danton's speech before the revolutionary tribunal word for word; he had learned it by heart as a boy. "They want to choke the republic in blood. How much longer should the footprints of liberty be graves? Behold the dictatorship—it has torn off its veil and carries its head high as it tramples our dead bodies."

The words had been burning his tongue, but the temptation lasted only a few seconds. Then, when he began his final speech, the tranquility had enveloped him. He had realized it was too late.

Too late to retrace the path, to once again stride on the graves of his own footsteps. Speeches could undo nothing.

Too late for all of them. Because none of them could turn the dock into a speaker's rostrum at their last public appearance, standing behind the courtroom barrier, and reveal the truth to the world, flinging the accusations back at their judges like Danton: "*Ma demeure sera bientôt dans le néant* . . . my residence will soon be in nothingness . . . and my name in the pantheon of history." Some, like young Misha, stayed silent out of sheer physical fear; some in the hope of saving themselves; others to free at least their wife or son from the clutches of the Gletkins. The best were silent so as to render the party one final service by offering themselves up as a scapegoat—and even the best had an Orlova on their conscience. They were too deeply woven into their own past, caught in the web they themselves had spun according to their circuitous logic and convoluted morality; they were all guilty, just not of those particular deeds to which they were confessing. For them there was no turning back. Their exit from the stage happened strictly according to the script of their bizarre play. History did not want to hear any swan song from them. They did not sing; their speech was the howling of wolves in the night.

So now it was over. None of it concerned him anymore. He no longer had to howl along. He had paid his debt and his account was settled. He was a man who no longer cast a shadow; he was relieved of all commitments. He had thought and acted everything through to the end; the hours that remained to him belonged to the "silent partner" whose realm began precisely where thinking-through-to-the-end stopped. He had christened this partner the grammatical fiction, driven by the shame instilled by the party when it inoculated everyone against employing the first-person singular . . .

Rubashov stood beside the wall that separated him from Number 406, which had remained empty ever since the departure of Rip van Winkle. He took off his pince-nez, looked surreptitiously around to make sure no one was watching, and tapped:

2-4 . . .

He listened, with a feeling of boyish shame, and tapped once again:

2-4.

He listened as he repeated the tapping once again. The wall was silent. He had never tapped the word "I" in a conversation. He listened. The tapping faded without any echo.

He continued his wandering through the cell. Ever since he had been enveloped in tranquility, he had been preoccupied with certain questions to which he would have gladly found a quick answer. They were naïve, childish questions; the most important had to do with the difference between suffering that served a purpose and suffering that was senseless. Purposeful suffering had a biological origin, senseless suffering a social one. The elimination of the latter was the sole objective of the revolution. But it turned out that eliminating the second type of suffering was only possible at the cost of a temporary but very severe increase in the first. The question now was whether such an operation was justified. When applied to "mankind" in general it evidently was; but when applied to the cipher 2-4, to a real flesh-and-blood human being, it led to absurdity. As a youth he had believed the answer to all such questions could be found in working for the party. That work had gone on for forty years, and right at the outset he had forgotten the question that was the reason for starting it in the first place. Now the forty years were over, and he was returning to the naïve question of his youth. The party had taken everything he had to give, and it owed him an answer. And the silent partner, whose magic cipher he was tapping on the wall of the empty cell next door, didn't know anything either: he, too, had no answer for these urgent, logical, or curious questions.

And yet there were ways to prompt this silent partner. The melody of "Come, Sweet Death" sometimes induced him to speak out, or the outstretched hands of the pietà, or specific memories of childhood. Certain tuning forks set off a resonance inside him, eliciting a state that mystics dubbed ecstasy and saints called contemplation; the greatest and most clearheaded of modern psychologists had acknowledged its existence and christened it "the oceanic feeling." When you were in this state, everything personal dissolved like a grain of salt in the sea, but at the same time, it seemed, the boundless expanse of the oceans was captured within a single grain of salt. The grain ceased to be locatable in time and space. It was a state in which thinking lost all direction and began to circle like the needle of a compass at the magnetic pole, until it finally broke from its axis and floated freely in space, like a beam of light in the night, until all thoughts and perceptions, joy as well as pain, seemed to be nothing more than the spectral lines of the same ray of light, shattered by the prism of consciousness . . .

Rubashov wandered through his cell. Earlier he had forbidden such naïve ruminations. Now he was no longer ashamed. His death was imminent. In death the metaphysical becomes reality. He stopped in front of the window. Over the machine-gun tower he could see a patch of blue. It was very pale but nevertheless reminded him of the particular shade of blue that he had seen as a boy when he lay in the grass on his father's estate, staring at the poplar branches as they wafted slowly overhead. Evidently, even a tiny patch of blue was enough to unleash the oceanic feeling. He had read that according to the latest cosmological theories the volume of the universe was finite—and while it had no boundary, it was closed within itself like the surface of a sphere. He had never figured out how this could be; now he sensed a burning desire to understand it. He also remembered where he had read it: After his first arrest in Germany some comrades had smuggled a scrap of the illegal party paper into his cell. Three columns at the top of the page reported a strike in an industrial bakery; below, as a filler in a single column, in tiny letters, was the discovery that the universe was finite, but at that point the page was torn. He never did learn what the torn lines contained . . .

Rubashov stood by the window and tapped on the empty wall with his pince-nez. As a boy he had actually wanted to study astronomy; now for forty years he had done something else. Why hadn't the prosecutor asked: "Accused Rubashov, what about infinity?" He would not have known how to answer, and here, right here, was the true source of his guilt. Could there be any greater?

Back then, when he read that notice in the paper, all alone in a cell just like now, his limbs still raw from the last torture, he had given in to a peculiar state of excitement—the oceanic feeling had carried him away. Afterward he had been ashamed. The party rejected such states, dismissing them as petit-bourgeois mysticism, ivory-tower escapism. Such states, they claimed, distracted from the task at hand and were a betrayal of the class struggle. The oceanic feeling was counterrevolutionary.

Because in the struggle one had to stand with both feet on the ground. The party taught how it was done. Infinity was a politically suspect quantity and the "I" a suspect quality. The party wanted nothing to do with the existence of such an entity. The definition of the individual was: a mass of one million divided by one million.

The party denied the free will of the individual—and at the same time it demanded that the individual bend his will to the party; it required absolute self-sacrifice. It denied the individual's ability to decide between two alternatives, and at the same time demanded that he always decide on the correct one. It denied his power to choose between good and evil, and at the same time it solemnly declaimed about guilt and betrayal. The individual operated under the sign of economic fatalism; it was a gear inside a clockwork that whirred without stopping, predetermined for all time and impervious to any influence—while the party demanded that the gears rise up against the clockwork and influence its course. Somewhere there was a mistake in the calculation—the equation did not add up.

For forty years he had struggled against economic fatalism. It was the central evil of humanity, the cancer gnawing away at its bowels. The need to operate was dire; the rest of the healing process would take care of itself. Everything else was amateurish, romantic quackery. You cannot heal the critically ill with pious exhortations and a laying-on of hands. There is only the surgeon's scalpel and his cool calculation. But wherever the knife was applied, in place of the old evil came a new festering sore. Once again the equation did not add up.

For forty years he had lived strictly by the rules of the party order. He had always followed its logical calculus, thought and acted everything through to the end. He had taken the caustic pencil of reason and burned the vestiges of the old, illogical moral laws out of his consciousness. He had rejected the temptations of the "silent partner," had placed his faith in reason and resisted the oceanic feeling with all his might. And where had he landed? Premises based in unassailable logic had produced completely absurd results; the irrefutable deductions of Ivanov and Gletkin had led him directly to the chilling drama of the court trial. Perhaps thinking everything through to the end was not a healthy thing to do.

Rubashov stared out through the window bars at the little patch of blue above the machine-gun tower. Looking back, it seemed he had spent forty years in a mad frenzy—in a rampage of pure reason. Perhaps it wasn't healthy for people to cut off the old ties, to disengage the brakes of "Thou shalt not" and "Thou mayest not" and go racing off toward their goal unchecked . . .

The sky had begun to redden; dusk was falling. A flock of dark birds was circling the tower with slowly flapping wingbeats. The equation did not add up. It was evidently not enough to give people a goal to set their sights on and a scalpel to hold. Experimenting with the knife was not a healthy thing to do. Perhaps at some later point. For the time being humankind was too young, too inept. And how had he himself carried on in this enormous field of experimentation! Gletkin's justification for everything that happened was that the bastion had to be preserved. But what did it look like from the inside? No—paradise cannot be constructed out of concrete. The bastion will survive but it can no longer serve as an example to the world; it no longer has a message to deliver. Number One and his regime had sullied the utopian promise of the future social state just as much as Rodrigo Borgia's papacy had sullied the concept of a Christian theocracy. The flag of the revolution was fluttering at half-mast . . .

Rubashov wandered through his cell. It was quiet and almost dark. It couldn't be much longer before they came for him. Somewhere there was a mistake in the arithmetic—no, in the whole system of calculation. He had suspected as much for a long time, ever since Richard and the pietà, but had never dared to admit it to himself. Perhaps it was all simply a gross error in timing. Perhaps the revolution had come too soon, a premature birth with stunted, monstrous limbs. Roman civilization at the time of Christ had also seemed doomed, rotten to the marrow, just like ours; at that time, too, the best had believed the time was ripe for the great upheaval—and then the old, antiquated world had gone on for nearly half a millennium. History had a slow pulse; humans calculated in years while it calculated in generations. Perhaps this was the beginning of the beginning. Oh, how he would have liked to live so he could develop his theory of the relative maturity of the masses . . .

Inside the cell was quiet: Rubashov could hear nothing but the grating of his steps on the tiles. Six and a half steps to the door, from which they would come to get him; six and a half steps to the window, behind which it was now nearly night. Soon it would be over. But when he asked himself, *What are you really dying for?* he could find no answer.

There was an error in the system, perhaps even in the proposition he had hitherto accepted as incontestable, in whose name he had sacrificed others and now he himself would be sacrificed—the proposition that the end justifies the means. It was this tenet that had killed the great fraternity of the revolution and had turned them all into mad, frenzied people. How had he put it at some point in his diary? "We have jettisoned all the norms and conventions of tennis-court morality, our only guideline is logic . . . We are sailing without ballast . . ."

Perhaps herein lay the core of the malady. Perhaps it was not healthy to sail without ethical ballast. And perhaps reason alone was a faulty compass, which indicated such a long, tortuous, circuitous course that the destination got fully lost in the fog . . .

Perhaps now came the time of the great darkness.

Perhaps only later, much later, would a new movement arise, with new banners, a new spirit that would understand both economic fatalism *and* the "oceanic feeling." Perhaps members of the new party would wear monks' cowls and teach that only purity of means can justify the end. Perhaps they will disprove the theorem that a human being is the quotient of one million divided by one million and introduce a new arithmetic, based on multiplication: on the merger of millions of *I*s to form a new unity that is no longer an amorphous mass but maintains its I-character, the oceanic feeling reinforced a millionfold, within a universe that was boundless and yet closed within itself . . .

Rubashov interrupted his wandering through the cell and listened. A dull, muffled drumming had begun outside in the corridor.

3.

The drumming sounded as though a wind were blowing in from afar; it was still distant but coming closer. Rubashov did not stir. Standing on the stone tiles, his legs suddenly felt strangely removed, no longer subject to his will; he sensed the gravity of the earth slowly rising inside them. Without taking his eye off the spy hole, he backed up two steps, toward the window. He took a few deep breaths and lit a cigarette. A ticking came through the wall beside the cot:

THEY ARE FETCHING HARELIP. HE SENDS GREETINGS.

The heaviness in his legs subsided. He went to the door and began pounding with both palms quickly and rhythmically against the metal. It made no sense to pass the word to Number 406; the cell was empty, the chain broke off with him. He drummed and pressed his eye against the spy hole.

In the corridor was the same dreary electric light as always. As always he saw the concrete doors from Number 401 to

Number 407. The drumming swelled; now came the footsteps, clearly audible on the stone tiles, approaching slowly, dragging. Suddenly Harelip was in his field of vision. He looked as he had in the glaring light of Gletkin's room, with quivering lips; his hands were cuffed behind his back and his arms hung down in a strangely crooked position. Unable to see Rubashov's eye behind the spy hole, he peered at the door with blind, searching eyes, as though behind it might be some last hope for rescue. Then a command was given and Harelip obediently turned away and continued his journey. Behind him came the uniformed giant with the pistol belt. One by one they vanished from Rubashov's field of vision.

The drumming subsided; once again it was quiet. The wall ticked beside the cot.

HE CONDUCTED HIMSELF QUITE WELL . . .

They hadn't spoken since the day Rubashov had told 402 he was planning to capitulate. His neighbor continued:

YOU STILL HAVE ABOUT TEN MINUTES. HOW DO YOU FEEL?

Rubashov understood that 402 was making conversation to ease his waiting. He was grateful for that. He sat down on the cot and tapped back:

I'D GLADLY BE DONE WITH IT . . .

I'M SURE YOU WON'T GO TO PIECES, tapped Number 402. AFTER ALL, YOU ARE A DEVIL OF A FELLOW . . . He paused and repeated the last phrase. A DEVIL OF A FELLOW . . . He was clearly at pains not to allow any break in the conversation. DO YOU REMEMBER? BREASTS LIKE APPLES, ROUND AND FIRM. HA-HA. DEVIL OF A FELLOW . . .

Rubashov listened for sounds in the corridor. Still nothing. Number 402 seemed to guess his thoughts and tapped again right away:

DON'T LISTEN. I'LL TELL YOU IN TIME WHEN THEY'RE COM-ING . . . WHAT WOULD YOU DO IF THEY PARDONED YOU?

Rubashov thought a moment, then tapped:

STUDY ASTRONOMY . . .

HA-HA, tapped 402. I MIGHT DO THE SAME. THEY SAY THERE MAY BE PEOPLE LIVING ON OTHER STARS. PERMIT ME TO GIVE YOU SOME ADVICE?

GO AHEAD, tapped Rubashov, puzzled.

BUT DON'T TAKE IT AMISS. TECHNICAL TIP FROM AN OFFICER. EMPTY YOUR BLADDER. ALWAYS BETTER IN SUCH CASES. THE SPIRIT IS WILLING, BUT THE FLESH IS WEAK—HA-HA . . .

Rubashov smiled. He went dutifully to the bucket. Then he sat back down on the cot and tapped:

THANK YOU. EXCELLENT IDEA. AND WHAT'S IN STORE FOR YOU?

Number 402 didn't answer for several seconds. Then he tapped, a little more slowly than before:

EIGHTEEN MORE YEARS. NOT ENTIRELY, JUST 6,530 DAYS . . . He paused. Then he added:

ACTUALLY I ENVY YOU . . . And after another pause: JUST THINK, ANOTHER 6,529 NIGHTS WITHOUT A WOMAN.

Rubashov was silent. Then he tapped:

YOU CAN STILL READ, LEARN THINGS . . .

I DON'T HAVE THE STRENGTH FOR THAT, tapped Number 402. And then, loudly and hastily: ATTENTION, THEY'RE COMING NOW . . .

He went silent, but then a few seconds later added casually:

PITY. WE WERE HAVING SUCH A PLEASANT CHAT . . .

Rubashov rose from the cot. He thought a moment and slowly tapped:

MANY THANKS . . .

The key grated in the cell door. The door flew open; outside stood the uniformed giant and an official in civilian clothes. The official called Rubashov by name and reeled off some words from a document. As they pulled his arms behind his back and put on the handcuffs, he heard Number 402 quickly tapping on the wall:

I ENVY YOU. I ENVY YOU. FAREWELL.

◇

Outside in the corridor the drumming began once more. It accompanied them all the way to the barbershop. Rubashov knew that behind each of the concrete doors an eye was pressed to the spy hole, watching him, but he did not turn his head right or left. The handcuffs chafed his wrists; the giant had screwed them on too tightly and wrenched his arms while pulling them back—they hurt.

The stairs to the basement came into sight. Rubashov slowed his pace a little. The civilian official stopped in front of the stairs. He was small, with slightly bulging eyes. He asked:

"Do you have any further wish?"

"None," said Rubashov, and began to climb down the stairs. The official stayed in the corridor and followed Rubashov down with his bulging eyes.

The stairway was narrow and poorly lit. Rubashov took care not to stumble, since he was unable to hold on to the railing. The drumming had ceased. He could hear the uniformed guard descending three steps behind him.

The stairs formed a spiral. Rubashov had to lean forward so as to see better; his pince-nez slid off his face and landed two stairs below him, then shattered after it tumbled down one more and stopped on the last stair. Rubashov hesitated for a moment, then felt his way down the remaining steps. He heard the guard behind him bend over and put the broken pince-nez in his pocket but did not turn his head.

Now he was nearly blind but once again had solid ground beneath his feet. He entered a long corridor, whose walls were a blur and which had no end that he could see. The guard kept three paces behind him. Rubashov felt the man's gaze on the back of his neck but did not turn his head. He walked on, placing one foot evenly in front of the other.

It seemed to him that he was walking through the corridor

for several minutes. Still nothing happened. He would doubt-lessly hear when the guard behind him opened his leather hol-ster. Until then he still had time, he was still safe. Or was the man behind him discreet, like the dentist who hid his forceps in his sleeve while bending over the openmouthed patient? Rubashov tried to think of something else, but he had to devote his full attention to not turning his head to see what the man behind him was doing.

Strange that his toothache had disappeared ever since that point in the trial when he felt enveloped in tranquility. Perhaps the abscess had ruptured at that very moment. What had he said then? "I kneel before the country, the masses, our whole peo-ple . . ." And what of it? What was happening to these masses, this people?

For forty years they had been driven through the wilderness, with threats and enticements, with bogus frights and sham con-solation; but where was the Promised Land?

Did such a destination even exist for this wandering human-ity? That was one of the questions he would have liked to have answered. Moses had not been allowed to set foot in the Prom-ised Land either. But at least he had been permitted to lay eyes on it, from the top of the mountain, spread out at his feet. It was easy to die like that, with the goal certain and in plain sight. But he, Nikolai Salmanovich Rubashov, had not been led to die upon a mountain; all that he could see was wilderness and the darkness of the night.

A dull blow struck the back of his head. It was long expected but nevertheless took him by surprise. He was puzzled to feel his knee giving way and his body spinning half around. *How theatrical*, he thought as he fell, *and yet I don't feel a thing*. He lay crumpled on the floor, his cheek on the cool concrete. It grew dark; the nocturnal sea was carrying him off, rocking him away. Memories wafted through him like flimsy veils of fog above the water.

They were pounding on the door to his apartment; he was

dreaming that they had come to arrest him, but in what country was he?

He tried slipping his arm into his robe, but whose portrait was that hanging over his bed and watching him? Was it Number One—or was it the other one, with the ironic smile—or the one with the rigid stare?

A shapeless figure bent over him; he smelled the fresh leather of the holster, but what symbol was the figure wearing on the sleeves and shoulders of his close-fitting uniform—and in whose name was he raising the dark barrel of his pistol?

A second, shattering blow hit him on the ear. Then all was still. The sea rushed on. A wave gently lifted him up. It came from afar and traveled serenely onward, a shrug of infinity.

APPENDIX

Excerpts from "The Case of the Anti-Soviet Block of Rights and Trotskyites," heard before the Military Collegium of the Supreme Court of the USSR, Moscow, March 2–13, 1938. Source: Marxists Internet Archive (Marxists.org), 2001; transcription Mathias Bismo; marxists.org/archive/bukharin/works/1938/trial/3.htm.

Bukharin's Last Plea

Before the Supreme Court of the USSR, Moscow, March 12, Evening Session, 1938

THE COMMANDANT OF THE COURT: The Court is coming, please rise.

THE PRESIDENT: Please be seated. The session is resumed. Accused Bukharin, you may make your last plea.

BUKHARIN: Citizen President and Citizen Judges, I fully agree with Citizen the Procurator regarding the significance of the trial, at which were exposed our dastardly crimes, the crimes committed by the "bloc of Rights and Trotskyites," one of whose leaders I was, and for all the activities of which I bear responsibility.

This trial, which is the concluding one of a series of trials, has exposed all the crimes and the treasonable activities, it has exposed the historical significance and the roots of our struggle against the Party and the Soviet government.

I have been in prison for over a year, and I therefore do not know what is going on in the world. But, judging from those fragments of real life that sometimes reached me by chance, I see, feel, and understand that the interests that we so criminally betrayed are entering a new phase of gigantic development, are now appearing in the international arena as a great and mighty factor of the international proletarian phase.

We, the accused, are sitting on the other side of the barrier, and this barrier separates us from you, Citizen Judges. We found ourselves in the accursed ranks of the counterrevolution, became traitors to the socialist fatherland.

At the very beginning of the trial, in answer to the question of Citizen the President, whether I pleaded guilty, I replied by a confession.

In answer to the question of Citizen the President whether I confirmed the testimony I had given, I replied that I confirmed it fully and entirely.

When, at the end of the preliminary investigation, I was summoned for interrogation to the State Prosecutor, who controlled the sum total of the materials of the investigation, he summarized them as follows (Vol. V, p. 114, December 1, 1937):

Question: Were you a member of the center of the counterrevolutionary organization of the Rights? I answered: Yes, I admit it.

Second question: Do you admit that the center of the anti-Soviet organization, of which you are a member, engaged in counterrevolutionary activities and set itself the aim of violently overthrowing the leadership of the Party and the government? I answered: Yes, I admit it.

Third question: Do you admit that this center engaged in terrorist activities, organized kulak uprisings, and prepared for White Guard kulak uprisings against members of the Political Bureau, against the leadership of the Party and the Soviet power? I answered: It is true.

Fourth question: Do you admit that you are guilty of treasonable activities, as expressed in preparations for a conspiracy aiming at a coup d'état? I answered: Yes, that is also true.

In Court I admitted and still admit my guilt in respect to the crimes that I committed and of which I was accused by Citizen the State Prosecutor at the end of the Court investigation and on the basis of the materials of the investigation in the possession of the Procurator. I declared also in Court, and I stress and repeat it now, that I regard myself politically responsible for the sum total of the crimes committed by the "bloc of Rights and Trotskyites."

I have merited the most severe punishment, and I agree with Citizen the Procurator, who several times repeated that I stand on the threshold of my hour of death.

Nevertheless, I consider that I have the right to refute certain charges that were brought: a) in the printed Indictment, b) during the Court investigation, and c) in the speech for the prosecution made by Citizen the Procurator of the USSR.

I consider it necessary to mention that during my interrogation by Citizen the State Prosecutor, the latter declared in a very categorical form that I, as one of the accused, must not admit more than I had admitted and that I must not invent facts that have never happened, and he demanded that this statement of his should be placed on the record.

I once more repeat that I admit that I am guilty of treason to the socialist fatherland, the most heinous of possible crimes, of the organization of kulak uprisings, of preparations for terrorist acts, and of belonging to an underground, anti-Soviet organization. I further admit that I am guilty of organizing a conspiracy for a "palace coup." And this, incidentally, proves the incorrectness of all those passages in the speech for the prosecution made by Citizen the State Prosecutor, where he makes out that I adopted the pose of a pure theoretician, the pose of a philosopher, and so on. These are profoundly practical matters. I said, and I now repeat, that

I was a leader and not a cog in the counterrevolutionary affairs. It follows from this, as will be clear to everybody, that there were many specific things that I could not have known, and that I actually did not know, but that this does not relieve me of responsibility.

I admit that I am responsible both politically and legally for the defeatist orientation, for it did dominate in the "bloc of Rights and Trotskyites," although I affirm:

a) that personally I did not hold this position;

b) that the phrase about opening the front was not uttered by me, but was an echo of my conversation with Tomsky;

c) that if Rykov heard this phrase for the first time from me, then, I repeat, it was an echo of my conversation with Tomsky.

But I consider myself responsible for a grave and monstrous crime against the socialist fatherland and the whole international proletariat. I further consider myself responsible both politically and legally for wrecking activities, although I personally do not remember having given directions about wrecking activities. I did not talk about this. I once spoke positively on this subject to Grinko. Even in my testimony I mentioned that I had once told Radek that I considered this method of struggle as not very expedient. Yet Citizen the State Prosecutor makes me out to be a leader of the wrecking activities.

Citizen the Procurator explained in the speech for the prosecution that the members of a gang of brigands might commit robberies in different places, but that they would nevertheless be responsible for each other. That is true, but in order to be a gang, the members of the gang of brigands must know each other and be in more or less close contact with each other. Yet I first learned the name of Sharangovich from the Indictment, and I first saw him here in Court. It was here that I first learned about the existence of Maximov, I have never been acquainted with Pletnev, I have never been acquainted with Kazakov, I have never spoken about counter-revolutionary matters with Rakovsky, I have never spoken on this subject with Rosengoltz, I have never spoken about it to Zelensky. I have never in my life spoken to Bulanov, and so on. Incidentally, even the Procurator did not ask me a single question about these people.

The "bloc of Rights and Trotskyites" is first and foremost a bloc of Rights and Trotskyites. How then, generally, could it include Levin, for example, who stated here in Court that to this day he does not know what a Menshevik is? How could it include Pletnev, Kazakov, and others?

Consequently, the accused in this dock are not a group. They are confederates in a conspiracy along various lines, but they are not a group in the strict and legal sense of the word. All the accused were connected in one way or another with the "bloc of Rights and Trotskyites," some of them were also connected with intelligence services, but that is all. This, however, provides no grounds for asserting that this group is the "bloc of Rights and Trotskyites."

Secondly, the "bloc of Rights and Trotskyites," which actually did exist, and which was smashed by the organs of the People's Commissariat of Internal Affairs, arose historically. It did really exist until it was smashed by the organs of the People's Commissariat of Internal Affairs. It arose historically. I have testified that I first spoke to Kamenev as far back as 1928, during the Sixth Congress of the Comintern, which I at that time directed.

How then can it be asserted that the bloc was organized on the instructions of fascist intelligence services? Why, this was in 1928! By the way, at that time I narrowly missed death at the hands of an agent of the Polish "Defensiva," a fact very well-known to everybody who stood close to the Party leadership.

Thirdly, I categorically deny that I was connected with foreign intelligence services, that they were my masters and that I acted in accordance with their wishes.

Citizen the Procurator asserts that I was one of the major organizers of espionage, on a par with Rykov. What are the proofs? The testimony of Sharangovich, of whose existence I had not even heard until I read the indictment.

The record of Sharangovich's testimony was submitted to me, from which it appears that I practically drew up the plan for wrecking.

SHARANGOVICH: Stop lying, for once in your life at least. You are lying even now in Court.

THE PRESIDENT: Accused Sharangovich, don't interrupt.

SHARANGOVICH: I could not restrain myself.

[Omission]

BUKHARIN: I want briefly to explain the facts regarding my criminal activities and my repentance of my misdeeds.

I already said, when giving my main testimony during the trial, that it was not the naked logic of the struggle that drove us, the counterrevolutionary conspirators, into this stinking underground life, which has been exposed at this trial in all its starkness. This naked logic of the struggle was accompanied by a degeneration of ideas, a degeneration of psychology, a degeneration of ourselves, a degeneration of people. There are well-known historical examples of such degeneration. One need only mention Briand, Mussolini, and others. And we too degenerated, and this brought us into a camp that in its views and features was very much akin to a kulak praetorian fascism. As this process advanced all the time very rapidly under the conditions of a developing class struggle, this struggle, its speed, its existence, acted as the accelerator, as the catalytic agent of the process that was expressed in the acceleration of the process of degeneration.

But this process of degeneration of people, including myself, took place in absolutely different conditions from those in which the process of degeneration of the international labor leaders in Western Europe took place. It took place amid colossal socialist construction, with its immense scope, tasks, victories, difficulties, heroism. . . .

And on this basis, it seems to me probable that every one of us sitting here in the dock suffered from a peculiar duality of mind, an incomplete faith in his counterrevolutionary cause. I will not say that the consciousness of this was absent, but it was incomplete. Hence a certain semiparalysis of the will, a retardation of reflexes. It seems to me that we are to a certain extent people with retarded reflexes. And this was due not to the absence of consistent thought, but to the objective grandeur of socialist construction. The contradiction that arose between the acceleration of our degeneration and these retarded reflexes expressed the position of a counterrevolutionary, or a developing counterrevolutionary, under the conditions of developing socialist construction. A dual psychology arose. Each one of us can discern this in his own soul, although I will not engage in a far-reaching psychological analysis.

Even I was sometimes carried away by the eulogies I wrote of socialist construction, although on the morrow I repudiated this by practical actions of a criminal character. There arose what in Hegel's philosophy is called a most unhappy mind. This unhappy mind differed from the ordinary unhappy mind only by the fact that it was also a criminal mind.

The might of the proletarian state found its expression not only in the fact that it smashed the counterrevolutionary bands, but also in the fact that it disintegrated its enemies from within, that it disorganized the will of its enemies. Nowhere else is this the case, nor can it be in any capitalist country.

It seems to me that when some of the Western European

and American intellectuals begin to entertain doubts and vacillations in connection with the trials taking place in the USSR, this is primarily due to the fact that these people do not understand the radical distinction, namely, that in our country the antagonist, the enemy, has at the same time a divided, a dual mind. And I think that this is the first thing to be understood.

I take the liberty of dwelling on these questions because I had considerable contacts with these upper intellectuals abroad, especially among scientists, and I must explain to them what every Young Pioneer in the Soviet Union knows.

Repentance is often attributed to diverse and absolutely absurd things like Tibetan powders and the like. I must say of myself that in prison, where I was confined for over a year, I worked, studied, and retained my clarity of mind. This will serve to refute by facts all fables and absurd counterrevolutionary tales.

Hypnotism is suggested. But I conducted my own defense in Court from the legal standpoint too, oriented myself on the spot, argued with the State Prosecutor; and anybody, even a man who has little experience in this branch of medicine, must admit that hypnotism of this kind is altogether impossible.

This repentance is often attributed to the Dostoevsky mind, to the specific properties of the soul ("*l'âme slave*," as it is called), and this can be said of types like Alyosha Karamazov, the heroes of *The Idiot*, and other Dostoevsky characters, who are prepared to stand up in the public square and cry: "Beat me, Orthodox Christians, I am a villain!"

But that is not the case here at all. "*L'âme slave*" and the psychology of Dostoevsky characters are a thing of the remote past in our country, the pluperfect tense. Such types do not exist in our country, or exist perhaps only on the outskirts of small provincial towns, if they do even there. On the contrary, such a psychology is to be found in Western Europe.

I shall now speak of myself, of the reasons for my repentance. Of course, it must be admitted that incriminating evidence plays a very important part. For three months I refused to say anything. Then I began to testify. Why? Because while in prison I made a reevaluation of my entire past. For when you ask yourself: "If you must die, what are you dying for?" an absolutely black vacuity suddenly rises before you with startling vividness. There was nothing to die for, if one wanted to die unrepented, and, on the contrary, everything positive that glistens in the Soviet Union acquires new dimensions in a man's mind. This in the end disarmed me completely and led me to bend my knees before the Party and the country. And when you ask yourself: "Very well, suppose you do not die—suppose by some miracle you remain alive—again, what for? Isolated from everybody, an enemy of the people, in an inhuman position, completely isolated from everything that constitutes the essence of life . . ." And at once the same reply arises. And at such moments, Citizen Judges, everything personal, all the personal incrustation, all the rancor, pride, and a number of other things, fall away, disappear. And, in addition, when the reverberations of the broad international struggle reach your ear, all this in its entirety does its work, and the result is the complete internal moral victory of the USSR over its kneeling opponents. I happened by chance to get Feuchtwanger's book from the prison library. There he refers to the trials of the Trotskyites. It produced a profound impression on me, but I must say that Feuchtwanger did not get at the core of the matter. He stopped halfway; not everything was clear to him, when, as a matter of fact, everything is clear. World history is a world court of judgment: A number of groups of Trotskyite leaders went bankrupt and have been cast into the pit. That is true. But you cannot do what Feuchtwanger does in relation to Trotsky in particular, when he places him on the same plane as Stalin. Here his arguments are absolutely false. For in reality the whole country stands behind Stalin; he is the hope of the world; he is a creator. Napoléon once said that fate is politics. The fate of Trotsky is counterrevolutionary politics.

I am about to finish. I am perhaps speaking for the last time in my life.

I am explaining how I came to realize the necessity of capitulating to the investigating authorities and to you, Citizen Judges. We came out against the joy of the new life with the most criminal methods of struggle. I refute the accusation of having plotted against the life of Vladimir Ilyich, but my counterrevolutionary confederates, and I at their head, endeavored to murder Lenin's cause, which is being carried on with such tremendous success by Stalin. The logic of this struggle led us step by step into the blackest quagmire. And it has once more been proved that departure from the position of Bolshevism means siding with political counterrevolutionary banditry. Counterrevolutionary banditry has now been smashed, we have been smashed, and we repent our frightful crimes.

The point, of course, is not this repentance, or my personal repentance in particular. The Court can pass its verdict without it. The confession of the accused is not essential. The confession of the accused is a medieval principle of jurisprudence. But here we also have the internal demolition of the forces of counterrevolution. And one must be a Trotsky not to lay down one's arms.

I feel it my duty to say here that in the parallelogram of forces that went to make up the counterrevolutionary tactics, Trotsky was the principal motive force. And the most acute methods—terrorism, espionage, the dismemberment of the USSR, and wrecking—proceeded primarily from this source.

[Omission]

It is in the consciousness of this that I await the verdict. What matters is not the personal feelings of a repentant enemy, but the flourishing progress of the USSR and its international importance.

◇

Editor's note: In the final verdict of this trial, on March 13, 1938, Bukharin, Rykov, Yagoda, Krestinsky, Rosengoltz, Ivanov, Chernov, Grinko, Zelensky, Ikramov, Khodjayev, Sharangovich, Zubarev, Bulanov, Levin, Kazakov, Maximov-Dikovsky, and Kryuchkov were sentenced to be shot, with the confiscation of all their personal property.